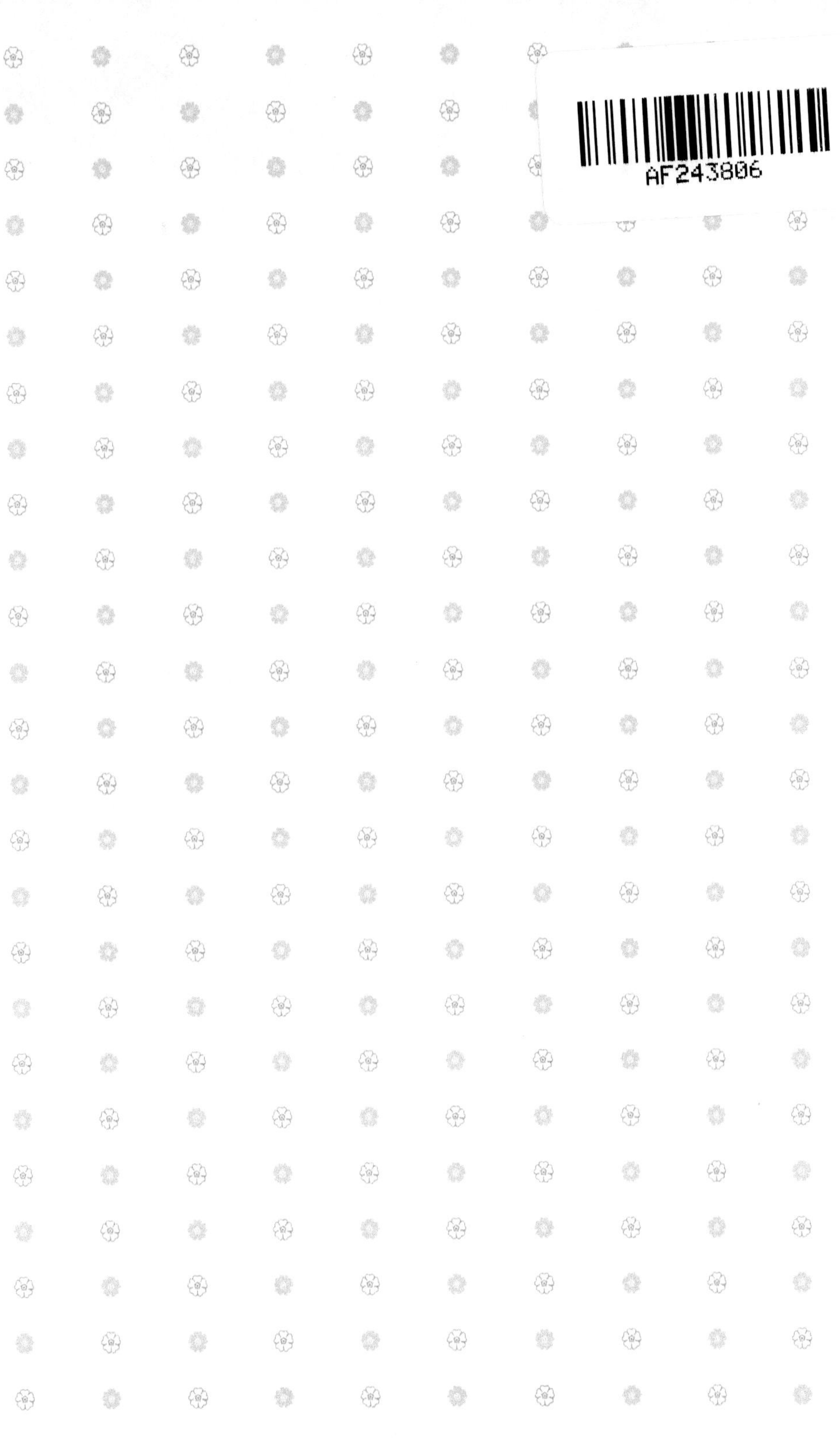
AF243806

in case of emergency press

We are proud to acknowledge the Traditional Owners of
country throughout Australia and to recognise their
continuing connection to land, waters, and culture.
We pay our respects to their Elders.

We support recognition, reconciliation, and reparation.

The Distance between Loves

Peter Farrar

in case of emergency press
https://icoe.com.au
Travancore, Victoria
Australia

Published by in case of emergency press 2026

ISBN: 978-0-6486111-4-1

Acknowledgements

Firstly I'd like to make my thanks known to Earl Livings and John Irving. Their encouragement and support has been like oxygen to me. Without them I'm not sure I would have persevered.

My thanks also to Howard Firkin who decided the book was worth publishing. I'll always appreciate his work and helping breathe life into the manuscript.

I'm grateful to the editors of the various literary journals who published my work over the years. They probably don't realise how much their emails accepting and appreciating my work meant.

Further thanks to my daughter Isabella for taking on the launch, especially involving a writer not keen on public speaking. Her invitation design, venue research and ability to cram this into her already accomplished life has been impressive.

Thanks as well to my wife Nina and other daughter Olivia who must have thought I'd left home when in fact I was just down the hall behind a keyboard.

There's the greyhounds and cocker spaniel that did shifts lying at my feet as I wrote this work. Whilst they may appreciate being mentioned, they'd probably prefer a treat.

Thanks Mason Murray for all the questions.

Dedication

To a world badly in need of a wakeup call.

Table of Contents

We made our final stop. The anchor chain rattled as it plunged into water. Sunshine lit the blue surface. My line dragged taunt, cutting into the skin of my finger. I tugged the fish in, a bream, left hand, right hand, feeling it drag and swerve. Lifted it over the boat's rail, fine water spraying me, tasting of brine, the silver body flashing and beating. It fell, slapping on the deck. I stared mesmerised at its fight and the moments of panic and dread I'd lived with for months welled up inside me again.

The Distance between Loves

Peter Farrar

The Shadows in your Face

The ions of a weather change shifted between us. Cooling, like your hand on my arm after dangling fingers out the car window as we drove through pine forest. Late afternoon light flared orange as sun dropped below hills. It had lit grey that morning like the skin of people in nursing homes. I'd noticed the shadows in your face at the time. Your features listless, purple hollows curving under eyes. You looked at me when I asked what's wrong. You used to sing inside rooms, your voice ricocheting off walls. I stood close to feel the press of your songs, to touch your shoulders, your warmth.

Later I listened to you sleeping. Soft rhythms of breath lifted and fell. Hail pinged off the windscreen, fragmenting before slapped away by wipers.

"It's raining so hard an inland sea will be here by morning." You never heard me or saw my head shake glumly. Rain cascaded down the windscreen, as if we drove underwater. I parked under the span of an overpass. The downpour eased, still sluicing past us in gutters, steaming off bitumen. You slept on. I watched your mouth, slightly apart as if you drew breath to whisper to me.

"Where are we?" you finally asked. Said I didn't even know what season it was here. Growing season, wet season, summer or harvest season. We drove to the next town, log trucks overtaking us, trailing tornadoes of churning wind.

"I don't want children," you'd said. Your feet painted with black nail polish planted on the glovebox. You told me we'd have to hate children to bring them into this world.

This corrupt, collapsing, over heated, doomed world. When you said that I felt a space in me, as if I'd coughed something up. Children meant hope and belief in the future I said. But you turned to the window, looking out.

We stayed in a caravan park on a cliff. The car banged over smooth rocks bulging from the dirt road.

I wasn't surprised by the strength of your hands. Yesterday you'd gripped my shoulder so tightly a line of yellow bruises pocked my skin. Delicate as dabs from finger painting. This morning we stopped to buy a small box of oranges. They smelt like sap and I inhaled them so their residue of coarse skins settled in lungs and blood. You sliced away the top of one, squeezing hard so your fingers turned white and juice dripped heavily into your mouth. Then you held the orange above my lips so I felt drops landing like rain tapping. Seeds pushed out and I swallowed them too.

That night I recalled when we met. Nervousness and yearning collided in my chest the first time we spoke. I'd followed your eyes, half smiles, shy looks into your lap, your head tilting up in laughter, neck round and smooth. Later I let you overwhelm me, your feet hooked behind my back like links in a chain.

Our caravan was last in the row. Brine smells and mosquitoes gusted through a gap in the window. I slept against your back despite the heat. Felt the stirrings of your dreams, the murmuring dialect of them. Northerlies blew and I noticed mangroves gusting wet earth odours as rain fell. A neighbour told us the wet was coming, batten down. We watched storms approach, light muted and grainy.

You said plans were more useless than superannuation. Hopeless as 7 AM to 7 PM jobs, mortgages, child bearing hips and a credit rating. That was all about the future. Who could see a future while the world collapsed? Future didn't extend beyond the next kilometre of road or tomorrow's meals. I'd looked up that road as you spoke, mirages rippling in distance. I went to ask about where home would be when this was over and what then. But I stayed silent. You'd given up on futures after all.

You took up smoking. It changed how you smelt. It replaced your mornings of peppermint toothpaste and afternoons of salt. You joked it stopped you swallowing mosquitoes. You kissed me, your chapped lips like paper cuts.

The café opposite the caravan park taped a position vacant sign on the door. It dangled crookedly, a corner fluttering every time the door opened. I enquired. The blackboard listed milkshakes, beef and red wine pies, toasted sandwiches with double cheese, and ice creams. Two petrol bowsers stood out the front.

"Kitchen hand work," the owner said. "Plus taking readings off the petrol bowsers. Receiving orders, processing payments. Washing floors when kids are car sick. Stacking stock. Cooking burgers after you've been trained. Being nice to people driving home to another year of boring jobs." He stepped back and appraised me. "Do you have any clean shirts? Give that beard a trim?"

Lightning twitched at night. Thunder turned along horizons. Channelled along my bones. Humidity dulled me like concussion. Our neighbour handed us three day old newspapers. Last year the fifth hottest ever recorded you read to me. Pacific islands inundated by rising seas. Landfill space running out. Old Beatles footage found. Your father used to own all their recordings you said. When he died your brother helped himself to the stacked vinyl records. Another reason not to believe in anything you quipped. Imagine your own flesh and blood stealing from you.

They provided an apron and gloves. I sliced lettuce into strips, sawed into over ripe tomatoes. Sprayed insect killer into spaces behind the vats and refrigerator. Topped up the ice block freezer.

"Where you headed?" I asked drivers.

"Cairns then a ferry to Thursday Island," one said. "Anywhere the fishing is good," another explained. "Why?" a woman who never looked at me asked.

The café was run by a couple. They barely spoke to each other but seemed in touch through a language of eye movements and routines set as dance steps. They lived in a shack behind the shop. Once they sent me back there to look for a notepad. Pictures of their children lined a wall, smiling but in a way where it didn't reach eyes.

"Can you slice that quiche?" the woman asked. "Make sure each piece is exactly the same size."

Afterwards I told you about my day. Right down to the condensation on lettuce and paper wasps hovering near the back door. About the Japanese tourist bus with people stepping off pushing up umbrellas under the burning sun. That the café owners showed me how to toss a burger and the woman said it was artistry. Then the man said he could feel rain coming. Approaching storms ached in his joints. I laughed when I wasn't meant to. You sat on the step, smoking and barefoot, listening but maybe not. I asked what you'd been doing. You said you'd been wondering how far to the Gulf of Carpentaria and what was beyond that. What was out past the ocean with its blue green furrows sweeping in?

That night rain hammered. I saw you singing softly in the gloom, stubbing out a cigarette with smoke that stuck to my sweat like glaze. Long curtains of rain fell off the roof. Damp mist seeped in from a hole I never found, layering over us. In the morning I stared at your bare limbs, sheets kicked off, your body stretched and deeply brown, hands flung above your head. And the shadows in your face, as if some parts of you were more alive than others. Casuarina trees dripped onto the roof. Walls ticked in the swelling heat. I dressed, shirt already sticking to my back. On the road dead cane toads scattered. Patterns of tyre tread squished through them. Others bloated, covered in green flies. More lay already leathery from roasting in the sun.

"It rained the bastards," the owner said to me, passing an apron. "You didn't hear them? Up the coast the storm front picked them up when blowing through. Peeled them off the ground like they were chip bags. Started falling from the sky down the road. Few lizards too. Probably lucky didn't get a hitch hiker crashing through our window. Rained cane toads right through here. Have to climb the ladder and hose their guts off the roof before they begin stinking."

I started cooking the first hamburgers. Geometry as well as artistry. Circumference of meat patties fitting the circles of buns. Corners of gently melted cheese protruding from the burger. Two rings of tomatoes with taste left behind in a cool room looping on top. People came and went. A German tourist left a half-eaten burger on one of the plastic tables.

"This meat is so pink it could be alive enough to teach circus tricks to!" the owner said. He peeled back the leftover burger insides as if standing over an autopsy. "That isn't cooked. It could be put on a leash and taken for a walk. Audrey! Come out here!"

I hadn't realised her name was Audrey. Or anything. She brushed through the fly strips, looking at me. Her skin mottled pink and brown from too many sunburns.

He said I couldn't keep working there. I'd poison someone cooking like that. He held up the patty to Audrey and a shape of pink meat drooped in his hand. He shook his head.

"Wait there. Give me your apron," he said. "How many hours you work today? Here's $28. Make it $30. Don't ever come back. Even to buy petrol." I looked desperately at Audrey. She squeezed eyes shut, inhaling unevenly.

"Just go," she said quietly. "I wish I could."

I explained everything that happened and you nodded lethargically. I felt humidity rising in my skin. You said you weren't surprised. Employment was like that. Job ads should say responsibilities included being taken advantage of, feeling bored and someone talking down to you. I said I wanted to go home. There was nothing past the next town except bingo nights and haze from burning cane fields thick as smoking a roll your own. You said no. Going back meant suburbs. Living meekly. I told you the world needed your activism. Make your anger soar. March, contact people, fund raise, sign petitions. You looked impatiently at me as if I was a child attempting adult conversation.

During evening I stirred vegetables through rice. Heat lifted from a gas jet. We ate outside, lightning cracking, illuminating us bloodless, like corpses. You asked if I wanted children. And if so, what did I feel so optimistic about that enabled me to believe they would be safe from the world's mounting horrors? Kids have closer relationships with mobile phones than parents. Did I want everything else in that life? A $3000 monthly mortgage and no goals beyond spending weekends catching up on sleep and standing in supermarket queues? I ate in silence.

I barely heard the knocking. The caravan filled with morning light. Yanked the sheet up so it billowed over you, drooping into your undulations. I grinded open the door. The site manager nodded at me. Looked past at plastic plates piled in a drying rack and mildew spotting walls. Remarked it'd been the hottest wet season he'd experienced. His eyes swung towards the sound of your breathing.

"Those storms, apart from dropping a few thousand cane toads, washed away part of the cliff." He looked into my eyes as if hoping I might finish his sentence. "It's not safe here anymore. State park people closing it down. They reckon the place could start tipping into the sea. Climate's gone crazy, I tell you." He turned, beginning to walk away. "Mango season up to March if you're looking for work."

I lay next to you. Leaned on elbows to study your face. Your shadows had changed, moving the way high and low pressure troughs cross maps. Green veins lined under your arms. I kissed the salt of your chest. You didn't move. I stepped outside into gusting sea breeze. Three caravans up a couple packed. Fishing rods strapped to the top of a jeep.

I cooked you eggs. Angled my body away from the spitting pin pricks of boiling fat. Eased the eggs onto buttered bread. You sat at the table, pushing the fringe from your eyes. You told me the life I'd spoken about returning to offered you the same emptiness as when people talked about believing in religion. You touched my face, stroking with fingertips before cupping my cheeks in your hands. You said quietly what I wanted seemed like a dying language. That one day what I now spoke of going back to would no longer exist in living memory, the way old wisdoms of growing vegetables, sewing, which winds bring rain, and kneading pasta would disappear. That night you pulled a singlet top over your head and your hair dragged up and toppled down. You nestled into me so that I absorbed your warmth and heartbeats.

I rolled into the bunched sheets and drifts of your body heat. Cool air filled the spaces left behind by humidity. I sat up, the mattress giving slightly under me. You'd gone. The caravan empty, no longer seething with your despair or passion. I followed your footprints in wet soil outside the door, high arches of your feet angling towards the highway. Even asked the site manager if he'd seen you. Did you depart on a bus or ask for a ride with someone else leaving? The manager shook his head, telling me he'd been watching greyhound racing so closely he wouldn't notice a tsunami arriving. I dragged my feet back to the van, opening the door so your smells and shadows wisped over me. Hauled up my bag and slid it into the car.

The car engine stuttered and I eased forward, yanking the steering wheel away from potholes filled with black water. The site manager waved half-heartedly as I passed. At the highway I stopped, looking towards where the road faced north like a line marking longitude and how it curved south. I waited a long time, motor idling, not knowing what to do and wanting to tell you that.

Home, with Arms and Legs

Bryce stepped away from his bed and paused where he used to stand. He imagined the carpet dented there, as if heavy furniture stood for a long time. But instead marks shaped to his feet—slightly pigeon-toed and in front of windows from where he once looked out. He pictured the dusty glass—pockmarked with long gone flurries of rain he used to gaze through to the front garden.

Bryce yearned to peer out past the fence. He wanted to see joggers trailing churning mists of breath as they thumped past. He longed to turn and see his wife's ruffled hair knotted and strewn over the pillow, the vast walls with hanging pictures too small for them and a half-finished book by the bed.

Last night Bec read to him. By the second page he nodded off. During the night he woke against the bunched edge of the pillow, then, later, along a dip in their mattress. Last week he said that dip felt as if he was sleeping in a dry creek bed, the uneven springs like angled stones.

Bryce imagined dragging himself up in the morning to five-day working weeks followed by television, before dozing off before the first ad break. He missed seeing the muted colours of his room, yesterday's limp clothes draped over the back of a chair, rows of letters on spines of books and the no spill straw standing from his cup of water.

Dreams cheated him into thinking he could still see. He dreamed of dawdling walks through his garden. Flowers drooped heavily with dew and mangled lines of beans and tomatoes stood half dead at the end of their season. At times, wrapped in a billowing coat, he strolled grey laneways with espresso machines hissing from cafes. The sheer joy of those moments brought him awake occasionally, feet jerking through the next step he was to take. Then there were the dreams he wanted to leach out of himself. In those he stood at checkpoints, squinting into the glaring distance at slowly approaching cars; his gun trained on windscreens; shallow breathing as he waited.

"We'll have tests done." Weeks ago a doctor said that. Bryce heard a pen picked up. Heard the doctor's chair tilt and sag as he shifted. Even listened to him write. Can you read by listening to handwriting? Was that the pen sweeping side to side to write an s?

Something clicked next to Bryce's face. He waited, guessing. Was it a pen? A surgical instrument? He sensed the slow passing of the specialist's hand across his face, only then deciding it must be a torch.

"Can't say what's wrong exactly," the doctor said. "No obvious external signs. No indication of a tumour or cyst. Even the tiniest fibres penetrating behind eyes would leave minute scratches." Again Bryce sensed the torch passing over eyes, peering into them: light sharp and brilliant like the arc of an eclipse. "Very unusual," the doctor added.

Bryce had been able to see during the evacuation. Six of them were airlifted. Their Black Hawk helicopter skimmed above sand dunes. The pilot half turned, shouting—above the sound of the rotor—that they were seeing what the end of the world would look like. They watched sand dunes sliding past as the helicopter thudded towards the base. Dust storms had almost buried abandoned cars and ruined walls of houses, as if the weather was trying to wipe away all the tragedy. His eyes worked long enough to last through the debriefing. Where did the firing first come from? Which house did you see activity in? How was confirmation to engage given? At what time did you enter the house? Who first rendered assistance to the wounded children?

Bec drove him home from the doctor. Bryce felt her hand straying from the steering wheel, touching his knee. He pictured her tears beading, smudging the broken lines marking lanes. He knew the streets they drove: plane trees, three quarters bare, lining the road; leaves like damped rags dragging along in the wake of passing trams; chairs grouped outside cafes.

Next to Bryce, Bec slept. She breathed slowly, rustling when turning over. He touched her. Had she lost weight? She was warm under his hands. Had that muscle in her upper arm softened? He lay against her so he felt the length of her down one side. Her breaths and trembles moved through his skin.

Bryce's clothes were left out so he could find them easily in the morning. He fumbled his way out of bed, feeling around obstacles. He felt Bec vault off the bed and hurry to him.

"It's okay," he said softly.

He brushed her bare skin, warmth lifting off her like steam after a shower. He sensed her fear, now as much a part of her as humour, caring, the want to have a baby, buy a bigger house, wear high heels, and love of his thumbs kneading into the dips of her shoulders.

Bryce asked Bec to pass his clothes so he could dress. A few minutes later he told her to go ahead and he'd follow her to the kitchen. He knew the way, right down to the angle of every step. Bryce was often content to trail Bec, listening to her slow steps and putting his feet where hers landed, as if fitting them into her footprints on the beach.

Carefully he edged down the hall. Walked so closely to Bec he smelt soap on her skin.

"Little more to the left," she said, but Bryce signalled her to silence. He pushed on, drawing back from a corner, sensing it there. Then five steps later he bumped a door.

"Shit!" he said.

Bryce stopped, rigid in mid stride, feeling Bec's hand cupping his arm, steadying him. Then he twisted away, taking clumsy steps until he arrived in the kitchen with its onion and curry sauce smells.

Bryce faced the direction of a chair scraping out from the table. He felt Bec guide him down to it. He sat tilted over the table. Listened to Bec make coffee, cocking his ear to her movements. A spoon rang when she stirred. The mug was set down in front of him. Her fingers closed warmly around his hand, guiding him towards the cup. A telephone rang in the next room. Her footsteps skittered away.

Bryce listened to her speak. Her voice was higher than usual, as if nervous.

"It's the doctor!" she called across the room. "I'll put him on speaker."

Bryce swung the chair towards her.

"Bryce can hear you," she said.

"We've concluded our tests," the eye specialist said. It caught Bryce out. The doctor's initial uninterested drawl—how cold it was; car windows being iced up in the morning; frost burning plants—had lulled him into thinking it would be a nothing conversation.

"We think it might be a psychological problem. Eyesight could have shut down because of something horrible that was seen or experienced. It's a condition we know little about. It's occasionally been found in refugees after long journeys. Cambodian boat people for example. I'd like you both to see a psychologist who works in this field."

Bryce heard Bec rummaging for a pen and taking down details.

Later Bryce glided his fingers over the table top as if reading Braille. He touched over crumbs, spills and coffee circles. His face lifted up to her as she came closer to him. His eyes followed movements as if watching her.

"I'm never going to see again, am I?" he said quietly.

"One day you will. I'm sure of it," Bec said.

Recently, he'd said now that he was unable to pick a lie by seeing her he could take her wrist in his hands to do so. He could tell from her pulse. Whether it would beat ferociously or calmly. Bryce knew she stood in front of him then, thin wrists extended towards him, waiting for him to take them. Instead he slowly reached up, finding her rows of knuckles, lines of veins and tapering fingers, until he slipped his hands inside hers. Bec swung her head down to his, kissing him so passionately she forced his head back.

Bryce used to fear going on the patrols and leaving the safety of the base. They drove down narrow roads— considered clear the day before, but by morning carrying the risk someone had planted a mine during the night. Once they found the remains of a missing journalist. One of his shoes lay well off the road. No one wanted to retrieve it in case there was a trap.

Last week Bec drove him to places they used to visit. Bryce knew where they were by how sharply the car cornered, the smell of fish and chips sweeping by, the long wait at a set of lights, and clinking of yacht masts. They drove with windows down. Sea air blustered into the car. It vibrated and howled. Bec took him out to the pier he used to fish from. Bryce listened to the water. Ribbed with small waves, the sea foamed and slopped into the wooden pier. Bec asked him to talk about fishing there in minute detail: catching a flounder, its body as narrow as flowers pressed in a book; the rush of line across fingers; the slow days when there was nothing but the smell of bait in the sun and tourists asking if anything bit around here besides teenagers on each other's necks. Bryce knew what she was trying to do; attempting to bring his eyes back to life, using smells and recollections while talking quietly to him.

"Here," Bec said, so close her breath layered over his ear. Bryce imagined touching his skin there, feeling the soft edges of her words brushing him. Bryce smelt toast as Bec pushed a plate towards him. He found his way to the jam and vegemite. His hands knew the shape of the jars. At times he smelt the contents. Bryce noticed smells more often now. 'Tree Dahlias,' he said yesterday and Bec said she'd seen their lilac petals feathering over ground.

Bryce could not help with directions anymore. He was unable to tell her to turn left here, or that there was a parking spot ahead. Soon they arrived in another waiting room. Bec commented on a line of French impressionist prints. A table of old magazines stacked with crosswords finished and recipes torn out. They waited. Cars wisped by outside. Bryce smelt perfume, probably from the receptionist, vapour burning inside his nostrils.

"What was the last thing you remember seeing prior to the blindness?" the psychologist asked once they were seated in the office. "Tell me about the two or three days before. Was there anything especially traumatic that happened leading up to losing your sight?"

Anything especially traumatic? Bryce could've laughed. How about that child so burnt her skin was leathery black? Would you settle for the taxi driver they shot dead carrying nothing more than cash and a picture of his wife? What about that bomb detonated in the market that Bryce couldn't stop replaying through his mind?

The psychologist wrote everything down. The pauses between questions dragged out. Finally, he told them he would be in touch. The psychologist said he understood it was difficult. They may well not be looking at an operation or medicine.

Afterwards Bec took Bryce for coffee. He listened to her wrap his latte in a serviette. He told her it was hopeless. Maybe he should count his blessings that he came home with arms and legs, or that he was not on a kidney recipient list because of shrapnel wounds. He heard her turn in the chair. From her breathing he could tell she was facing away. Probably towards rows of shop windows where the layered reflections of passing people glided by.

When they went home Bryce knew what Bec would do. She often hurried to a small space behind the shed. It was a narrow shaded area, damp and overgrown by clover. Bec once told him it was her crying space. She said it was where sobs came up lumpy and hard. Between creepers dangling from the shed and the splintering fence she recovered and found strength, steadying herself and finally retracing steps to the house. Bryce sometimes picked the difference in her voice when she returned inside. It croaked and broke before she cleared her throat and repeated the words. Bryce concentrated on her. He could sense her change in how she walked, her skidding hurried steps when trying to keep herself busy, her heavy, pausing steps when she was preoccupied.

They finished their coffee in silence.

Bryce had called out from his bunk at the base. Somewhere between confused dreams of running, crouching and taking cover jammed against the walls of shattered houses. When he cried out his voice echoed back to him, pinging between beds, floors and walls. "Can't see! Can't see!" he shouted over and over, until rushing steps crowded around him. Someone told him to calm down; another asked what happened. Bryce sat up, blinking, wiping the heels of palms through eyes. Within an hour he was lying on a stretcher in a helicopter, feeling a draught as heavy as bad breath across his face. Someone's voice he'd never heard before kept reassuring him.

In the afternoon Bec read to Bryce. He sat rigidly. Lately he noticed her changing her voice at times, letting it lift and fall, depending on which character's lines she spoke. During her pauses he wondered if there was more to her words than the characters she brought to life, that there was also the texture of her own pain. Eventually Bryce slumped, dozing. The puff of air from the closing book briefly roused him. He heard Bec stand. Her steps seemed so quiet they were weightless. She eased through the backdoor. He imagined her crossing the cracked back path, passing stunted roses towards her space. Bryce gave her the moments he knew she needed.

Later Bryce stood and the chair wobbled under him. He walked unsteadily, arms floating sideways for balance. He approached, step after tentative step, off concrete onto grass, just missing the possum-scratched trunk of the gum tree, a hand brushing the old metal clothesline. He knew where she was in the same way he had learnt to locate his way to the sink, to stand in front of music or find her hands.

Bryce heard her say his name quietly. For a second he paused, suspended in the late afternoon cooling sun. He heard Bec leave the space, her next steps coming closer to him.

He moved towards her.

Unchanged Skin

For a long time I'd wondered if her skin was the same. I still owned an old photograph of her. I'd snapped it kneeling on the bed, rocking slightly, trying to still the camera. Photographed Tina's back tapering over sheets. A white seam crossed below shoulders, dipping where she flexed. That line reddened when she lay on a towel sunbaking in the crammed square of my patio. But the picture was black and white, unable to reveal her nut brown skin, how perspiration lay like dew on her, the way grains of sand salted over shoulders.

The south wind brought sea breeze. Brine smells gusted, enough for me to picture the bay rumpled and heaving. But this summer smoke coursed in, inhaling like rope burn down my throat. Smelt it in the morning air, how clothes stunk after sitting around campfires. Sunlight shone faintly orange. At work I arrived coughing.

"Listen to you," one of the managers said. "That's eight on the Richter scale."

I worked silently at my desk. Stopped for instant coffee or to spend a few moments wandering through another department, eavesdropping on gossip. Tinny golden oldies played from a radio behind my desk. My manager stood next to me, looking over my shoulder into the computer screen.

"We're looking okay for Thursday? Need all this wrapped up by then."

I hated Thursdays. Imagined the early scent of a weekend floating in on Thursdays. If I turned my head a few degrees, could smell Saturday and its freedoms dawning somewhere.

"You're a battery hen." That's how my wife described my workplace. She'd stopped by for lunch. Vietnamese rolls and long silences. She leaned on the empty reception desk texting someone.

"How do you work in such a tiny space?" she said as we left. "It's worse than a phone box. Is there enough oxygen to go around for all those people?"

Kate was right. My window looked out to an alcove of clumped plants. Walled in, the wind barely reached them. Those plants stood like artificial flowers.

"This weekend can we go shopping for outdoor furniture?" Kate said.

"Great. Five days trapped in an office before one more stuck in shops."

I swayed back in the chair. A waiter quickly gathered our bowls, rattling away. I followed Kate out.

"Hope you're in a better mood tonight," she said over a shoulder.

The message on my mobile felt nervous. Barely heard the first words, the way long distance calls used to sound. Then her voice went through me like ultrasound. Played it over and over. 'It's been a long time. Saw your name on LinkedIn. Was wondering about you. You can call me if you want.'

I carried the mobile delicately. How I'd carried that picture of her bare back, her face sideways on the pillow, turning to whisper in her low breaking voice. I'd always been careful not to crease that photograph, not wanting to bend the image where I rested a cheek or lay my chest.

At first was too nervous to return her call. Once or twice thought my mobile hummed in a pocket. Took it out, peering into dead blue light.

"It's winter right there," I'd said to Tina once, hand between her shoulders. She felt chilled in that place, despite the warmth I knew pooled under skin like bore water. I glided my hand along her spine, knots of bone sweeping through my palm. Body heat glowed lower, in the small of her back. She suffocated her smile into the pillow, the slightest laugh like hiccups. "Here's where it's summer," I said, my hand lingering close to her hips.

Her fingers tapped on my skin the way loud music drummed inside me.

I finally rang Tina from a meeting room at work. My voice soared around walls in the closed spaces. She asked if I remembered her.

"Yes, I said. "Of course I do. What've you been doing?" Immediately I felt embarrassed by the question, how it amounted to nothing but small talk after all we'd been through years ago and what I once felt for her.

"Not very much," she said. We fell into silence. I heard background noise of traffic grinding and sputtering.

"If you want to go for a coffee," Tina said. "I mean, you might not want to. But if you're interested. We can meet in a cafe. Let me know if you like."

After dinner Kate slept on the couch. Her legs drew up, arms crossed, nail polish flaking or bitten off fingers. She murmured in sleep, indistinct and mysterious as another language. Lately she'd started learning judo.

"Don't ask me to spar with you," I'd told her. "Take up shadow boxing. You'll get a better opponent."

On the weekend Kate walked around the house to break in a new pair of shoes. I listened to her measured steps, her sitting down to rub blisters. Once she shouted across rooms whether I knew where the band aids were. I heard a shoe wrenched off.

I lied at work. Said I was seeing a dentist.

"Receding gums, receding hair. What's next?" someone said. I drove to the cafe. Inside coffee smelt like approaching downpours. I missed Tina at first. Searched for how she looked thirty years ago. She sat alongside a wall, six tables back. Her top strayed off a shoulder, grooves of bone like rafters.

Tina cut my hair once. It fell in dark clumps. She'd angled over me, fingers slow and deliberate on my scalp. Her ribs slotted against the length of my arm, breath weaving around my ears and neck. I didn't want her to stop.

"Cut until I can join the marines."

"I found two pens and an old sunhat in there," she said.

Now she was shy with questions. Peeping into my life rather than examining it. Tina asked if I still photographed landscapes, wrote poetry and grew vegetables. She skirted if I married and had children. I said I wouldn't have been surprised to find she lived in France or Italy. That she'd completed a thesis. Taken up life drawing or singing.

"None of those things," she quietly said.

"We're learning throws," Kate said during a break in the evening news. "Have to learn how to land without injury. I'll show you when I know how."

"Can't you just go back to kicking me in your sleep?"

"Are you interested in anything I do?"

"I'd feel safer if you'd taken up learning guitar or speaking Japanese."

We'd driven to the shops earlier in silence. Years before I'd pointed out to her on that road a prunus plum tree, explaining it'd blossom at the end of July. I'd asked her to look at the mist hushing in, rubbing her hands between mine at a red light until skin turned warm and pink with friction. Now I asked her if we needed milk, what aisle low fat ham was in, should we just pick up one of those barbecued chickens rather than cook.

The second time we met I kissed Tina's cheek. So lightly I barely brushed through her aura, over pores. Trailed her inside the cafe, faintly remembering that skin, shoulders tacking towards the direction she'd take. Tina slid her chair out, smiling that uncertain smile that flooded back to me when I recalled all the times I'd seen it when things started ending between us.

We didn't know where to start. I spoke about trips I'd been on. Recalled Paris for her, surging cold winds off the banks of the Seine River, turning from them like side on against waves sweeping in at beaches. Disgust at politicians, smoke like dirty rain in my neighbourhood and dead end jobs.

She concentrated as I spoke, intently enough to be lip reading. Close enough so I could watch her swallowing, see one eyelid hanging slightly lower than the other. Tina's voice sounded the same. Even the same pauses, plus how it changed with laughter. Wanted children but an aunt at least. Cared for an ill mother and it occupied four sad years. Abandoned a Psychology degree. Preferred cold weather, loving the short days and thin light of July.

After the café I'd followed Tina in my car, driving to her house. Now and then I nearly swerved into side streets, expecting to pull over and text sorry, I can't do this.

"Hope you find varicose veins attractive," I said in her hallway. "You can change your mind anytime between my shoes and shirt coming off." Tina smiled, shucking out of her top. We didn't meet each other's eyes, the room rustling to clothes peeling and falling. Didn't say I remember your back exactly like that. Avoided telling her those old chicken pox marks still reminded me of the space a raindrop leaves. That I occasionally carried that photograph around. How her breathing still quickened the same way.

She whimpered softly. Just once. Her ribcage strained and gave like the timbers of a small boat pressing through waters.

How might we have lived? I imagined that, lights out in my bedroom, curtains drawn as if eyes already closed. I didn't picture a suburban home. I never heard our voices discussing interest rates and if a fireplace might be nice. There was no immaculate lounge room or fridge magnets with glittered lettering announcing "Noosa Heads" or "Trump Tower." I expected books on the floor, haphazard like patio tiles kicked up and left loose. Saw our hands in mixing bowls, still smelling of fish sauce the next day, the crinkling turn of newspaper pages. I lived our lives together every night before sleep.

Kate watched me in that way that made the side of my neck burn. As if her stare heated air between us. She told me I'd changed. Distracted, as if living somewhere else.

"We never do anything," she said.

It was true. Our last outing to a beach was months ago. I'd breaststroked out, tugging through an undertow pulling me like gravity. I'd swum so far Kate was lost amongst the other bobbing heads and flotillas of parents guiding thrashing children through waves. At that moment we'd separated, the gap between us far more than a stretch of water.

Tina wrote me a letter once. It'd be tucked inside a book somewhere now, perhaps nestled with Gatsby as he tried to win Daisy back. It was short. She had looping handwriting on crooked lines as if words might fall off the page. "I've been aware of certain feelings towards you" was the first sentence. It'd sounded formal, almost corporate. Yet I'd remembered it word for word, carried that line around like lyrics from "Khe Sanh" I'd belted out at nightclubs, my throat sore as if the higher end notes were something burning I'd swallowed. Words on that letter eventually harmed me, aching the way old injuries did before weather changes, always reminding me of what might've been.

Our skin grazed at the cafe table. Particles of warmth remained on my arm, how fine sand stayed on me when lifting off beach towels.

"I still want to be with you," Tina said. "Even after all this time. From the first sight of you again and the first word you said. I knew."

"I can't." I couldn't look at her when I said that. But even staring into the outline of a heart melting in the foam of my coffee I noticed her flinch, her arm retreating.

"The timing will never be right for us," she said.

I sat in the car with what I nearly said, so heavily inside me it was like I'd heard it from someone else. I think I've always loved you. I was loving you when I didn't realise it. I loved you so that I thought of you when I walked, when I turned on the hot water tap at 6 AM, when I scraped pebbles and clay from a hole to plant an apple tree. I loved how you spoke to my eyes, sometimes to my pain. You made my mistakes lighter, my triumphs larger. I cried when you left, sobs so wet and gulping they were like my final breaths ever.

I didn't have the courage. I couldn't upend my predictable life of Friday night watching football, able to finish Kate's sentences, knowing how long her sulking would last and her absorption into online shopping. It was easier to live the pretence. As well as the other lies where I loved my job, was fulfilled in our listless suburb and feigned a happy marriage to our friends. At least I'd been honest enough not to promise Tina I'd one day leave everything for her.

I kept seeing Tina in the rear vision mirror of my life. How she twirled a straw while ice chinked around her glass. Her grasp on my arm that left the silhouette of fingers. Her hands when rolling on lipstick. Her thumbs in the gaps of my shoulders when I complained about bad days. One of her legs draped casually across my back so a strip of warmth still lay across skin when it lifted off. Her throat when her head tilted back laughing.

Next to the bunched credit cards in my wallet I glimpsed that photograph, bending slightly so her back was at that angle when she used to half lean out of bed to pull back a sheet for me. That last morning when she stretched a particular way to retrieve clothes before leaving. I watched it long enough to see it fold into darkness as the wallet closed.

Sirens

The sirens start across the city. They wail through distance, lifting until they hum behind my ribcage. Then they fall as if running out of breath. The sound settles over the drumming traffic and the voices of neighbours upstairs. We have ninety seconds. That's the recommended time to find shelter. Outside doors slam. People clatter down fire escapes. They don't panic the way they used to when the attacks started months ago. Yvonne and I stand from our table. I go to the sink to rinse out a coffee cup. Yvonne snaps at me, asking is a clean cup more important than being blown to pieces.

We move into the stairwell. Others gather. They stand around. Some smile and nod at us. The sirens fall silent. I hear people's breath, soft as waves falling from a long way off. Body heat warms the space we share. Not far away two explosions thump. Shockwaves roll through me and the ground lurches slightly. People look at each other. One man has an unlit cigarette in his mouth. When he swears it bobs between lips.

We are meant to wait for the all clear sirens. That ensures the danger has passed. Everyone ignores the rule. We hurry back to our lives. Yvonne and I go outside. There's hardly any traffic. A single taxi noses past.

"Death wish," Yvonne mutters, nodding towards the car. In the sky vapour trails slowly dissolve.

Yvonne and I are always walking out in the middle of something. Some mornings the sirens begin and we leave behind toast. Yvonne's slice has the symmetry of an orthodontist corrected bite in it. We leave coffees cooling, the brown suds of our lattes melting away. We walk out on cold meat on slabs of heavily buttered bread. Last week we nearly left our bed. Our bony chests wedged together with Yvonne's arms flung above her head. She whispered into my ear, her voice low and thick, breath bitter and warm, lifting gently onto me. She said let's stay like this, the sirens make it dangerous. I tried to peel off her but she gripped me with her legs, rolling me onto my back and laughing. I loved her high pitched laughter, her head thrown back so I could see the folds in her neck.

Last week we stood in the stairwell. I held her hand as an explosion boomed from blocks away. We always stood where there were no windows so there wasn't a risk of being sprayed with shattered glass. Most people boarded up their windows by now. I told her let's not have children. Let's not bring anyone into this life. She looked at me, sad and conflicted.

The sirens are like opera voices. They control us more than calendars or clock alarms. Hopes for peace dashed the headlines say. There's never been peace. There never will be. If I'm out driving and the sirens start, I check the GPS for one of the shelters. Quickly I park, even blocking a laneway or mounting a kerb. Shelters are underground. I glide my palm along a hand rail as I descend into them. Greenish water seeps down walls. The government announced the shelters would survive a direct hit. They also protect us against shrapnel. We pile out after the explosions, checking the sky for the vapour trails of any new rockets. Then we search for what directions the exploded missiles took. Once a woman next to me became hysterical, convinced the direction of the trail meant it'd landed in her neighbourhood. Her crying was so loud I felt it in me, as if I was also sobbing.

The rockets are small. Their explosive is fertiliser. No one knows where they will come down. At night we sleep fully clothed, shoes next to the bed to leave quickly. Yvonne sometimes sleeps through the sirens and I have to rouse her awake.

"I'm not going. I'm tired," she said in the darkness last week. The sirens soared, soprano like. I couldn't blame her. Our sleep was often interrupted. Perhaps one of their weapons was sleep deprivation. For a moment I begged but her head lolled to one side, eyes heavy. "Please," she whispered. I nearly argued but then there was the sound of her breath in sleep, that inhaling I'd watched many times, swelling her ribs towards me. I went to our small bathroom window, the only one not boarded up. Tiles chilled the soles of my feet. Through the grimy glass I saw two rockets floating soundlessly, arching over the city before falling gracefully. There was a flash of orange light but no noise. It must be far away. The second fell too, picking up speed as it descended. Then there was nothing. Many of them never exploded. They slammed into walls or crashed through cars. One exploded recently when a person started touching it. Later someone said the victim was a child.

At times I examine their anger. Who hates us so much to do this? Someone we don't know killing people they've never met. How do you become like that? When I used to want children I never imagined them on my knee teething as I told them about the people across the border they must learn to hate. My uncle once told me he covered my head in a wet towel when I was a child. Bitter breezes of tear gas innocent looking as rain clouds wafted towards us during an anti-government demonstration. I still carried a faint recollection of my cart wheeling breath in that damp darkness.

Yvonne's sister visits us late the next afternoon. She jokes about how long we'll be able to sit before the sirens start. We eat eggplant tossed with pasta. After dinner we go into the street. Some boys are playing soccer, jostling and taunting each other as someone kicks madly at the ball. It zooms away crookedly before bouncing and rolling down an alleyway. They tear after it. We laugh at them and see others leaning over balconies watching. I put my arms around the shoulders of both women. I face Yvonne and kiss her on the mouth, tasting the pinot wine we've been drinking. Her lips are liquid and warm. She turns and goes inside, telling me she will be back in a moment. I glance at her sister Maria and see her staring at where the boys had been. I hear them down the alleyway, bantering. Now and then there is the muffled thump of the ball being kicked. Maria asks will the troubles ever end. She wishes she had the money to leave this place. People in other countries didn't realise how fortunate they were. They visit shops without wondering whether bread will be in stock. They go to see a film without fears of being killed. Their biggest problem was a weather change, not rockets.

"At times I wish those rockets would blow up in the faces of the people who make them," I say. Maria turns towards me and I shake my head, ashamed of telling her that. "See what it turns you into? I'm becoming like the people who want to kill us."

We watch the boys return to the street. Some file past us, one has the ball under his arm. A couple of them say hello politely.

"Last week I was visiting friends," Maria says quietly. "One of the rockets landed a couple of streets away. After we left the shelter we went straight there. Followed the smoke. The house was gone. Nothing but broken concrete. We started going through the rubble because people said the family had been inside. Fire fighters arrived. They found them all where they'd been sitting around a table." I stare at her. Maria's eyes scan across the skies. "I saw them. Every single body. There was a baby." She looks at me. "I have never been filled with so much sadness. And hate. I don't know what to do."

Behind us I hear the door open. Yvonne comes out. Maria touches my arm.

"Please don't tell my sister," she says quietly.

Yvonne stands with us. Together we watch two jet fighters black and shapeless streaking soundlessly across distance. She asks if we had a nice talk. I smile thinly. We face the horizon turning a burnt orange colour. After a while Yvonne says it's becoming cold and we should go inside. Mechanically I turn back to the apartments and follow them.

The Cherry Orchard

That cold entered Ross like illness. A bone scan would've revealed it grey and still, lying through joints and marrow. He looked through the kitchen window fogged dirtily by last night's burnt sausages. At times sleet slapped the ground before rain set in again. Water coursed between rows of cherry trees. Last night he'd driven home, car sliding slightly on black ice, drifting off the road like being caught in an undertow.

"Coming in from Bass Strait," Ellie said beside him. She understood weather maps, familiar with the wandering circles of high pressure troughs and sharp triangles of cool changes. Ross used to joke she must've swallowed a barometer. She could face winds, look at the shapes of breaking cloud or study the glow of sunsets and predict the next day's weather. He used to love lying his head on her stomach at night, her breath quiet, heaving slightly like a gentle swell in the ocean.

"We need the weather to finish its tantrum for the cherries," Ross said. "It's knocking the flowers to the ground. Can you forecast any dry weather for us?"

Ellie looked away, as if listening in to a different conversation.

Ross walked hunched into the shed. A mist of rain wafted over him from where it floated from gaps in the roof. He stood in the doorway. He'd slouched there often early last summer. Sometimes drinking a beer so fast it plunged coldly through him. The casual pickers had started, trooping up from accommodation in three old caravans parked across the back of the property. It'd been hot from last November. Heat scalding as touching a hotplate and needing to run cold water over singed skin. Ladders balanced against trees and pickers climbed them with plastic buckets. Ross was always lecturing them. Leave the unripened cherries. Don't squash them. And you can't eat any cherries unless you want pest spray coursing through your veins.

A couple of pickers were university students. There was an older man still fit enough to lumber up paths, shoulders dragged down by the weight of buckets. Ross warned the pickers on working holidays from England about sunburn.

Ross wasn't sure where Robert came from. Someone said he migrated from Argentina, others that he'd deferred a PhD and was spending a couple of semesters travelling and working. He was the best picker. He moved over the eroded ground easily. Other pickers stumbled and tripped where paths washed away. Robert tipped the buckets of cherries onto a conveyor belt transporting them to where they'd be washed. He was the kind of worker Ross wanted back during July for pruning. Ross considered inviting him for making jam in late summer or bottling their cherry and chocolate sauce.

"He's a natural," Ross told Ellie. "He ran orchards in a previous life. There must be a cherry tree somewhere on his family tree. Perhaps there was a Lapin cherry that was his great aunt."

The next day Ellie said to point him out. Robert was on his own amongst the trees. That was something Ross admired about him. He could complete picking a tree alone in the time it took two others to finish it. And he worked without gossiping. Ross noticed a couple of the women flirting with him. They sidled up to Robert, laughing towards him so that he must have felt their breath lightly buffeting him. Ross couldn't remember the last time Ellie looked at him like that. Probably during that period before marriage, their first drought, last year's burning late frost and Ellie's miscarriage.

"Like watching a machine," she said. "He's muscled, isn't he?"

Ross didn't answer. It was as if she'd said he wasn't muscled enough. He was muscled on his fingertips from all the time on keyboards he thought bitterly. Eyes muscled from having to keep watch over everything. Voice muscled from reciting over and over what had to be done.

Last summer seemed it would never end. Eventually the days shortened but the heat didn't stop. At times Ross stood in the breathless shade. He stood for such a long time the sun moved and he had to shift to stay in shadow. Most of the pickers had moved on by then. Four of them remained, working in the paddock furthest away. Robert worked amongst them. Ellie carried down iced teas twice a day. Even she seemed unsteady on the ground gouged up by downpours. Ross stood at the kitchen window watching her. He even took out those old military style binoculars. He zoomed in on her, right down to her bunched calf muscles. They used to leave containers of iced water and cheap cordial down there. The pickers then served themselves. But now Ellie traipsed towards them. The pickers took drinks off the tray she carefully balanced. Robert was always last Ross noticed. As if Ellie could pass his direct to him with her hand. Robert descended the ladder, balancing on the first rung to drink. He performed mini acrobatics on the ladder, holding a rung with one hand before slowly lowering himself, then pulling back up. He sipped while smiling at whatever Ellie said to him.

The season ended. Faint oranges and reds started running through leaves. Ellie announced she wanted to ask the last of the pickers up for a meal to thank them for all their work. She said there weren't enough thanks in the world. Thanks was a word slipping out of our language, the way 'pigtails' or 'typewriter' had. She said all Ross had to do was light the barbecue, incinerate the spiders and cook the meat.

Deep down Ross didn't want to. He wasn't interested in hearing about people returning home or their life plans. But he was no match for Ellie's enthusiasm. She'd decided the food, wine and to hold it outside before he grumbled there wasn't time. He was surprised at how she turned on him then. After all, he'd barely responded, his voice meek and flat under her loud planning. We never go anywhere except the supermarket Ellie said. When was the last time we visited anyone? Always too tired to even try for a baby.

Ross froze to the spot. He watched the deepening red around Ellie's neck, vivid as a tattoo. She was so still he thought she'd stopped breathing.

Someone knocked at the back door. Ross felt the sound, hard and rapid through him as if bones broke. Ellie turned, slowly at first, walking to the door.

"Hi," Ross heard from out of sight. The voice became louder as it came inside. Ellie re-entered the room still flushed but somehow radiant. "I was going past," Robert said, stopping at the edge of the room. He flinched when he saw Ross. "Heard shouting. Thought something may have happened. An accident maybe. Sorry. Just thought I should come and check."

Mind your own business and bugger off Ross nearly said. He couldn't comprehend how Ellie spoke ahead of him next. He'd even had his first word out and it'd hung in the air alone. If Robert could lip read surely he'd understood it.

"No it's okay," she said quickly. "I only had a few hysterics over something I dropped. But it's fine now."

Ross watched her. He'd never caught Ellie lying. But now he stared at her doing it with ease. Her face gave nothing away, unmoving under their scrutiny.

"But while you're here," Ellie said. "Ross and I were talking about a little thank you lunch. For all the work. The others as well. Now that the season is ending. We thought we'd have a barbecue. We'll eat outside. I can see we have a few warm days coming. What about Thursday?"

Ross glared at Robert. Directed his stare point blank at him, anger sweeping through his body as if transmitting it through ESP.

Robert smiled. He said he'd love to. And he'd let the others know. As he replied he never looked at Ross.

The house filled with silence. Like the way air sliced open for lightening. Ross retreated to the study, paying invoices and shredding old credit card statements. He heard Ellie trooping through the house. She folded out the trestle table. Knives and forks clinked together. Bottles chimed as they were stacked in the fridge.

Ellie was right about Thursday. Skies clear while heat built. The table was set early. Off to one side the barbecue stood. Please at least cook the meat she'd said. I'll do the rest. Black on the outside, pink in the middle.

Only two pickers remained. Others had moved on, headed for the apple and pear orchards to the north. Robert led the way, for once awkward as he walked, probably because of the smart casual clothes he wore. He perspired above his top lip Ross noticed. Good, he's not so perfect, he thought.

The other picker was quiet. Ross watched Robert and Ellie opposite each other in their seats. Imagined their feet touching, ankles weaved together like thick strands in a tapestry. She nodded as Robert spoke, sometimes throwing her head back laughing, showing the faint veins in her curving neck. Ellie hung on to his conversation, patient as he searched for a word or in the seconds his Spanish accent lifted and fell through his conversation. Ross overcooked the meat so that it was brown and dry in the middle. Eventually a puddle of salad dressing and a few wilted lettuce leaves lay in the bottom of a bowl. A red residue dried in the bottom of the wine glasses, grubby with fingerprints and lipstick. Robert said he was a little bit drunk and returning to the caravan to nap.

"Just leave all this," Ellie said, standing. "Ross will hose it down later."

The other picker stood, thanked them and followed Robert. Ellie went inside, saying she had stained her top and was going to sleep. A post Shiraz siesta she said.

"Sure," Ross said. "Your hormones could use a rest." He waited for a reaction but she kicked off shoes and flopped onto the bed. Ross undid his belt and eased off shoes, lying with his back to her.

There wasn't the twilight found in cities that lasted all night where they lived. No light lifted from highways and shopping centres. On moonless nights a distant halo layered the sky faintly, towards the city. It was like that time she saw a shimmer of the southern lights on a holiday in Tasmania Ellie once said.

Through touch Ross realised she wasn't there. He sat up, eyes adjusting so that he could see the rumpled bedspread from where she had moved off. He stood, flicking on lights, striding through the house and checking rooms. Outside the table wasn't cleared. Chop bones lay on the ground, picked clean by crows or red ants. Down through the corridors of cherry trees Ross noticed an orange light glowing in Robert's caravan. He hurried back into the house, rummaging in a cupboard for a torch. Finally he found one, testing it against his hand so that his palm briefly shone luminous.

Outside Ross stumbled on the crevassed paths. Stones scraped underfoot. The torch beam bounced around, lighting tree trunks and catching the silvery walls of caravans. He walked so that hard stones cut bluntly into his feet. He reached Robert's door, climbing the two steps and flinging it open. Torchlight pushed into gloom, lighting the cramped kitchenette before falling on Robert. He snapped up, the sheet dropping from his chest.

"Who is it?" Robert said.

Ross kept the torch on him. Dust turned through the light.

"Pack up your shit," he said. "I'll leave your pay in the meter box. Be off my property tomorrow."

The rain didn't let up. Ross had stood daydreaming for too long under the leaks. Now he felt the cold damp of them through his collar and down his back. He returned to the house, breaking into a run. Ellie was at the window, scrubbing the greasy swirls of smoke off glass from the burnt sausages. She barely looked at him as he came inside, stomping boots on a mat.

"Hardly believe it will start being hot in a couple of months," he said. "Will be swapping a waterproof coat for sunburn cream."

Ellie smiled slightly. She scrubbed the window in uneven circles that smeared over the glass.

"I'm looking forward to harvest time again," she said. "When the pickers are around and you hear them chatting and laughing. It brings the place alive instead of all the silence we have. I hope Robert comes back this year. He never really said goodbye."

Ross looked at the reflection of Ellie's face in the glass and how it strained as she cleaned the window. She sprayed on more liquid and her face distorted under the foam. He stood next to her, looking through the part of the window that was now clean. Still the rain fell, drab and heavy, coming in at angles. He willed it to never stop until every single bud that would become a cherry was smashed off those trees.

An Aircraft Flew Over the Sun

Curtains dragged open, clacking into position. Outside a helicopter flew by, rotors trembling through window panes. Off to one side a vase wedged amongst dirty cups. Carnations tipped against the rim. They had an odour like rot, coming from water needing changing. Miraculously, I still had a sense of smell.

Fiona fed me. Leant so closely breath pooled against my cheek. I glimpsed where fair skin on her chest met brown, the way wet sand on a beach borders powdery white. I'd been unable to turn towards her as she came through the door. Couldn't smile back when she joked I was dribbling more than a teething baby. Fiona shifted on the bunched up sheets. She said the heat outside was unbearable and blackened leaves fell from a fire so far away it glowed at night like sunset.

I wasn't meant to smoke. Last week Fiona came in and shoved open a window. Heat swept in. She told me not to tell anyone. Wished I could, wished I could utter just one word. She sat on the bed and said we didn't have much time. The air conditioning police could be here in a few minutes. She lit a cigarette, drawing heavily on it herself. Then she passed it to me, easing it into my mouth. Her fingers lay along my lips. Smoke coursed into me. It tasted silky and bitter.

Fiona congratulated me for almost finishing breakfast. I'd eaten three quarters of a bowl of cereal. She wiped around my mouth. The serviette traced my laugh lines. She asked if my wife was visiting today. Would Thea read the newspaper to me? Fiona helped me into a wheelchair and angled it so I could see out to where the stretching half dead lawn stopped and bitumen started. Two weeks ago a storm broke. Dark as a nuclear winter the cleaner said. I would've rushed out into it, rain thrumming against skin. Now Fiona quickly ran a comb through my hair. It snagged on knots and I was unable to ask her to be careful.

Thea came into the room later. She bent to kiss me, exhaling a faint coffee smell. She drank coffee with too much milk and it curdled on her breath. She dragged a chair to the edge of the bed. Thea told me our daughter was going to visit on the weekend. She said rates were paid and plants watered. Perhaps I could be home in time to see leaves turned orange for autumn. Massage my back I wanted to say. Warm my skin under the friction of your fingertips. I admired the way she was still happy to touch me. Even my heart bypass scar. Before the stroke I'd asked if she preferred my incontinence pads to take her out to dinner as they seemed more alive than I was.

I often thought back over our lives. Recalled images of our suburb as if I turned the pages of a photo album. The houses all squatted with the same design. Our neighbours probably ate the same mixed grills every night, watched the same police shows and planted identical rows of flowers through our graded flat front yards. Thea and I used to walk on Sunday afternoons, our palms suctioned together. We sat outside cafes, always on the side where sun landed on her back, skin sometimes blotching pink on shoulders. Last year she said our suburb smelt like quarrels and credit card debt. That was when I felt it. Lost feeling on one side of my face. As if my bones disintegrated.

"It can be years for a stroke," I remember a doctor said. "He may not ever recover. Some do, some don't."

Kill me, I wanted to tell Thea. You know how ashes are scattered at sea? Wheel me to the edge of that cliff with the view I've always loved. Push the wheelchair to the edge. Then let me go. Anything but this half-life.

Janine did not like visiting. Even the new staff guessed she was my daughter, our faces shaped the same. She often sat, complaining how the place stunk like a hospital. Sometimes she told me about her week. Traffic becoming worse. Should be happy I stopped driving. Had I seen that television show about weight loss? It was inspiring. There was a new machine which reduced time slicing fruit. Researchers found drinking coffee improved memory.

Thea shaved me gently. One of the nurses had already done it that morning. Thea snapped they'd missed around the dimple in my chin. Little clumps of hair also protruded like wires from my nose. She found the razor in a cabinet, gliding it down cheeks before rinsing blades under jets of water. I could tell from her uneven breaths she cried. An occasional sob hunched her shoulders. I heard each one and it went straight through me.

Thea fed me and left. The food was so mashed there was no need to chew. One day they hoped to try me on solids. Probably carrots diced into overcooked pieces. Afterwards I was alone with television glaring in the muted light.

People came and went in the morning. Occasionally someone greeted me. Water in the vase changed. Dead carnations removed. A window sill wiped down. When they saw me they noticed a man needing to have sheets changed. Who had to be helped in the toilet. Someone needing to be washed. They couldn't know the other components of me. The part that used to launch myself at Thea on Sunday mornings so that our ribs slotted together like pieces of Lego. A man who built an outside sunroom that became our favourite place in winter. That person who looked at Thea so deeply during wedding vows she had to say "I do" through tears. They lifted me carefully from the bed and eased me into a wheelchair. I looked down at toe nails flaking away.

Fiona arrived after breakfast. She nestled a hand over my arm and smiled. Her warm skin radiated into mine. She said some of the residents would go on an outing today. Would I like to go? I answered, transmitting it to her as if by telepathy. Of course, I would love to, anything to leave this room. Take me to a public toilet, a war zone, jail or a sewerage treatment plant, as long as I can escape this place. Perhaps she recognised my face flinch. Her hand lifted off me. She said Thea could come along. Fiona would also take care of me.

They wheeled us into a mini bus. The wheelchair was locked into place. Thea sat next to me, her fingers twined around my arm. A driver climbed on and called back, asking how we all were. A couple of voices answered from behind us. Fiona stood at the front. She said we were visiting the beach. We should all smell the sea and enjoy a little sun. She added we weren't allowed to do belly flops or start racing on jet skis. She laughed at her joke and sat down.

Thea and I used to visit these beaches. Water rolled in with crests and troughs shaped like ploughed land. We lay on beach towels with colours washed out. We leapt from the pier, water fizzing around us from our clumsy dives. Some days we walked, kicking through shallows and sitting on warm rocks. At times we were caught in slashing rain pocking sand like lines of acne scars. All our decisions were made in view of the sea. The decision to have a child, buy our house, drive through Spain and return to university.

Now beaches skimmed past the bus window, knots of people here and there, oil tankers out to sea and occasional palls of smoke from park barbecues. Eventually we stopped in a car park at the end of a pier. The door slid open and I smelt brine. They wheeled me out onto a platform that lowered me to the road. Fiona moved in behind me and eased the wheelchair forward. Thea asked if she could wheel me and took her place. Her hands briefly rested on my shoulders. I knew they were Thea's, her palms and loose skin briefly on the hard edges of my joints. The wheelchair bumped along the pier. Blood stains from cut up fish shadowed sections of the ground. Behind me broken pieces of conversations from the others drifted past.

"I want to dive in," I tried to say. Behind me Thea couldn't see my attempt to pronounce the words. Wondered if she may have felt their intensity as they blew back onto her. If she felt them as certain as my hands on her. They may have gone to her as a current in the sea breeze or arrived so quietly it was as if she thought of them herself. But she kept talking softly, at times bending down to me so her breath rushed warmly over my skin.

"Remember how hot the car was when we would go back to it?" she said. "There was so much sand on the floor you said let's go beach combing where the brake and accelerator are."

We reached the end of the pier. Fiona and the others had dropped back. Thea pushed me right to the edge so that I could feel cool ebbing off the grey waters. I sensed her half turn, looking back the way we'd come. I held my breath so that salt and breeze stilled in my lungs. Then I went to lunge forward, closing eyes so that it was briefly dark as if an aircraft flew over the sun. I would tumble turn, dropping to water slapping into the pier. I surged so hard it was as if my soul left me, ripping away and out towards white ribbed sea. As I opened eyes I was still wedged in the chair. Maybe something of me had broken free, like spittle or a breath, whisking away over light brown sands and the half circles left by high tide. Thea started turning the wheelchair around. Along the pier I saw Fiona, distracted and gazing towards seagulls wheeling down to the sea. I hadn't been able to take my own life. And now they led me away, as if it was still a beautiful day and it'd been wonderful at the beach. All my face would let me do was cry silently. By the time we reached the bus Thea said the wind must've made my eyes water. Then Fiona flicked a switch and they stood back watching as the platform shuddered slightly before lifting me up into the bus.

Dead Star

You step down from the bus. Thick air heaves. Heatwaves wrinkle behind rushing semi-trailers hauling pine logs. You barely recognise the road now. During childhood it'd been one lane north, hair pin bends and car sickness. And glimpses of ocean. Water crinkled blue from a side window smudged with sketches drawn by your fingertips through condensation. Now holiday apartments line the road, windows dark tinted like port swirled in a glass.

You queue three people back from a cash drawer tinkling open and slamming shut. Ahead you glimpse a man taking orders, turning towards a kitchen, pressing post it notes to a window. You order an espresso and gulp its heat. The bus driver speculates how long it'll take Cyclone Deborah to make landfall. That at night high beams bobbing the other way could have a UV rating.

The bus drops you. Somewhere past shredded banana palms and pineapple plantations. Opposite a silky dirt road meandering towards sand dunes. You can't see water but smell mangroves, the way you used to as a six year old when your father roused you from sleep, announcing the fish are biting and you're old enough to dress yourself. Now you imagine tourists in those fishing spots, stroking through tepid waters during box jellyfish season.

Your father drove you up here with the rest of the family once. He kept to the speed limit all the way to the Gold Coast in between taking his eyes off the road and telling you to shut the hell up. You'd been complaining about how far to go. He stopped so you could eat a burger and empty your bladder. He drove through a town with a war memorial listing names in metallic paint. Four surnames the same. You wonder how much of that town all these years later you'd remember. Would memories flood back to you, even though the town could be gone, the way light from a dead star can still be seen?

He pulls up as you begin thinking he won't come. Veers off the road where you wait, gravel skidding and chipping by. He's slow out of the car, straining his body so you know he has a bad back or hip. The same problems you'll most likely suffer if it's true what they say about inheriting genes. He shakes your hand. The skin in his palms is calloused as if dead. You glimpse it yellowed and creased as he picks at nails while asking how you've been. Hands gnarled, as if stricken with arthritis. Same hands that used to gut the silvery bream caught off the pier, tossing intestines towards sea gulls circling the way they do over garbage tips. For a second you wish he'd hug you, his ribs probably like blunt knives through your shirt.

Your father drives down an old miner's road, narrow enough for branches to scrape sides of the car. At times the car whooshes through shallow creeks at the bottom of hills. You pass those mangroves and their deep brown mud, recalling losing your size four shoes when attempting to cross them, their peculiar sucking noise when dragging your leg out that years later reminds the sound of tongue kissing.

The house is a Queenslander, up on stilts, elevating into humidity and mosquitoes wisping around an outside light. Haul your backpack out of the boot. Insects shrill from trees trembling veined leaves. He asks if you're hungry but walks ahead as if your answer doesn't matter. On his fridge a shopping list hangs, precise handwriting like embroidery.

"You should see the stars," he says. "Too much light pollution in the city. Out here they're incredible. You know looking at them is seeing into the past, right?"

You nod and stare outside. Gloom gathers but you make out the house lies in a valley, as if a glacier carved its way through ten thousand years ago. He grinds at a can opener, pausing and shaking his hand, inspecting fingers.

"Cut off me circulation," he says. "Can you finish it?" You take the half opened can, reinserting the opener, turning the stubborn handle so the tin spins slowly in your hand. As the top buckles you smell watered down tomato sauce and broiled sausages.

"How many chef hat awards for this?" you ask.

Your father takes the can, reading the label. Then he tips it into a saucepan. He says two more should be enough and if you wouldn't mind opening those as well. Gas flicks on and in a few minutes the saucepan sizzles. Cooking smells push through whiffs of rain. Your father says it's falling two valleys away.

He spoons the meal into two bowls. You see they used to be patterned but now only faint colour blurs where a picture used to be. Your father eats quickly, sauce spotting his chin.

"She still waiting on a grandkid?" he says. "So long since I've seen her. Not sure I'd pick her face in a line up. Barely remember being married to her. The way your life falls into a lot of small memories. Being bashed at school, failing university, first car accident, getting married."

You ask why they stayed together as long as they did. Remaining in a marriage the way people keep living in earthquake zones. Hoping for the best even though every plunging temperature, every once in a century high tide or relentless burning drought could start the earth reeling. You recall that day sitting in memory so vividly it's like touching scar tissue with its scratchy pain and knotted surface. A day that made you forever hate August in Melbourne. Winds swelling, parched and weighted with dust and pollen. Surging through streets, tumbling rubbish. Skies bitumen grey. Light so weak it belonged in a different hemisphere. His two backhanders that afternoon. First you. Then your mother.

Your father looks up from a chunk of bread wiped around a bowl. Lights a cigarette soon as his meal finishes, flicking ash into a coffee cup. Sizzles when he drops the butt in. He asks about your mother.

"Roast with her on Sundays," you say. "Sprinkle of rosemary and pink salt rubbed into meat. Hour thirty at 180 degrees. Ice cream and tinned peaches afterwards." He nods. Tells you she'd hate it up here anyway. Too many snakes. Humidity so thick you need gills to breathe. Further north you travel the bigger everything becomes. Bugs, spiders, hats, thirsts and loneliness.

"I used to want her back you know. Move up here. But not the version that I left. I mean the earlier her. The person singing at Kiss concerts. Who read headlines out loud because she thought you had to know. That made coffee leaving you sleepless for three days. Where's that person?"

"She left at the end of your fist," you say.

Your family holidays always lay to the north. By Port Macquarie he'd be saying we should move up here, find a view of Flynn's Beach, watch the jellyfish rearing up through waves, dangle a handline off the wharf. Bring home a couple of undersize flathead. Your parents argued until Nambucca Heads. Your head burrowed under sheets, blankets, pillows and whatever else they gave you to sleep. When silence returned you stretched out, looking up through the rear window, stars visible but their twinkle lost behind mottled patterns left by dust and dew.

"Maybe one of them is a star called Sirius," he said once, voice thin and alone. "Takes four years for its light to reach us you know."

He drops you at the bus depot. Watches you boarding, trailing behind a family trying to decide where to sit. As the bus lumbers away he faces you, half waving. When the bus U-turns you glimpse stars, faint through windows, turning slightly as if in a kaleidoscope. You wonder how old their light really is and if might have first shone before all this.

King of the World

He had brown teeth. It almost made me feel sorry for him. Espresso dregs, cask red wine, cheap sugary chocolate or cigarettes smoked down to fingers probably to blame. He smiled the same way at everyone who came through the door. I sauntered down the first aisle. Slipped hands into pockets, flexing fingers to keep them nimble. It was all newspapers and magazines. Nicole Kidman and the Duchess of somewhere smiled from the racks. I glanced up to him grinning at a customer. Coins tinkled. I u-turned into the next aisle.

The chip bags were too large to steal. I picked up a chocolate bar, dropping its weight into my pocket. The next one had caramel centres. Tucked it in beside the other. As soon as the shop assistant's eyes went to the cash register, I picked up the strawberry centres. He looked in my direction, still smiling but no longer like he meant it. I strolled to the top of the aisle.

"You don't have any of those chocolate truffles?" I asked. He shook his head.

"No. Sorry. Only what is there."

"Never mind," I said. I walked out, hand squeezed in with the chocolate bars, steadying them from falling out.

A warm breeze threaded through the car park. A car pulled in, handbrake dragged on. Behind me the shop's automatic door rolled open and steps clicked out. I started peeling back foil.

"Not bad," someone said behind me. Before I looked around I heard his breath, deep and slow next to me. "It's all in the timing isn't it? Wait for them to be with a customer, then make your move. Of course you'll be on their CCTV. So you can't go back. Unless you grow a beard. Dye your hair maybe. Although you'd have to go back to steal the hair colour wouldn't you?"

I tried to walk ahead but he drew level with me. I stopped suddenly so that he slightly overtook me.

"Are you a security guard?" I said.

He pushed out his bottom lip as if thinking about it.

"I never went into that profession. Personally I don't like jobs where you have to wear a uniform."

We took window seats. They looked out onto the street. Cars passed soundlessly behind glass. He tore the corner of a packet of sugar, pouring it into coffee. I never went into cafes. I was so out of my depth I watched him to copy how to pick up a latte using a serviette.

"Bruek," was his next word to me. I thought it was a greeting in Dutch until he said it was his name. He explained he watched me the whole time. Knew which pocket I hid the chocolate bars in. What flavours I chose. The headlines I paused to read. How my jaw grinded when I picked up the chocolate. Now he was asking what I thought of his offer.

"Look at it like a promotion," he said. "Today you're stealing chocolates. Tomorrow you're delivering packages and being paid. The day after you aren't going to worry about governments wanting you to work until you're seventy or putting up your university fees." He reached into his back pocket, taking out a wallet. It flipped open. I glimpsed a picture of a woman, smiling so that she could've been laughing. Two smaller pictures of children positioned side by side with it. "I'm so sure of you, I'll give you this." Bruek folded a fifty dollar note, tucking it into the palm of my hand. He wrote a telephone number on a serviette, pushing it across the table. "That's where you'll find me."

It was easy. Every morning I walked down a laneway. Bluestone pavers cobbled ground. Sometimes dogs stuck snouts under gates, snarling as I passed. Bruek met me at a rear fence. The first time I greeted him I asked how he was. From his face I realised it wasn't a time for small talk. As far as I could tell the package he handed over was nothing more than newspapers rolled up and tied together. I took a tram across suburbs. Those suburbs changed from wall to wall houses with occasional spindly trees into sweeping front yards with vivid bursts of petunias. I left the tram at the bottom of a hill. By the time I reached the top it was as if my lungs weren't large enough to hold the amount of air I needed to breathe. From there it was always the same. I walked through the front gate that shuddered like a stutter in speech. Headed down the rounded pathway beside garden beds topped with mulch. Left the package on the porch, concealed behind a wall. Sometimes I lingered, wondering who might be inside. Even listened for the treading of footsteps towards the door. At times I sensed someone behind curtains, shifting slightly. Then I left, descending the hill. Oncoming trucks whipped hot bursts of wind over me.

I did that for months. Through the heat of late summer. Autumn came, laneway buried under drifts of leaves shaped like children's hands. Each morning Bruek was there, face deadpan, handing over the package.

"Ring me when you've finished," he said one morning. "Will meet you at the cafe." He shoved the package into my hands and swung away.

I had money now. Ate take-away and owned new t-shirts. Sometimes I called into a beer garden, drinking pints and feeding salt and vinegar chips to the sparrows. I'd even been into cafes on my own. When Bruek sat opposite me I ordered his coffee for him.

"Look at you," he said. "Six months ago you had to eat your own skin flakes for protein. Now you're the king of the world." I dipped my spoon into the coffee, lifting out froth and sucking it off.

Bruek asked how I'd come to live the way I did. Told him my father used to move around the house always looking like he'd received terrible news. Whether I scored an A in English or been caught removing screws from a school desk, his reaction was the same. My mother lay on the couch after dinner, sometimes dragging off a bra from under her blouse, slapping it over the arm of a chair, leaving it to dangle there. She sighed with relief as it came away. She only spoke to tell me to clean up or bring her headache tablets. If a week went by and I wasn't on the end of a drunken beating I could convince myself life was normal. But it never lasted. Months later I wondered if they noticed I'd left home.

Bruek said it was time for the next stage. Think of it as another promotion he explained. More responsibility but extra money. He added I'd proved myself, especially by never asking what was in the packages. He asked me to meet him outside the cafe at 9 PM.

I'd heard it was the warmest May ever. If I'd been visiting from another country I would've thought it was spring. I stood next to the cafe but away from the security cameras as Bruek instructed. Eventually a car pulled up beside me.

The window slid down. Slightly illuminated by dashboard lights Bruek grinned at me.

"I've come for the king," he said. I climbed in, the car's warmth layering my skin. We drove through the city. People queued outside nightclubs. "That's your next life," Bruek said. "Out of shoplifting into the VIP lounge. Except you won't be waiting in line only to be told there's too many males inside already or your pants are too casual. It'll be welcome with your hand shaken. Have a seat at the front. What can we get you to drink? On the house of course. I'm taking you the short route to that life."

Slightly out of the city we parked in a street so long and dark I couldn't see where it ended. I followed Bruek out. We passed doorways to abandoned warehouses.

"I'm going to show you what I need you to be able to do," Bruek said. He was grim, looking left and right, rubbing hands together. It made a sound as if a generator was running. I spotted a man reclined against a wall smoking a few doors down from us. His cigarette smelt putrid, as if a roll your own made of chop-chop and weed killer. Bruek deftly unbuttoned his shirt. He shouldered out of it, passing it to me. There was a whiff of musty aftershave from the material. The smoker barely had time to take a second drag. Bruek swung a punch that blurred through air. I heard it thud dully, tipping the cigarette from his mouth. Embers lifted from the ground as cigarette ash broke against pavement. He gasped, tipping forward.

"That's how you do it," Bruek said. "Hit him on the right hand side of his body. About three quarters of the way down. Just here." Bruek pointed to a spot on him. "That's where his liver is. A solid hook into there can find it. Make it short and fast. Your opponent will often twist away to avoid you but end up exposing the spot, making it easier to hit. Or they don't protect their head, giving you another target there." He tapped fingers on my arm as if checking whether I was hollow. "Shirt please," he said. I handed it back and he pushed into it.

"Why do you take your shirt off?" I asked.

He shrugged.

"In case they cough up blood. Or throw up."

I looked at the man crumpled on the ground, trying to hoist himself up on a hand, then falling spread eagled.

"Watch," Bruek said. "Aim for the same area. If you have any luck he'll be an alcoholic so the grog would've already done some damage to his liver. Given you a head start so to speak." He took a measured step back, balancing, then launching into a kick. His victim grunted and started groaning.

"Please," he said from the ground and it came out like a sob.

"Go on. You do it," Bruek said. He moved back to give me space. I watched the man grovelling on the ground. He crawled a short distance away from us. Bruek rubbed hands together, cupping, then blowing into them. He glanced up and down the street.

"You won't kill him. But you have to feel like you want to. Bonus points if you crack a rib. Put everything into it."

"Please mate, I'm homeless," the man said. I hovered there, watching him curl up to protect himself. At first I wasn't sure. I had no argument with him. All he did to me was give off a terrible smell. But it was exhilarating too. There was this power I'd never experienced. The man started pleading again and I lashed into him, kicking him so hard he rolled over. He gripped his stomach. I kicked him again, this time in the back; the sound could've been the low note on a bass drum. He was crying and it made me angry. Adrenalin surged hotly through me. Bruek's hand clamped over my arm.

"Enough," he said quietly. His voice soothed me, helping my heart fall into a slower rhythm. Bruek stared at me, ignoring the barely moving body. His hand lightly patted my back. He led me away.

The bar was packed. Bruek set two beers in front of us. Foam trailed down condensation on my glass. I drank, wiping the back of my arm across my mouth when I set the glass down.

"The spoils of a consumer society," Bruek said. He raised his glass towards me. "You've made the leap from the have nots to the haves." He drank his beer quickly. In the glass liquid lifted and fell in time with his gulps. When he set it down his eyes roamed the room. Now and then they paused as he lingered on something. "Going to the crapper," he said, standing. "Will bring back another beer."

I lounged back. The place was loud with end of working week revelry. I had no idea what working must be like. Perhaps people left their desks, loosened a couple of buttons and walked a block or two to celebrate their lives being their own for the next two days. A couple of people asked me if the seat where Bruek sat was free and I shook my head.

"I saw you looking," she said. She sat down opposite me. I glanced around, half expecting to see Bruek returning from the bar. I told her I hadn't been looking but couldn't help it now. Tattoos swirled down from her neck. In the light I couldn't make out what the shapes were. She lay her arm next to mine. "You're a blank canvas," she said. "I'd like to write '*Audacia*' there. That's Latin for courage."

I would've asked what made her think that was relevant to me. But instead I asked whether those tattoos had hurt. Right then Bruek arrived, setting down a beer in front of me and a wine next to her.

"You'd like something dry?" he said to her before winking at me. "From the Barossa Valley? With a hint of peach aromas? Am I right?" He laughed. She smiled up at him then at me. "I'm going," Bruek said. "Stock market is like a friend you can't trust. You have to keep checking it. Make sure it hasn't been up to anything." He told me he'd be in touch and left us.

She told me her name was Sienna. She slipped fingers around the stem of the glass. I braced myself for the questions a couple of friends I used to have warned me about. Questions about what I did, was this a place I came to often, was I with anyone at the moment.

Even in the morning I couldn't take my eyes off her. Her tattoos flexed. Roses and birds lay along her chest. There was a heart drawn so it appeared to quiver. Butterflies with patterned wings trailed her stomach.

"You've looked at my secrets," she said. "Tell me one about you."

There was the obvious me. Struggles with conversation. My hair uneven from hacking it shorter myself. Silvery scars under arms where I once self-harmed. But I only had one real secret. I'd never spoken of it. Yet with Sienna I told her. She weaved her arms and legs around me so that she must have felt my quiet voice pressing through her.

"I once went home from a hotel with a woman who worked in a shop near where I lived. I stayed the night with her. Months later I went to the shop and could see she was having a baby. Left before she saw me. Was it mine? Maybe.

After that if I needed to buy something, I went long distances so I didn't have to go into that shop. One lunch time I saw her in a park. She was pushing a pram. You should've seen the way she looked at that baby. So much love. That really defined love for me. I'd never felt it or seen it before. But seeing her showed me what it was like. Started going to that park. Every day. Just to watch. Always staying out of sight. Kept it up for about three weeks. Then one day she wasn't there anymore. I kept going. Even went past the shop. But never saw her again."

Later Sienna slept. Her eyelids twitched and I wondered if they were giving off a Morse code that explained her dreams.

The cafe stayed open late on Saturdays. Light resembling what flicks on inside a fridge came in from the street. We sat as usual by the window. Soft rain fell, angling through headlights. Bruek paid me. At first I thought he'd given me too much.

"Works out to about thirty dollars a kick you gave that guy," he said. "If you care about the maths." I stuffed the cash into a pocket as the coffees came.

"When was the last time you were happy?" Bruek asked. "I mean really happy." I thought about it. Almost had my life flashing by my eyes, the way people describe what it's like before you drown. Told him there was that time my father lit me a cigarette when I was about eight years old. He'd laughed, throwing his head back when I started coughing. But I was happy he'd given me his attention for once. Also remembered being happy when I stole for the first time. It was a half loaf of bread. A few minutes down the road realised I needed butter too. Hid the bread inside someone's hedge before returning and stealing two tubs of unsalted butter. Was proud of my two crimes in five minutes.

"Sometimes I envy the people you see walking around," he said. "They don't expect anything of life. Just go off to work and feel numb from the shoulders up. Receive a modest pay and live a modest life. They aspire for nothing more than a nice car and stained floor boards."

Bruek tipped sugar into his coffee. He said debt collection was my new responsibility. He explained not everyone paid on time and some did not pay at all. He visited those people. Sometimes to collect money, at other times to remind someone to pay. He told me it's how you remind them. Tone of voice and use of eyes usually more effective than fists. He said he was always polite, unless they behaved badly. I just needed to go with him.

"Two people make the point better," he said.

"What are they paying you for?" I asked. Bruek glanced around the cafe.

"That's your next promotion," he said.

Sienna had large Latin letters tattooed across her back. The letters were jet black and in medieval writing. I don't remember what they meant. Probably something about resilience or strength. When she was under me I could watch the words moving and straining, like newspaper headlines bobbing and contorting in moving waters. After two weeks together I was scratched, bruised and the serrated line of her bite bruising over my collarbone.

It was straightforward. We arrived at houses during the time between people finishing dinner and going to bed. We walked down front paths and stood away from peepholes. Porch lights flickered on over us. Sometimes money was fumbled towards us, the person speaking in a low, humiliated voice so others inside wouldn't hear. At other times they stood stunned and quiet, barely making eye contact.

"I enjoyed our visit," Bruek always said at the end. There was no mistaking the threat in his voice. They stood in doorways as television voices droned from somewhere behind them. "Who is it?" someone called out from other rooms at times.

Within a few months I had a car. It was about seven years old but I polished it and blackened tyres. Bruek found me a place to live and I moved in with two others. We hardly saw each other. I assumed they were working for Bruek too. A few days later at the cafe Bruek said his dream was to live in Paris. He said he wasn't suited to the sport and celebrity worshipping culture of Australia. Feeling like you were really French but stuck in Australia must be something like those people who say they are a man trapped in a woman's body he said.

"Do you have to stand by the window without any clothes on?" I asked Sienna in her house. "What's out there to look at anyway? It's darker than being locked in a cupboard."

Sienna crossed the room towards me. She pulled back the sheet, shimmying herself down into the depths of the bed. I leaned over her and kissed her, slowly at first until I lay on her and felt the hollow down the centre of her chest.

"Shit! Let me go!" I cried out and jolted my body away from her. Sienna released her legs around me. They dangled mid-air like a Praying Mantis ready to strike. I collapsed across her before bracing hands either side of her shoulders and lifting myself off. "Not so tight. Are you trying to kill me? There's no point, you're not in my will."

"Maybe you should start doing push ups or weights," she said.

Sienna propped on an elbow, looking at me curiously. It could have been the same look I sometimes had when studying a fly manically spinning circles after spraying it.

The next day I rang Bruek as I always did to check if there was a job and what time to be ready. He gave me a much earlier time. I dawdled through the afternoon, watching television and snooping around in the other's rooms.

I watched out the window for him closer to the time. Almost to the second he pulled up outside, motor idling in the quiet street. I hurried out, sliding in next to him. He gestured towards the smoky distance, saying suburbs were one of the worst inventions of the human race. He asked me to imagine what an archaeologist might dig up around here in a few hundred years. They might uncover a television. They could find antique furniture. Probably a rusted out computer. He said they'd find items that demonstrated how superficial we were and how we filled our lives with rubbish.

Bruek eased the car away from the kerb, accelerating so that I sunk into the seat. We drove as it became dusk, street lights indistinct in fog. Lights floated by the window like distress flares. Bruek turned up the radio, turning the dial to keep the signal as we left suburbs. I asked where we were going. He said he didn't know the name of the area, only the direction there. He said our destination wasn't a place that deserved naming anyway. Eventually we turned off the main road, nosing along a narrow track where headlights lit the trunks of low growing gum trees. Then he turned again, this time the car bumped onto a dirt road. Bruek dimmed the lights and we drove slowly. His face was close to the windscreen concentrating, breath misting glass. He switched the lights off completely.

"Nearly there," he said. "Why would anyone stay out here? It'd be as remote as living in a space station."

In the gloom I saw the outline of a house. Yellow light shone from behind one window. Bruek turned into the property, easing the car over uneven ground. We bumped up and down before stopping. He turned off the interior light and opened the door.

"Usual routine," he said. "Just a house call. Who knows, we might all end up sitting around smoking cigars and drinking port."

I tailed him through grass, long and sharp so that its edges sawed against hands. We paused behind a tree before easing forward. Then we slowly climbed steps, settling our weight carefully on each so timber didn't creak.

He signalled me to one side of the door and knocked. We heard steps. They took a long time to reach the door. It opened slightly. Bruek leaned into the space.

I was at the wrong angle to see what happened. I heard something and he reeled back, holding his head. Between his hands blood trickled through. Someone followed him out. They took a single, wide step towards Bruek and he fell. I stood so still it was as if I had no breath or heartbeat. The man turned towards me, hesitating, before running back into the house.

"Jesus, quick!" Bruek said, standing with a hand out for balance. "He'll have gone to get a gun. Or something. Get back to the car."

I ran to the car. A heated friction of breeze streamed along my face. Bruek stumbled, veering away and straightening back. He held his head. Torchlight from behind us flashed through the trees, swinging, sliding, illuminating tree trunks before finding then losing us.

"You drive!" Bruek said. "See if you can get that much right."

We drove off. Stones flinted under the car. The torchlight found us, turning the inside briefly silver. Bruek pressed a fistful of tissues to his head. Long grass swished down the side of the car. We lurched onto road and the car surged forward.

"Are you okay?" I asked. Bruek dabbed at his forehead.

"You'd better hope I don't need any kind of a transplant because you'll be the donor. You fucked up. Unbelievable. You just stood there. He hit me with something so fast I didn't have time to see it. And you didn't move as if you were waiting for a bus." Bruek yanked another tissue from the box. "How bad is it?" he said, facing me.

The wound needed stitches. It lay open like a gill in the side of a fish.

"It isn't bad," I said. But something gave it away, my eyes, how I spoke, maybe the way my shoulders slumped. Bruek turned from me, folding down the visor and gazing into a mirror behind it.

"Drive to Sienna's," he said. "I'm not going to have some medical student practicing on me in an emergency department. You'll have to do it."

"What?" I said. "How come you know Sienna's place?" But he only spoke to tell me where to turn next. Eventually I recognised the road and we continued in silence. Bruek rang ahead. I recognised Sienna's voice, small but still velvet on his phone. We parked outside her unit. Dull light shone behind curtains. She was at the door before we reached it.

"Squizzy Taylor over here stuffed things up," Bruek said. "And he's no Sherlock Holmes either. Hasn't even worked out how I know you. I'm going to need him to do some surgery. Can you swab me and give him the needle and thread?"

Sienna whisked away. She was quickly back, dunking cotton wool in warm water and sponging blood off Bruek's face. She passed me a needle and thread.

"Don't muck this up," he said. "I don't want to be reminded of you every time I see a scar in the mirror."

I pinched my fingers around the needle. The end of it trembled.

"I can't," I said. "I couldn't even replace a button on a shirt."

Sienna reached across me, taking the needle. Her hands were controlled and still. Bruek tilted his head back. She hunched over him, backs of hands obscuring her work.

"Were you a nurse?" I said after a few moments, trying to break the silence. She ignored me. Finally she drew back.

"You're really going to look like a gangster now," Sienna said. Bruek touched a fingertip to the scar. "You should have antibiotics you know. Maybe you were hit with a used toilet brush." She smiled. Bruek stood, walking to a microwave oven, studying his reflection in the door.

"Perfect," he said. "You could have a career remodelling people's faces so they can change identities." He glanced at me. "Don't worry. I wasn't going to let you do it. Only wanted to see if you were prepared to. Looks like you failed that test too." He stood, crossing to a window and peering out. "Looks safe to go. No one hanging around." He told me to make my own way home. Sienna walked with him to the front door. I heard them talking, voices hushed and monotone. She came down the hallway, stopping at the table to clean up tissues and stray pieces of thread.

I asked how she knew him. Through her top I saw the letters, towering on her skin. Told her it seemed strange he knew what drink to buy her in the bar that night but I thought it was only a good guess. Stood so close behind her saw the tight curling wisps of hair down her neck.

"Would a little angry sex make you feel better?" Sienna asked. She unbuttoned her top with one hand, spaces to her skin springing open one at a time. She lay slightly against a wall, shoulder balanced across it as precisely as the arms on a set of scales. Her tattoos moved as if independent of her.

I stood from the bed, approaching her slowly. I can cross examine her later I thought. Sienna barely smiled. I stood over her, bracing an arm against the wall either side of her head. Then I lowered through the heaviness of her breath, the softness of her heat and how her perfume tasted as I inhaled it. She watched me evenly.

Sienna's weight changed as she tilted to one side. Her hands cupped my shoulders and her knee vaulted up, crunching into me. The pain was instant. I collapsed, falling from her and across floorboards. I jammed into a ball, sliding a hand between legs, gripping myself as if squeezing out pain. Sienna stepped in front of me, positioning feet in front of my face. I whimpered. Her toes were close enough to see the diamontes glued onto her nail polish.

"Why'd you do that?" I eventually said, my face bunched.

"Get out," she said, taking a step back. She brushed her body down with hands, as if flicking pieces of me off her. "He said I should hurt you before you left. That you deserved it. He had such hopes for you. You were going to be the next ...what's it matter now? In the end you'd be better off going back to shoplifting or Centrelink. All the things he gave you are gone. You don't have a house to stay in any longer. He won't ring you with jobs. And don't ever come here again."

I slowly dressed, straightening clothes that now felt clammy on me. Sienna sat on the bed and pulled a pillow across her chest. I walked to her bathroom, sliding my toothbrush down into a back pocket. Tucked a small bottle of aftershave in next to it. In her mirror spotted with soap I still had the same innocent, bland expression Bruek once told me meant I could get away with murder.

The Gift

An aftertaste of bushfire smoke salted rain. I opened my mouth. Rain tingled, pocking lightly on my tongue. I stopped at the rear of a crowd waiting to cross the road. In front of me a man draped his arm around the shoulder of a woman. I felt an arm land on me lightly, knot of elbow pressing below a shoulder. I inhaled deeply, filling lungs with humid air. The arm lifted slightly, settling again as I breathed out. Across the road drizzle swirled, billowing like sheets straining from pegs on a clothes line.

My brother lived in the northern suburbs. It was hotter there, as if I'd crossed the Tropic of Capricorn rather than Bell Street. The tram's rolling sound had a soothing rhythm, slowing my heart and thoughts. I stopped in a park, leaves sparking silver in glare. People reclined under trees. I sat, shadows jittering in breeze. Not far away a man reclined in someone's lap. Fingers glided through his hair. I felt each stroke, every trailing fingertip.

My brother's front garden barely clung to life in the heat. Mine was meticulous. Right down to planting to the phases of the moon. I'd added lime to soil the way some people sprinkled truffle salt into pasta. Crushed aphids between thumb and fingers, forming a sticky paste of wings and bodies. Mulch tucked in like bedspreads around the trunks of trees.

Janice met me at the door. She placed hands on my shoulders when she kissed me. Her fingers found gaps between bones the way a masseur finds sore spots. She kissed each cheek, so slight it was like breath. I followed her inside. My brother's heavy steps approached from the sunroom. He often dozed in there, snoring like drowning.

"You made it," he said. "Must feel like we're so far away it's a different time zone."

Janice sat opposite. I liked her. Probably too much. I wondered if she knew. Had any intuition about me surfaced through her mortgage struggles, near separations and dull evenings in front of reality TV? Truth was I only stared at her when she wouldn't notice. When she gazed out a window, read a magazine or slowly stirred gnocchi through bubbling water. The last time I visited I'd heard her play violin. Her wavering music eased from the room like light under a door. It was the music of yearning. Wanting to be somewhere else. Music pacing alcoves and hallways. When it stopped the last note hummed, hanging in mid-air as softly as a word spoken in love. It was like her own voice she explained once. She stroked the violin at the time, studying its neck. She said it was as if the music came from her vocal chords, that she was singing every note.

My tea still had the bag in it. I jiggled it, thin string over the join in my finger where fishing line often went.

"We'll snap freeze that tea bag when you're finished," my brother said. "Money has been classified as an endangered species here. Save it for next time."

Janice smiled but so emptily it may as well have been drawn on. She asked what I'd been up to.

"Cleaned out the shed," I said. "Found some of Dad's old stuff. A crowbar that if pushed into ground would come out in China. So many dead spiders they must've turned cannibal during a famine."

Janice watched me. I wanted my brother to leave the room. Just long enough to lean over and kiss his wife. Feel the heat coming off her face as we propped together. Be stroked by the tip of her nose, her smooth cheeks. Then watch her draw back reluctantly and see if she again put on that bland smile when he returned.

"Have you had any…you know. Episodes?" he said.

"One or two," I said.

He grinned. You had to know him to recognize the sneer in it.

"You don't know do you?" my brother said to Janice. "He has this problem. Although our mother told him it was a gift. In the same breath she said to him never talk about it. That he'd have a lifetime of people telling him to get help if he did. Everyone saying see a psychiatrist. What's it called again?"

"Synaesthesia."

'That's it! Sounds like a sinus condition. Go on. Tell her. What is it?'

I looked at Janice. I couldn't tell if her gaze was sorrow or love. Her eyes roamed over my face. She said I didn't have to talk about anything I didn't want to.

"When I see people touch I feel it," I said. "A hand shake. Slap on the back. Kiss. I just feel it. Heightened senses or something."

"Imagine that," my brother said. "If you stabbed me right now he'd feel it. No blood or stitches. But the pain."

Janice gazed at me.

"What I want to know," my brother said. "How come I never received this ability? I mean, I can build a letterbox. Put up a picture. Why didn't I inherit anything besides hair growing out of my ears and dislocating knees?"

I sipped my tea. The teabag label tickled a cheek so I pinched it out, squeezing at the top of the cup. I lowered it sodden and crumpled to the saucer.

My brother reached over, gathering Janice's hand into his. His face exerted as he squeezed it hard. Janice winced, snatching her hand away.

"Feel that?" he said. "Maybe next time you visit your hand will be bandaged." Janice examined her fingers. Colour returned to where they'd turned bloodless. "What about this?" He stood. The fatty tissue of his chest drooped through a t-shirt. He placed hands either side of her face, roughly angling her up to him. Then he kissed her messily, exaggerating his movements so that her head tilted and strained involuntarily under him. He pulled away, staring triumphantly at her. Janice wiped the back of a hand across her mouth.

"She's a great kisser. Then again, you'd know."

I stared at him. Janice reached across the table, seizing my tea. For an instant I thought she'd throw it over him. But she drank deeply, probably rinsing away his taste.

"How would I know?"

My brother winked at me.

"Can't you feel these things? Isn't that your gift? Unless of course you've cornered her when I didn't know. But you're not the type. You're like a voyeur. Except you experience everything in 3D."

I thanked them for the tea. Said I should be leaving. Finish cleaning out the shed. Digging through the rubbish in there was like archaeology.

"Is that why you never did anything with your life?" My brother said. "You didn't need your own experiences because you took them from other people?"

They trailed me to the front door. He said we didn't need to shake hands. He could join his so I'd feel like we had anyway. Janice opened the door. A strap on her top fell away, dangling in a loop down her arm. Had I known she loved me I would've gently threaded it back into place, smoothing it over the undulations of her shoulder. Instead I turned and left them.

I walked towards the tram stop. A passing car thumped through a pothole. I looked around for couples, languishing in shade on verandas, touching with fingertips, talking so softly and closely that their words landed gently on each other. I searched them out so I could feel what they did. But there was no one. I pressed on, feeling nothing but dripping humidity and the dread of arriving home.

The Photographer

It's difficult to say when it started. Perhaps between the third and fourth coffee that Friday morning. It could've been as I rasped the broom around ceiling corners where cobwebs swirled and bent in draughts. I may have felt it lying bare backed on floorboards trying to cool down. I started counting the seconds between. Lightly touched the tip of each finger in time with whispering numbers. It was four. Sometimes it seemed longer and I became nervous, as if waiting for a heartbeat that wouldn't come. I went out into heat, blistering like I'd brushed a hot surface. Around me the streets remained still except for the twitching in my corner vision every four seconds.

"I had these... I don't know how to describe it. Ticks I suppose. Like a nerve jumping," I said to Lindy. She looked up from dinner. She asked what I meant. I shrugged. Her gaze stayed on me for a second. She turned pasta through her fork. Lindy said it was probably nothing.

"Could we take down some of those photographs?" she said. Lindy looked past me towards where they hung. "It's not that I don't like them. It'd be nice to have different pictures. Paintings even."

I left the meal half finished. I might return to it later when the food was cold and clammy. For months every meal was like that anyway. I stood from the table.

"You know how important those pictures are to me. They reveal more of me than if you put up my x-rays."

Down our hallway the pictures hung in a straight line even though one or two tilted at times. I often tucked a finger to a corner, straightening them. Lately they seemed to become uneven every couple of days, perhaps shifted by the moon's gravity the way tides are. In the narrow space I passed the pictures in close up. Windows blown out in a shop front. Ambulances queued outside a mosque. Burnt tarpaulin of a market after a fire. It was sanitized now, no smells, no screams, no heat or panic.

"I stood there," I sometimes said to Lindy, nodding towards one of the pictures. "Off to the side. You can't see the spot. But that's where I took it from. I used to worry people would hate me for photographing them at a time like that but I realised during all the destruction they didn't even notice me."

How often had I walked past those pictures? Sometimes oblivious, biting out the corners of marmalade on toast on my way to morning television. At other times passing slowly, reliving tornados of billowing smoke from one, shrieking heat from another. There were places where I was cut by fragments of stones from the dull thump of a falling mortar, left deafened in a doorway, head bowed down and camera tucked into the hollow of my stomach to protect it. People ran past, hysterical, reaching back to each other while I pushed my spine into the wall, sighting them in through a lens, taking photo after photo, cutting off legs, heads, arms, front half of faces until I could only hope there was one image in there good enough. I never checked the pictures until I was back in my room. Never looked at them until my hands stopped shaking. When I returned home from Afghanistan Lindy brought me back to life with curries. Thai Green, Penang, Madras and Moroccan. Spice odours stood in rooms like apparitions. Brine ran off my skin. At night I perspired chilli and cumin.

I arrived at the last picture on our wall. It was the only one that was peaceful. Men sat around sipping coffee, heads back, laughing.

"That one," Lindy said from behind me. I hadn't noticed her trail me but now we stood shoulder to shoulder. "I want to change that one." She pointed to the picture hanging next to the men drinking coffee. I stepped back to examine it, even though I'd gazed at it hundreds of times. I went to ask her why, even had the first syllable out so that she looked sideways at me, waiting for me to finish. But I knew she'd say it was too upsetting, none of them fitted with creating a happy home but that one especially. I said let's take it down. Before she had a chance to respond I lifted the photograph off, wire twanging behind it.

"No! It can stay for now!" Lindy said. Her arm jerked out, hand gripping above my elbow, fingers not quite fitting all the way around. I pulled away, telling her it was fine. Swung towards the door to a cupboard under the stairs, yanking it open and sliding the picture into a space.

"What will you replace it with?" I said sarcastically. "A print of a bowl of fruit? Watercolour of a cat chasing a ball of wool? Crucifix?"

Lindy went to touch me again but her arm fell away. She often retreated from my voice like that.

After returning I was lost. Sometimes I saw an image from Afghanistan in a newspaper that made me want to go back so I could photograph it, except better. Otherwise I mooched around, taking aimless walks down streets. Everything reminded me of Afghanistan. Heavy traffic, exhaust fumes sputtering, storms ghosting in, the still air before their arrival amplifying every sound until the thunder moved through me like blood clots. In my front yard I lay on the dirt after the walks. Crew cut grass sawed into my ear, that slight seismic movement regularly twitching in my eye.

More photographs were taken down. My past removed, picture frame by picture frame. They formed a rickety pile, rattling if the cupboard door was closed too hard. Slowly other pictures replaced them. Lindy came home from artists' markets, shopping bags clattering slightly as she hauled them up onto the kitchen bench. A black and white of the Eifel Tower, picture of orange skies over Uluru, a restored wedding day photograph of Lindy's parents and two water buffalo standing in a rice paddy.

It'd been hot. Told Lindy tap water was like warm packet soup. The doctor took my blood pressure and said I'd better give up everything except breathing. He shrugged when I asked about the eye movements. Asked if I noticed them now. I shook my head.

One night Lindy came home as I lay shirtless on the couch. She rubbed my back damp from perspiration, her hands pushing rolls of skin towards my neck until she said my skin was coming off in tiny scrolls like unbaked loaves. She said her hands were tired and I listened to her flex them. Then she leaned over me, her voice heated and whispery next to my face. Her breath touched my skin with the tickle of that pen nib when I wrote her telephone number inside my arm years ago. Lindy asked if there was anything wrong. She realised it was going to take time to adjust to life back here. That it couldn't be easy to come home and do everyday things again, like lighting barbecues and raking leaves.

"Do you mean that feeling I sometimes have every four seconds? Maybe it's the clicking of the photographs I haven't taken."

Lindy was silent. She moved on the cushions.

"Give it time," she finally said, so quietly the words were fading before I understood them.

That afternoon I pulled on a t-shirt and we drove up Mount Dandenong to escape the heat. Cool shade fell across us like rain. We found an enclosure and lay on the grass. Lindy sprawled with her head in my lap. I told her we should move up there. It might be the last frontier of our city that wasn't ruined. Always stepping over syringes in our local park. Graffiti swirling and cramped over walls. Glass in bus shelters kicked out, glittering over pavements. Let's get out of the rut we live in I told her. Lindy smiled up at me before pushing herself up. She looked out at plains stretching until they ended in heat haze and glare.

"You just need time to relax again," she said quietly.

During nights in Afghanistan Lindy and I spoke on Zoom. I balanced the laptop on tops of legs. Sometimes I adjusted my position, pins and needles numbing muscles like fine, cold rain landing on skin. When I moved, lamps at the back of her room tilted and swayed like lights on a heaving sea. Lindy asked when I was coming home, her voice gentle as if afraid of my answer. Did I still want to start a family with her? She said I'd be a great dad. Told me I'd never forget the smell of a newborn, breastmilk and swaddling. Come home to me she begged.

When I returned I left the camera behind when attending weddings. I didn't take pictures of beaches or puppies. Instead took photographs of people arguing in a shop, screaming at children or unhappy on their way to work. I'd become attracted to anger and misery, as if I'd picked it up in Afghanistan like illness. Once I went to a boxing match, paying too much to sit in the front row to be brought a cardboard plate of mixed sandwiches. I photographed the cut face of one of the men in close up, capturing him reeling against ropes, face cowering behind gloves. When I came home I was proud of the images, calling Lindy in when they flicked up on a computer screen.

"He's bleeding," she said. "Such a disgusting sport. People lose memories and end up with Parkinson's disease because of being hit like that. Why'd you take those pictures? They're repulsive."

I'd watched Lindy's neck as she spoke. Her neck was what first attracted me to her. People tell you it's the eyes you first notice or perhaps the mouth. Or it could be the sound of a voice. For me it was her neck. I could see the slight tendons running down like strings in a harp. I never told Lindy I loved her but whenever I wanted her to know, I kissed her there, gently amongst the warm crevasses or on the down faintly over skin that I only noticed when the sun angled past her a particular way.

I bubble wrapped the old camera. Drew the wrap around as lovingly as dressing a baby. Lindy cried softly from the bedroom. Her sobs pushed wetly into the pillowslip. It was better this way. Better that I stayed strong against her crying for twenty minutes now, rather than for an hour on the way to the airport plus during the farewell outside Customs. I nearly broke down when I went in to kiss her goodbye, her arms so powerfully around my neck I thought she might cut blood flow off in my arteries. But I knew it was what I had to do. Nothing had changed, yet everything had. I shuddered awake in darkness nightly, ran to the television when a few seconds of Kabul footage screened and hated the blandness of the suburb where I lived. The part of me who held down a steady job, washed the car and planted a vegetable patch was as dead as my mother and father. I'd given up trying to understand the movements in my eyes. During my last visit the doctor suggested it could be early stages of PTSD and did I want to see someone? I shook my head, surprised he hadn't prescribed antibiotics and sent me away.

Slowly Lindy's arms weakened and she left me, shoulders first, the hollow down her chest next and her hands last.

"You have to be embedded," they announced at a briefing in Kabul. I sat with other journalists who looked as bored as me. "You can only be given a media permit that way. We'll have you chaperoned around. Keep you away from danger." I barely listened, able to recite their instructions from last time. "You'll still be able to take pictures. We have school kids you can photograph. There's also a bridge almost finished construction. You can photograph women going to university for the first time. No one has ever done wedding photography until they've photographed nuptials here. We'll have you back in your motel with the palm trees outside bouncing around in the wind like belly dancers in a seven courses for fifty dollars Turkish restaurant. You'll be in your room in time to lie in warm waters and bath salts. There's even a few mysterious oils they pour in that leave your skin as young as a twelve year olds. Can arrange to have a bottle of port smuggled into your room too. Just don't tell anyone. A lot of money will have to change hands if you're caught with alcohol. Although we understand you need it in your line of work. Oh and one other thing. Don't take any pictures that aren't authorised. We don't want any images that harm morale. Or jeopardise security."

I shrugged in agreement and sat through more briefings where we were told victory was near and help yourself to coffee.

I didn't lie in baths to recover from a day in the desert. Changed my shirt and scrubbed dust out of folds behind ears with motel oatmeal soap. Then I went out into the evening coming in as abruptly as darkness thirty seconds into one of those sand storms blowing in from the Arabian Desert. Was always trying to photograph that time when daylight bleeds into dusk, when the light is like smoke haze, where cold travels through my body like borer trails in tree trunks. But I never captured it. Every day I closed eyes and recalled it perfectly but never once did I photograph that time of day the way I wanted.

Tangled with Line

$50 the sign said. It must've been written with the flat side of a piece of chalk. Letters chunky but pocked, as if a few drops of rain pitted them before swirling across the bay or along streets dark as mineshafts. I stood next to the sign, muted light beaming over it from an overhead lamp on the pier.

"Fifty dollars for two hours plus bait. We supply a hand line." She barely glanced at me from the boat. Rummaged in a fridge. I said it sounded fine and made my way over a short gangplank. On the boat she briefly took my arm. "Steady," she said. "Bit choppy today."

By the time we left, four others joined us. She'd introduced herself as Torren and pointed out her father, the skipper. He unhooked a rope, inhaling from a wet looking roll your own. He half turned and nodded in our direction.

Under my feet motors chugged. We eased away from the pier. At first I thought sun was coming up as the boat turned but realised the silver half-light was an aura over the city from lit up office towers. Ocean frothed dully. Vibrations hummed through me, in joints and ligaments.

I hadn't done this in two years. Lara came with me then. She was confident in the boat. From all those trips with her father on his runabout the 'Suzie Bell.' His outboard motor spluttering around the estuaries near Port Macquarie, searching for blackfish. She'd become expert fetching another stubby for him as he'd pushed the boat full throttle to reach the next secret fishing spot. Behind mangroves cicadas throbbed from treetops, an occasional orange one drifting by in the muddy waters. Lara said she rescued them when she could, placing each one on the rear of the boat to dry.

"Here's your bait," Torren said. The bag she passed dripped condensation. Even in this light I noticed how brown she was. Skin colour I normally associated with people returning from places like Bali or Cable Beach. She'd kicked off shoes and I saw them under another seat, dirty tennis shoes with backs broken down. Her father called from the helm but the words seem to blow back along with cigarette smoke. "Okay, I'll get it," she called up to him.

I looked ahead. Lights twinkled along the shoreline. A radio played indistinctly from the cabin, part static, part seventies music. Lara caught three flathead and one flounder that last time. Triumphantly hooking a finger through the gill later to pose for a photograph. The flounder looked so thin, like flowers pressed in a book although no one did that anymore. My mother used to leave rose petals in thick, heavy books containing histories of World War 1. As if offering something gentle amongst the images of muddy trenches and gaunt soldiers. I'd find petals brittle and dark when looking up the battle of the Somme.

The skipper cut engines. I listened to the hollow slap of water against the hull. With engines off, new sounds emerged. Already a low grind of traffic and clacking of trains from far off. And conversations from other boats transmitting to us as if on wires. I couldn't recognise the words. Hand lines from the others plopped into water. Torren paused near me.

"Ready? Good spot for flathead usually. See how it goes. They've been on the small side lately."

I watched my line unfurl into water. Lara half hung over the side when she fished. As if she might dive in to catch them with bare hands. Sometimes a crew member asked her to sit back. I couldn't imagine her ill then. Her strong body jogging, even when we took holidays. Running along bush tracks, grunting as she hurdled rocks. Still having the breath to laugh when I asked her to pick me up on her way back. The day we found out Lara was sick we drove home silently. Blizzards of oak tree leaves slapped over the windscreen. Road slicked wet by rain sticky on tyres. We went inside stunned. Lara sat on the couch, stroking our greyhound's round forehead. His eyes followed her everywhere. I cooked a Thai red curry, a meal I'd made so often it was virtually prepared with reflex movements. Yet it sat in bowls cooling as we picked and eventually left it. Rang our daughter and listened numbly to her small talk about how hot Brisbane was until I broke the news. Told our dog too but he already somehow knew.

Torren pulled up the anchor. I'd offered to help but she brushed me away. Wondered if she'd be the same if I opened a door for her or stood back to let her walk in somewhere ahead of me. Her father watched her, chain smoking, wet cough rasping. Light was coming up. From the cabin another cigarette butt flicked away, floating down like landing lights on a plane in distance. Felt gnawing on the end of my line and yanked it towards me. As the line wisped up it floated in without sinker or hook.

"Let me," Torren said. She reached past me and took the hand line. Backs of her hands were scratched as if she played with cats. "Haven't really done this before have you?" I said I'd forgotten. It'd been awhile. Nearly added I'd been trying to forget all kinds of things. The light in x-rays. Taking the diminishing body of someone you loved into your arms. How they felt lighter week by week. Changes in their voice. At that time Lara and I still slept without clothes. Drew her so close could feel the vertebrae of her spine. But the symmetry of her bones seemed to have changed. Pieces of her jammed into me like a stone in my shoe. At times her pain must have eased and she'd sigh quietly, breath soft and deep before her body stilled.

Torren threaded line through the hook. It moved in her fingers like sewing. Across the boat someone shouted 'got one!' and we watched them haul it over the boat's side, dropping it writhing on the boards. A flathead, it flexed side to side, gills opening and closing desperately. A man hunched over the fish, wrenching at the hook.

"Hello main course!" he said. "Been marinating in sea water for tonight's meal. How the hell do you get the hook out?"

"Hope he knows how to eat a fish better than how to catch one," Torren said quietly, winking at me. I sat back while she baited my hook. "This prawn is from my personal supply. Not that pulp we sold you earlier. You could land a whale with this." It threaded onto the hook, curling neatly around, guided by fingertips. I glanced up at the skipper. His face glowed dimly behind a flaring cigarette lighter. In the gathering dawn I glimpsed him watching his daughter affectionately, tiredness briefly lifted from his face. Torren went to where the fish now lay tangled with line. The boat shuddered forward.

I still memorised football scores and recipe ideas to tell Lara. She inhabited spaces. Next to that wall when deciding the framed black and white of an abandoned railway station should hang there. Beside the window where her raucous laughter at our greyhound's antics echoed. At the timber table where she arm wrestled my younger brother, beating him twice, bending back his straining arm until it thudded dully, wrist first into the table. Outside around a small glass table, sharing sports lift outs and reading articles to each other over coffee. The house felt like a display home now.

We made our final stop. The anchor chain rattled as it plunged into water. Sunshine lit the blue surface. My line dragged taunt, cutting into the skin of my finger. I tugged the fish in, a bream, left hand, right hand, feeling it drag and swerve. Lifted it over the boat's rail, fine water spraying me, tasting of brine, the silver body flashing and beating. It fell, slapping on the deck. I stared mesmerised at its fight and the moments of panic and dread I'd lived with for months welled up inside me again.

"Let me," Torren said, voice hushed, crouching next to me. She freed the hook, working it out from where it punctured through the side of the fish's mouth. Cupping it between hands she passed it to me and as I grasped it, the fish squirmed and twisted in my palms. Bracing against the boat's rail I let it slide from my hands, nose diving to water and streaking away. From the corner of my eye I saw one of the others shaking their head but Torren looked at me differently, as if she'd seen something she wasn't expecting.

Three Paintings

From the start I want to say I liked my job. They gave me a uniform. Provided an ear piece as light as Cooma's fingertips tracing the veins in my arms. Tea and biscuits. Morning tea break 10.15 AM. I was happy there.

Not much happened. Time passed slowly like lying in bed when you can't sleep. Occasionally a tinny voice with a background of static crackled through my ear piece.

"Missing child reported in red top. Last seen in the cafeteria."

"Assistance required for an elderly person on a walking frame in the Picasso exhibition."

"Could we have someone guide visitors in the walkway of the bohemian art area? Clean up underway following a vomiting incident."

I watched the visitors. Mostly retirees, pausing in front of pictures, stepping forward, then back. Perhaps critics writing for the retirement village newsletter, or merely changing positions from being long or short sighted. Later I'd see them in the cafeteria, angling forks through flourless orange cake. They probably smelt of our barista-made coffee or money.

I watched the students more closely. In high school uniforms they seemed contemptuous, at times laughing at the exhibits. They weren't ready to appreciate works of art. They'd rather be watching YouTube or gaming.

Personally I hated many of the pictures. Picasso's Cubism? Monet's lilies? Superficial and meaningless. I could do better. Cooma told me so. One day I would.

I had my own studio. Well, I called it a studio. In the garage where we rented, at the cold end, next to the cans of lawn mower fuel, weed killer and broken rakes. My jars half filled with water and streaked with paint lined along a table. Brush handles poked out. Finished paintings stacked tilted against a wall. Landscapes illustrating the sheer distance of places, plains disappearing into an infinity of heat haze, the way the universe has no end. Dying towns at the end of avenues of honour. Cooma's face, her arms at angles as she tied back hair. My paintings spoke to you. Maybe in whispers, but you still felt their language, the ripple of their broken dreams or lost hopes. On days off I painted until oils spotted my face and congealed like wounds on my apron.

Last Tuesday I took my portfolio to a small gallery. It was so quiet in there. You could bottle that silence and sell it alongside those jars of skin creams and Vitamin D supplements. Pour it out when the kids were too noisy or the staple guns banged next door during the renovations. I drifted around the gallery, pausing here and there. A painting featured sea shells adhered to the picture. On another tinsel sprinkled where a river turned through the painting, as if sparking in the light. I was above this tackiness.

"Can I help you?" I heard behind me. Had my best smile on as I swung to face her. The smile Cooma said made her want to sleep with me. It wrapped you before my arms she said. I liked that.

I announced I was an artist. Could I show her my portfolio? She glanced at me the same way I had looked at the gallery's pictures.

"You realise people come in here all the time wanting to show me their work?"

I said I did, trying to hold up my smile.

"Lucky for you I'm feeling generous today," she said. "Show me your best two."

I flopped the folder down. Turned to the portrait of Cooma. With all its wispy, pencilled lines. The circle of her belly, tapering fingers, floating hair. Watched the woman's face as she appraised it. Her frown folded into a pattern of tyre tread.

"And the next?"

I called it "Avocadoes in autumn". Their reptile skin, deep green leaves, a row of trees straight as a fence stretching to where skies dulled.

"Have you done any art classes?"

"No."

I didn't need classes. Cooma told me. That time she held me, arms joining across my back like rope. When she spoke so loudly her words flinted off me.

"You need to," she said. "Honestly, it's not what we're looking for. Thanks."

She was four steps away before I could reply.

"What... exactly... are you looking for?"

"I can only tell you it isn't what you're offering."

Watched her go. Like I'd watched so many girlfriends before Cooma. Leaving me without once looking back. No goodbyes or wishing all the best. Just swerving away from me in the middle of my sentences, sometimes as my arms dangled mid-air ready to hug, my buttons already undone as I believed they liked me enough to love me, even a little.

On the way out I wanted to smash a vase. That particularly pretentious one near the door. Speckled with pink rose petals down sides. But as a security guard, I'd been trained to show restraint.

"I know where you live," I called back into the gallery as I left. I didn't mean any harm. Only to have the last say. To hand back a small cruelty. It was worth it. Behind a desk her face twitched, the way a baby does before howling. And I'd seen plenty of that.

Cooma asked why. Had I been too demanding again? Which pictures did I show? I stood mute in the downdraught of her disappointment.

"Which ones?" she said again.

"Of you. Reclining on the couch."

"It doesn't even look like me. If you're going to show a picture of me, take a photo."

Bent my head and cried. Heat and tears burned out of eyes. Tasted it like that lingering salt after gagging on sea water while signalling for a lifesaver. Sobs hiccupped from me.

"Please don't leave me," I said, choking.

Cooma hugged me. Or at least leaned into me. Wasn't sure where her arms positioned. Hanging loosely as empty sleeves possibly.

On the morning of the Andy Warhol exhibition I delayed outside. Water cascaded down the gallery's front window; rivulets, textures and often hints of colour depending where the sun was. I placed my finger into it, water curling over my skin. It always provided comfort before the long hours of standing, occasionally asking someone to step back or not to touch the exhibit. I removed my finger and shook water from it.

Inside I gazed at the Warhol prints. Plus photographs of him with that straw blond hair. A woman stood next to me.

"Do you believe he was applauding or satirizing a consumer society with those Campbell Soup cans? And would you say it's abstract?" she asked.

"I just do security."

"Doesn't mean you can't have an opinion. Was he suggesting capitalism is a positive force with soup a metaphor for everything we consume?"

I stared stonily ahead. Like those Buckingham Palace guards in London. I could've told her his prints were pointless. He'd turned art into something resembling a television advertisement that you took a piss during. She should see mine. One day it'll be on these walls instead of the hoaxes hanging now. That the only way to enjoy these was to slash their canvas corner to corner so the true emptiness of the world would be exposed underneath. Make that your metaphor.

In bed my legs ached from standing all day. Sometimes I didn't want Cooma touching me. Telling me about her job. Threading her netball hardened legs around mine. That she'd had enough of wheeling patients back to recovery wards with their ghastly white complexions and strange mutterings as they emerged from general anaesthetics. When she spoke her voice trembled into me.

"Your art work. People will want it. They just have to see it."

Cooma tried to roll me towards her. Hooked an arm through mine and pulled me onto my back.

"Look at me when I talk to you!"

"You're hurting," I cried out. Cooma went limp. Started untangling herself from me. Drew limbs away, sliding to the other side of the bed so only a pool of her body heat remained.

"You need to do something," she said.

In the morning I drank a long coffee, dull heat sluicing through me. Took it outside into the watery light, shoving at the garage door so it squealed open on hinges. Strode to my studio where fragile sunshine hazed through windows. Reviewed pictures, letting each one tip against the next after I'd evaluated it. I selected three. That'd be enough, I didn't want to be greedy.

I approached the art gallery feeling the lurch of passing trams in the pavement as they ground past. Took my place under the Marilyn Monroe prints. The first of the visitors started arriving. Their small voices cooed and murmured from across the room.

I lifted my mouthpiece to speak.

"Mr Barnes? You can put me down for the evening shift tomorrow. Sure, I don't mind. I'll lock up after the Warhol exhibition as well. No, a double shift is fine. Just as long as you keep the tea and biscuits topped up." I laughed at my joke, hoping he found it funny.

I rarely volunteered for the member nights. When they brought out the canapes and glasses of champagne. When an art critic spoke and everyone nodded along during their speech as if to music. 'Stay invisible' I'd be told. That was fine, I wanted nothing to do with these people.

A steady stream of visitors sauntered through. Occasionally someone glanced me up and down, as if I was an exhibit. The day passed smoothly, the only problems a half finished coffee left next to a sculpture and a crying child. A man close to me shook his head as if I was to blame. I nearly asked him if he'd like the toddler capsicum sprayed.

Cooma was out playing netball. She often returned home angry with umpires after receiving a caution. I'd watched her play a couple of times. Her shoes squeaked and skidded over the smooth floors. Last time her opponent playing Goal Attack fell heavily and the game was stopped. An argument started that Cooma tripped her.

While she was out I stepped through damp darkness, groping for the garage door handle. Heavy dew layered over trees, tapping faintly as it dripped onto the roof. I hauled up the three pictures, clamping an arm over them and straining along the path to the car. Slid them one by one onto the back seat before throwing a sheet over them. I looked at the sharp angles of frames poking through the material. My pictures on the verge of greatness.

Cooma sat heavily on the couch after returning home. She began flicking channels. A light smear of perspiration lay across her forehead the way dew speckles a windscreen. I microwaved our frozen dinners and passed her one. She said they'd lost by one goal. Someone must've bribed the umpire. I asked why but Cooma said she didn't want to talk about it. In some ways I was relieved.

Before bed I told Cooma I'd be driving tomorrow. Was working a double shift and I'd use the car as I'd be coming home late. She nodded, not looking away from dinner or the television. Later she lay face down in bed and asked me to rub her back. I massaged around the bones of her shoulder as if modelling something out of clay.

I left home early. Peeled off Cooma's back. Watched faces in traffic already jaded passing the other way. Mists slung low in parks and joggers exhaled veils of steam. In distance the outlines of grey buildings towered. As I drove my paintings rattled in the back. At red lights my arm strayed back to them, touching their frames gently as if calming the lives I'd painted into them.

Parked downstairs next to a skip piled with rubbish. Locked the car and took the lift upstairs. I had an urge to go outside and stand next to the waters swirling down the window. Feel their rushing cool over my fingers until I'd lift them slightly blue and numbed, a few drips glinting and wobbling before sliding off. But I went to the tearoom. Dunked a tea bag into my mug of hot water, knowing its taste would be bland as always, nothing more than something that woke me up and meant I'd need a toilet break in about an hour.

Took my place in the Andy Warhol exhibition. Under the Elvis Presley pictures. I hated that, knowing they'd attract a lot of people who I'd need to tell stand back. My ear piece crackled.

"Be on the lookout everyone. We have intel climate change activists may stage a protest and attempt to vandalise a picture."

Nearly said I'd like to help activists but watched the first arrivals spreading through the room. Some of the older visitors surged towards the Elvis portraits as if mobbing him, remarking how young he seemed. I asked them to stand back. Someone asked me how old Elvis was in the pictures. I told them to join the escorted tour at 4.15 PM. A man started eating chips and I told him no food was allowed. He told me the gallery was part of a nanny state and threw the bag on the floor. I called for a clean-up.

Mr Barnes radioed to tell me to take my break. The gallery was closing for member's night. I ushered out a few people who sat on couches. Passed caterers arriving, carrying trays of cheese and grapes. Other guards sat in the tearoom eating sandwiches and reading newspapers.

"Should be an easy shift," I said to one of them. "Hopefully no one collapses from too much champagne."

I returned to the Elvis Presley pictures. An escorted group shuffled around the room. The leader's voice was muffled as he spoke and guffaws of laughter followed one of his remarks. I watched them closely as Mr Barnes was likely to come through and check we weren't stealing any cheese or not paying attention. The evening passed slowly. To avoid boredom I guessed people's names and ages. I was going to try guessing professions but member's night was mostly doctors and lawyers.

Eventually people started leaving. A few chatted, voices hushed. Sometimes I envied the security guards at the football, intervening in fist fights or frog marching someone out. It looked thrilling and occasionally dangerous. But I was an artist and couldn't risk injury, especially if it meant I'd be unable to paint. Still, it was a shame a climate activist hadn't shown up, it would've passed the time and created excitement, at least for me.

My ear tickled with the sound of Mr Barnes' voice.

"Secure the rear doors. Then make your way forward, locking each door as you go. I'll leave you to close the last one. Just scan your way out when you're finished."

The other guards started leaving their posts. They would lock up elsewhere. Made my way to the back of the gallery and turned off lights before closing the first doors. They whooshed shut behind me. My footsteps echoed around cabinets and sculptures. Turned off the next set of lights and again closed doors.

Out of respect I didn't take down Warhol's Marilyn Monroe pictures. Left her pouting in that way I wished

Cooma would. I chose Warhol's self-portrait with green hair, a maze of flowers and the Elizabeth Taylor picture. Unhooked and laid them carefully against the wall. But as I left I propped his self-portrait against the fire escape door to keep it ajar.

Corridors felt larger and more airy as I hurried through the building.

I swiped my card in the lift and clunked towards the car park. My car stood alone and I stayed in shadows. Vaulted open the back door and slid the pictures out. A corner snagged on a gap in the door and I pushed them back in before drawing them out again at an angle. This time I took the fire escape upstairs so there'd be no record of my card swiped a second time. The pictures jammed awkwardly against ribs. I kept pausing to adjust their angles and ensure they weren't dropped.

I had an impulse to change Andy Warhol's name to mine where it stood with dark letters above the entrance to his exhibition. Quickly I hung each of my pictures where his had been. Wires stretching across their backs twanged as they settled. I stood back for the moment I had planned and yearned for. I kept going to my paintings, easing a corner up to straighten one, sliding another along the wire to better centre it. At last they were ready. I returned to the self-portrait holding open the fire escape door and removed a shoe, wedging it against the door to keep it open. The door closed on it, squeezing it out of shape. Carefully I placed the Warhol pictures in a storeroom but right at the back where they'd be difficult to find, covering them in my sheet. Then I returned to my pictures, slowing down to inspect them a final time. I'd even considered what order to hang them, dullest to brightest, sombre to joyful. I retrieved my shoe. It had twisted, my toes now unnaturally bunched together. I barely noticed because my time had come.

Streets were mostly empty. I ran two orange lights and laughed out the window into blustering wind. Knots of people stood at tram stops. Lit windows of the St Kilda tram passed, people mesmerised into mobiles. If only they knew. If only I could shower them with brochures. Announce the inaugural exhibition of an exciting new artist who would challenge the musty boundaries of traditional painting.

At home I wetly kissed Cooma's ear. She arched away from me.

"Yuck!" she said, wiping the palm of her hand across it. "Feel like I've been attacked by a slug." I laughed louder than necessary and it seemed to ring amongst the saucepans stacked for washing up. Said I had a surprise for her.

"Is it you'll stop snoring?" I laughed heartily again. Told her she needed to come with me to work tomorrow. She stared at me sceptically.

"I'm doing the evening shift tomorrow and would like some sleep beforehand," she said.

"It'll be the best sleep you ever have," I said. "You have to come. Let's say you're about to witness one of the greatest events ever."

In bed I could barely contain myself. Kept imagining the faces of visitors to the gallery. How they would gather in awe and ask about the artist. How I'd eavesdrop on their praise. See the way they halted in front of my pictures, unable to move on, eyes following my sweeping lines, experiencing the grief, exuberance and magnificence expressed in my art.

In the morning I passionately kissed Cooma. Our mouths turned dryly against each other and she bucked me off.

"Too much," she muttered. I made her coffee. Lovingly spread her toast. Carried it all in to her. She sat up in bed, looking at me oddly. I asked her to hurry as of all days, today I didn't want to be late.

We drove to my work. Held her hand when I didn't need both on the steering wheel. Cooma said I was cutting off her circulation and snapped a hand into her lap. I parked near the skip bin. We walked towards the lift and again I took her hand.

"You're clammy," she said and yanked her hand away. The lift shuddered us up to the Andy Warhol exhibition.

"Andy Warhol?" she said. "Who's he? Do you know him or something?" I told her to follow me. As we entered the hall I slipped behind her, placing hands over eyes. The softness of eyelids pressed into my fingers. We faced the wall. At first I thought it was the wrong wall. My pictures were gone. I felt the hum of a migraine starting. I lifted hands off Cooma and she asked what we were looking at. For a few seconds I expected it was what people suffering a stroke feel. Trouble speaking, unable to understand speech, vision lost. I stood motionless beside her.

"Mr Barnes here," came over my earpiece. "Please attend my office immediately." Another of the guards approached me, herding me towards the lift.

"What's going on?" Cooma said. I wanted to answer but was pressed forward, seeing her recede in my corner vision like something in a rear vision mirror. "You know, I think there's something wrong with you," she called after me.

I'd only been in Mr Barnes' office once. When I was recruited. Facing his questions about how I handled anger and conflict. Now he met me at the door and stood back to let me in. Directed me to sit. Asked the other guard to join us. Mr Barnes sat across the desk and swung the computer screen towards me.

"Is this you?" he said. We watched a hunched figure pushing a painting into the space next to a fire escape door. "This picture...this beautifully expressed and historical work of art now has a scratched frame because of this."

I watched speechless. The cameras turned off in the exhibition area but must've been left on in the main thoroughfares because of closing late. If only I'd worn a hat, pulled low over my face. Possibly worn a climate protest top so they'd suspect an activist.

"Is it you?" Mr Barnes said, except this time in a way that made the other guard flinch.

I remained silent. Mr Barnes exhaled slowly.

"You're lucky," he said, turning back the screen. "We aren't making this a police matter. Personally, I'd like to. But the powers upstairs don't want the publicity. Another reason you're lucky is that you'll be paid two weeks salary. You just need to sign this. It's your resignation. I've completed everything. You also say in here you'll return the uniform within twenty four hours. And make no further claim. Do you understand?"

I nodded. My headache had worsened, especially on the left side. I signed, making my signature different in case I needed to claim someone forged it. Mr Barnes said to remove my ear piece and leave.

"Where are my pictures?" I asked. He leaned across the table. It was the closest I'd seen him to smiling.

"In the skip. Where we saw you park."

The other guard escorted me out. Walked me down to the car park and I noticed the car was gone. Cooma must've left to get her sleep. The guard watched me as I went to the skip and peered in. My pictures lay tangled with the sheet. As I lifted it I saw they were matchwood. Splintered into pieces with jagged edges. I stared in horror.

"What happened?" I said.

"You'll have to leave through the front entrance. Come on."

We took the lift to ground level. A large photo of Andy Warhol stood near the entrance, matted hair hanging into eyes. The guard stood back and a glass door rolled open. I walked out, as composed as I could. Circled around to water wrinkling down glass, splashing lightly at the bottom. Kids flexed hands under its rushing. I slowly inserted my finger into the hurrying waters, watching them slip over and tip off my skin. From the glass I saw the guard, watchful, alongside visitors clamouring in. Through the water their images shifted, the way a mirage moved on bitumen.

I thought I'd paint that scene one day.

The Specimen Jar

I don't remember hearing the thunder. I felt it, swelling and buffeting close to me. Noticed skies, shades of grey and purple, colours streaking like healing bruises. Lay dazed on my back, seagrass wisping dryly over me. Waves broke behind where I lay, spray hazing over skin, numbing with cold. I couldn't pinpoint the pain. Maybe it tremored in a hip. Scents of ocean floated as if someone held smelling salts under my nose. I couldn't move.

"Are you okay?" she said next to me. "Thought you were dead. My boyfriend's calling an ambulance." She bent down, gusting wind layering hair like bandages over her face.

I'd noticed it coming. The freshly turned earth smells, odour of downpours on steaming ground, rain angling, swishing through leaves and across bitumen roads radiating the day's heat. Watched people rolling up towels, hunching and dashing towards cars. But I walked on, light dimming and clouds clumping by. Later I recalled a crackle in air like breathing through bronchitis. The woman knelt next to me on the sand, taking my hand.

"You're going to be fine," she said and I searched her eyes.

The interior of the hospital reminded me of a whiteout. Bleached walls, cream sheets and pale complexions of ill people filled it.

"One in half a million," the nurse said. "Those are the chances of being struck. About the same odds of my kids sleeping in on the weekend."

They wheeled me outside. Felt the difference in air like changing into clothes already stretched to my shape.

Oxygen now thin and weightless, not bending with humidity. We bumped over pavements cracking from tree roots. Cara hurried ahead, yanking open a car door. Hands gripped under my arms, hauling me up. Bodies strained and manoeuvred me into the car. The nurse hung in the opening.

"Couple of days rest and you'll be fine. And let me know if you get any strange magical powers out of this," she said.

We threaded along streets. At red lights the car engine trembled through seats. Said I was sorry for spoiling our holiday. No tang of white vinegar smells in our nostrils as we unwrapped fish and chips at the sea's edge. No burnt orange sunsets as we reclined back in bars looking out over lucent water. No barefoot walks through sand patterned by tides under the shade of banksia trees. Cara concentrated on the road, asking how I was without looking at me. Told her a few aches and pains persisted.

We headed inland. Basalt plains crumbled and eroded behind fences. We drove roads, log trucks blustering past the opposite way. Nearing home grass tinged brown from early frosts. We fell silent before arriving.

Cara touched my hip. Felt her fingers barely on me, soft as exhaling. She said she'd never seen anything like those marks before. I glanced at where she touched, nails broken and uneven from her work. Spindly lines fanned out on my skin. Like tree roots Cara said. She tilted her head, examining me.

"I never knew lightning could do that," she said.

"Let's hope it's true about not striking twice," I replied.

I sat up, gazing outside. The window looked out to a plunging valley. At times winds came through like sirens, shearing through twisted trees. Moss furred their lengths of branches twitching in blizzards. I again told Cara I was sorry about the holiday. Shouldn't have walked the beach before a storm. Was distracted. Stepping into someone's footprints. Pretending to be a tracker. Seeing if the footprints led to a hidden fishing spot or camping ground.

Cara switched on a laptop. I walked through the house. My joints ached, pain heavy and pooling. At the end of the hall I flicked on a light in the last room. One year ago we'd stood in there, mapping out where a crib could stand, discussing wallpaper Cara wanted to buy with leaping baby lambs and vintage prams. She'd gestured along a wall that caught rare sunshine in winter. Said wallpaper would look cute there. Perhaps if we put up the right design it'd will a baby into our lives. By summer we both wanted to board the room up. But now Cara's specimen jars stood on a shelf. She'd built it herself, hammering early one morning. The blows broke in me like heartbeats too big for my chest.

"If you hammer any harder you're going to change the axis of the earth!" I'd called out to her.

"Lucky there's no baby then!" Cara shouted angrily across rooms. "You wouldn't cope with crying!"

An overhead fluorescent light ticked on. In each jar lay a small yellow body. Some curled up, brittle looking, legs folded. Yellow bands circled abdomens. I picked up the first jar. "Female European Wasp, (*Vespula germanica*), October 2023. Near Mansfield." Cara's meticulous writing printed across a label. 'Scientist's writing,' I'd said when we still smiled at each other's jokes. I held the jar above me, staring up into small wings and segments.

Winter had arrived abruptly. It usually did. Dinner Plain faced northwest, cool changes channelling in, snow dusting bush trails and car windscreens. My skin blemishes faded.

But the aches worsened, serious enough for me to lie motionless, popped foil of painkillers strewn around. One night lightning jagged and rain pelted, setting off agony in my hips and back, as if joints conducted its surging electricity. Cara came in, her hand briefly touching where pain heaved. She watched me impassively.

I later woke when rolling over, splaying across cold sheets. Morning light was grey, holding mist and exhaust from tourist buses idling in town while people queued for coffee. Through windows mist slunk close to ground as if it might be too heavy to inhale. I stood, stretching through where pain ebbed. Called out to Cara, my voice humming along walls. The kitchen smelt of coffee grindings and burnt toast. I strode out into chilling air. Then circuited the house, slipping on frozen ground. Eventually I spotted her in a blue waterproof coat. I'd often seen Cara turning its pockets out onto a table, pebbles, lichen and leaves scattering. She'd stand back before fossicking through what she'd collected. I headed towards her.

"Discovered anything?" I called. "Don't mean the remains of a woolly mammoth. More like how to save a marriage. Any fossils of that lying around?"

Cara looked around from a tree trunk. Faint green streaked down its column. Her breath turned and faded.

"Female wasps becoming more conditioned to the cold," she said. "More of them this year. Tucked in crevasses. Under bark. Found one that'd crawled through a crack into a fence post. Imagine the ingenuity of that. One day this country will be populated entirely by invasive species. Foxes, carp, cane toads, rabbits."

"Happiness," I added. "That's an invasive species around here."

Cara glared at me before facing back to the tree. She gouged at it with a blade, bark shredding. She unscrewed a jar, picking up something with tweezers and dropping it inside.

"Wish you were as forensic about you and me with your research," I said.

Cara's hands wrenched as she cut into the tree, her body shuddering a split second later as if a delayed reaction. As I walked away I knew instinctively she'd turned, glancing after me as if checking whether I headed towards the house or taken one of the muddy pathways leading towards the bunched trees covering hills. I wanted to turn around and look back at her to see what was in her face at that moment and if it was something I could live with.

I returned to the house. Squalls of heat fanned from ducts. I strode the hallway to Cara's room of specimen jars, snapping on light switches as I went so glaring light burst through the house. Taking down the first jar I shook it violently so the wasp inside pinged against glass. The insect careered around, as if alive and desperately trying to find a way out.

Away From It All

Heat fractured pavements that year. Leaves crisped on coarse winds blowing in flies and smoke. At night car alarms shrieked. During mornings Warren lay motionless in bed before sun came up. At times he stood restlessly at the window. His body left behind a damp outline on sheets, as if his shadow cast there. Through windows the neighbourhood glowed luminous. Air conditioning clunked and trembled. He smelt wet earth from sprinklers as if rain poured somewhere.

In the dawn Warren went outside. It felt airless. He marvelled at the quiet. Occasionally a car swished down the street. He drank two coffees down to a sugary sludge.

"It's coming up to a year again," Zack had said that evening on the phone. "We're due for our annual trip. Let's go next weekend. Pack a dialysis machine and colostomy bag considering the damage we do to ourselves. Add some clothes in camouflage colours. In case we have to hide from family. We might not want to be found until the red is out of our eyes and back in our cheeks."

Warren joked about being too old for this. Said he'd been around so long you could carbon date him. See all the moults he'd been through. The university student Warren, barely managing a pass after final exams in his Bachelor of Commerce. The accountant Warren helping others claim tax for dry cleaning and the just married Warren, honeymooning in Thailand. There was the Warren working years in an office wondering what he'd done with his life and the Warren wanting nothing more than to catch a couple of Murray cod and find time away from everything.

Inside Warren itched from heat and mosquito bites. He sat in a corner and waited on Angela to wake up. Above her a fan turned at the lowest speed. Under the light he'd watched its slow shadows swinging across her chest. In the dawn her skin shone slightly, sloping down to her waist. Warren moved, making a noise he knew would wake her. Angela was a light sleeper. Her head lifted from the pillow, messed hair across her mouth.

"What're you doing? Why are you over there?" she said.

"Too hot to sleep. Do you realise our combined body heat is about seventy five degrees? That means our bed is hotter than any place on earth."

Angela asked if he'd woken her for a science lesson.

"Only trying to have a conversation before global warming makes it too late," he said. She dropped her head back on the pillow.

"Zack rang," Warren said. "Our annual weekend is coming up again."

"So you're telling me whilst my defences are down. Fine. Just let me go back to sleep."

In the morning he found an old list in a coat pocket. He unravelled it and scanned the items. A fingerprint smudged across the top of the paper. His hand writing then was identical to now. Perhaps hand writing and your voice were all that didn't change. Tent pegs, hurricane lamp, beer, food and Band-Aids scrawled in a column on the page. Warren started rummaging through boxes storing equipment from previous trips. Weathered blades of grass stuck to objects. A torch and a cracked piece of soap tipped out.

A few days later they gathered. The friends shook hands, laughing at the idea of mischief ahead. Phil tied fishing rods to the roof rack. Zack packed the boot. Angela came out, barefoot on the top step, waving to them and bending to kiss Warren. He curved arms around her, lying against the grid of her ribs.

The car reversed out, slewing in a half turn before straightening and driving away. On the main road wind shrilled through the fishing rods. They joined lines of traffic across suburbs, tailgating cars taking kids to sport. Zack joked about last year's trip. That fart of Phil's more potent than a compost bin. The cans of beer they buried to keep cool but couldn't find again. The car bogged after a downpour with rear wheels spinning mud over Warren and Phil. Forgetting where the car was parked after endless billiards games at the local hotel.

Zack asked Phil how work was. He smiled bitterly.

"Feel like I live between doses of general anaesthetic. They put me under Monday morning and I come out of it Friday night. After the weekend they knock me out again. Sometimes I wake up in the middle of it and wonder where I am. But I'm quickly sedated again. It's what sales does to you. The way you appear on the outside has nothing to do with how you feel on the inside."

It was a yellow light day. The highway circled through hills before running a flat line into distance. Phil slept against the passenger's side window, cheek flattened to glass. They stopped at a service station. Warren filled the car, the petrol hose vibrating slightly in his grip. Phil woke, walking drowsily into the shop, stopping to rummage through a display of chip bags.

"He doesn't say much," Warren said. "Is he okay?"

"I'm guessing he's just tired. Who knows?" Zack said.

They arrived in the afternoon. Light glared off rushing brown waters. They fished from fold down chairs that strained and ticked whenever someone shifted. Now and then one of them leaned forward, tensing after feeling the fishing line touched. The lines stretched silkily towards water. Phil landed a carp. He stared disdainfully at the fish while it flopped around on the river bank.

"Even cats won't touch them," Zack said. "You'd have to love the taste of mud to tuck into one of those."

Phil removed a knife with a serrated edge from a cane basket. He pinned the fish with a boot across its body. The carp writhed under him. Sawing roughly, he hacked off its head. When he stepped off its remaining body arched and convulsed on the ground. The others watched impassively.

"Its own fault," Zack said. "Should be swimming around the canals of Venice. Where it belongs."

"Not like it could book a flight over the Internet to go back there," Warren said.

Phil resumed his seat. He cast out again, line whipping through air. He relit a half finished cigarette, flinching from the lighter's heat. Grey smoke twirled around him as he breathed out noisily. Warren watched the waters. He knew that river. Last year he dived in between the dark rocks, cheeks stretched and ballooned, holding breath. He swam down. Warm waters became numbingly cold. They rolled over him like taunt air before a storm. Deeper he swam, so that rocks on the bottom became outlined. A string of bubbles seeped from his mouth, winding and twinkling upwards. Eventually he stroked towards the surface, into shards of light and water the colour of tea.

Next morning air inside the tent was stale. During the night there'd been a dry storm. Warren heard its faint thunder like the rumble of water trapped in an ear after swimming. He squirmed out of his sleeping bag. Inhaling that air was like swallowing something whole. On all fours he stretched towards the entrance, dragging down a zipper. Towards the back of the tent Zack lay rumpled, deeply asleep. Warren stepped outside, squinting into sharp light. Just out of sight the river tinkled along. He shoved hands into pockets, crunching over gritty sand, making his way to the edge. He expected to find Phil already there. Phil was a serious fisherman, rarely talking after casting out.

Those were probably Phil's boot prints in the river sand. There weren't any other campers Warren had noticed. Gaps between strides were wide. The indentations of some prints were lighter, as if feet barely touched ground. Warren followed them to the river. The trail turned ahead of rocks eroded smooth and followed the water. Warren called out ahead. Through a clearing he came across Phil's shoes. He recognised them from the times they'd been left outside the tent the previous year when Zack complained about their fish gut smell. They stood neatly side by side, the way feet might be together before diving into a pool. Leading away from the shoes into water was a short trail of barefoot prints. Warren called out again but louder this time. He ripped shoes off and waded in, arms out for balance. Hurrying water pressed against him.

A camper found Phil downstream. Rinsing cups on the riverbank they spotted the body snagged against a log. The police questioned Warren and it wasn't difficult to see what they were trying to work out. Was there anything in his behaviour that suggested this could happen? Was Phil under any particular stress or strain? They wrote down the details of Phil's family. Zack came over and watched them scour around the camp site.

Wordlessly Zack and Warren dismantled the tent. Warren returned to the river, tipping in the bait. It floated away, speeding up as it went. They packed slabs of beer into the rear of the car. Warren folded up the gas cooker, metal hinges squealing shut.

The heat built up. Heatwaves lifted like isobars off the car's bonnet. Warren stood over dark deep holes left in earth by tent poles. He listened to the gurgle of the river for the last time.

In the car Zack asked did he think Phil had done it deliberately.

"It's a question we'll be asking ourselves forever," Warren said.

"Not like he was unhappy," Zack said. "Couple of kids. No problems at home as far as I knew."

Ahead above the road skies glazed brown. Warren said it was topsoil carried along by winds. If the weather changed the rains would be red.

They barely spoke on the drive home. They drove through the signals of radio stations crackling with static. Crossed bridges over low murky water with flourishes of green on the banks before paddocks became flat and brown again. At last the city reared on the horizon, smoky and almost transparent.

Warren dropped Zack home. Zack reefed a bag out of the back seat and dragged a slab of beer from the boot.

"Have to visit his wife," Zack said.

"Don't worry. I'll take care of it. I'll take Angela with me."

Zack nodded, relief crossing his face.

They embraced. None of them had ever done that before. It was always handshakes and banter. Zack's bones cut into Warren as if his body was all right angles.

"Stay in touch," Warren said, unsure they would.

Warren parked in his driveway. With engine off and windows down heat scorched the way indigestion sometimes burnt through him. He went inside, half way down the hallway before seeing Angela glance around a corner. She asked him about being home early. Wasn't it tomorrow they were due? Had all the fish gone to South Australia because the bait was better there? Warren guided her to a couch, feeling the shape of her small shoulder muscle under his hand. He explained, stopping and starting with what he had to say. Angela sat, at times standing to go to him but he signalled her to sit. She shook her head now and then, disbelieving. When he finished he stood lopsided in front of her.

They were half way down the front path leaving Phil's house when Angela commented the garden was immaculate. That it was lined with those roses that drifted a sweet scent inside on warm, wet evenings. Warren knew what Angela would say next. It was the question about whether Phil had worked on the garden as part of preparing to take his life. Had he made it perfect so there was one less matter to worry others?

"We don't know that he took his own life," Warren snapped, pushing through the gate. "Christ, he could have gone wading for all we know."

"What?" Angela said, half under her breath. She stood on the other side of the gate as it grated shut. "I didn't say anything."

"Sorry," Warren said. "I thought you spoke."

At home Angela said how stoic Phil's partner was. Warren had to ask what stoic meant. After that he stood over the sink, forcing a knife through a sweet potato before shredding skin off its sides. Later they ate together. Angela asked if he was okay. After dinner he said he was tired. They cleaned up, angling plates under steaming jets of hot water. Angela went ahead and Warren heard pipes shudder as the shower turned on. By the time he walked upstairs she had finished. From the shower to their bed her watery footprints trailed. For a long time he stared at them.

Goodbye Opa

The house stank of medicines. I checked around, making sure there were no break-ins or the mildew I scrubbed last month hadn't returned. The odour lingered around the entrance where bay windows jutted into the front yard. It channelled down corridors. It was especially heavy in my grandfather's bedroom. Whenever I inhaled in there I tasted the salt of that time he kissed me. He had aimed for a cheek, one of his dry pecks that had less feeling than his cuffs across the back of my head while growing up. On one occasion I turned my head and the kiss landed on my mouth. I wanted to spit it out. Now I worried about breathing the spores inside the house. Always threw my clothes in the wash when I returned home.

"He's so pale," my brother said at the end of one of our visits. We stood in the car park at the back of the nursing home, air grainy with mist. "If a mosquito bit him he'd need a blood transfusion. Switch on a torch behind him and he'd look like an x-ray."

I nodded. Asked what he expected from a ninety eight year old. Cigarette smoke sputtered with my words. I ground the butt into loose gravel.

At home Rita asked how my grandfather was. I looked silently at her. She smiled quickly, stepping forward into me. Her chest pressed into the hollows and lines of my body.

Sometimes I dropped into the nursing home after work. Those were fleeting visits. Long enough to see his hand with the intravenous drip half-heartedly wave. He had about four weeks left, or thereabouts, the doctor said.

"Don't give up on buying a one hundredth birthday card yet," my brother told me. "He's indestructible. Nicotine bounces off him. Can't believe he outlived both his kids. Especially after the life he had. Second World War. Then escaping East Berlin. Searched for by the Stasi."

I often visited when coming home from the football. Clomped in with a woollen scarf prickling my neck. At times the faint chill of swirling drizzle dampened my shoulders. I also called in after going out for coffee. Breathed espressos over him while he asked me to suck a mint next time. A few times held his hand. Skin squeezed between my fingers like wet sand.

"Listen to me," he said last week. He gestured me over. I sat on the bed, wedging against his hip under sheets. "Go to my house. Look in the bottom of my wardrobe. There is a box. On the outside I've written *Bucher*. It means books. Bring me some. Only three or four. They came with me from Berlin. I would very much like to have them with me."

I kissed his forehead. Lines criss-crossed his skin like stitches in a jumper. A nurse came into the doorway.

"We have chicken for you today," she said loudly.

"Tell these people," he said, eyes widening. "I am not deaf."

I stood, smiling at the nurse and shrugging.

"Goodbye Opa," I said. The nurse stood back to let me out.

I rang my brother to tell him our grandfather wanted some books. I imagined them carefully boxed up decades ago for his voyage to Port Melbourne.

"What for? They've been in those boxes for years. Probably turned to dust from weevils by now. He can't feed himself. Can't even pick his nose. How's he going to read?"

I explained he probably wanted them close by. Maybe for nothing more than to see them lined up next to the bed. Perhaps there were old memories of reclining in armchairs reading.

"Fine," my brother said. "At least he can't ask us to read them to him since they're probably in German."

The next day I drove to our grandfather's house. Soggy rolls of junk mail hung from his letterbox. I shook them out and went inside. The house was cold and I pulled the lapels of a coat together. Inside it was dark as if underground. I yanked a curtain open.

I once played in those rooms. On my knees in front of the gas fire I jammed pieces of Lego together. Drew stick figures on envelopes Opa had torn open so they would lie flat. Looked down an old microscope at a hair or fingernail. Watched his black and white television.

The wardrobe doors clicked open. They creaked on old hinges.

I dragged out a box. It grated against floorboards as it slid out. The flaps were taped down and I reached into my pocket for car keys, hacking at the tape with them. Eventually they tore open and the flaps sprung up. I peered in. Where are the books I almost said out loud. There were only papers. Written in German. I reached in, feeling around for the covers of books, expecting them to be under the papers. Towards the bottom I felt the sharp corners of what I guessed were photographs. I scooped a few into my hand and drew them out.

The first two could have been anywhere in Europe. They were gloomy black and white. Ground covered with snow undulated into distance. Blackened trunks of trees stood here and there. There was a picture of a house, snow cleared from the front footpath. In another picture a tank was stopped on the side of the road, fog of smoke pouring from it. The next picture stopped me. Our grandfather wore a white coat, stethoscope dangling around his neck. He smiled confidently into the camera. It was the smile we'd all fallen for at times. He won arguments with that smile. Charmed strangers. Received twenty per cent discounts and had people stand back to let him through. In the next picture he posed with two men in suits. I reached into the box again. Pulled out as many pictures as I could hold, placing them side by side like cards in solitaire. At first I thought he was assisting a surgeon helping war casualties. It was nothing he'd ever told us about. We only knew him as someone forced to serve in the German infantry, surviving a few months on the Russian front. Years after migrating he became a tip truck driver, dumping topsoil in new estates so home buyers could plant vegetable patches or grow roses. In another picture he posed with a scalpel, wearing a surgeon's mask. He was poised above someone while making an incision. It didn't occur to me at first. In each picture his patients were trussed down. In one someone restrained the patient from behind, hands on their shoulders. His patients were awake.

"Two phone calls in two days. Anyone would think we're related." I listened to my brother speak and walk around the house on his mobile. I could tell where he was; passing the television, shutting the cutlery drawer and dragging out a chair in his study.

"You'd better get down here," I said.

"Only if you found a fortune in cash," he said. "It'd be worthless anyway. They use Euros instead of Deutschmarks now don't they?"

After I hung up I stood outside the room. Light shone weakly down walls. It wasn't strong enough to see the squares where pictures once hung, the holes from picture hooks and lines of smudges and fingerprints. I stood motionless in the chilled air. I wasn't going to go back in until my brother arrived. I concentrated for the muted slam of a car door or a flare of headlights through curtains. Even when I faced down the other end of the house I was still seeing the pictures. I could stay out of that room forever but those pictures would always be with me now.

I met my brother at the front door.

"Must be four below in here," he said. "Need my fingers amputated for frostbite after five minutes inside this place."

I led him through the house. I heard him stumble over uneven carpet behind me. He asked if I'd found a body or a treasure map.

We walked into the room. The photographs crookedly lined up, as if the people in them had moved. My brother stepped around me, looking down at them.

"Find some memorabilia did we?" he said. He folded arms and glanced around. I told him to look closer. Slowly he lowered to knees, delicately putting weight on them. I watched him scan over the pictures. I told him there were others I hadn't looked at yet.

"Shit. He was a Nazi," my brother said quietly.

"One of those doctors doing experiments," I added. "Look at those people. Their faces. They aren't under any anaesthetic."

He touched the photographs lightly, as if comforting people in them. His gaze went from one to the next. I kneeled next to him, studying each picture also. Some were joyful. People were around a table in one, toasting glasses. In another he posed next to an early Mercedes Benz. In one picture he stood in a hunting party, gun pointing down and tucked under an arm.

I lit a cigarette, holding the thick warmth inside me.

"Do you have to?" my brother said.

I blew smoke away from him. Asked if we should tell our grandfather. Let him know we knew his secret. My brother shook his head, muttering he didn't know.

Slowly I picked up the pictures, one at a time, fitting them into the palm of my hand. My brother picked up only one, looking at it intently before slipping it into a pocket. I returned the others to the box, jamming the flaps down. Pulled out the next box. It was heavier. Again using car keys I sliced open the flaps, taking out the top three books.

"Look at us doing what he wants and making him happy despite what we know now," I said.

We walked out, sound of our steps ricocheting off walls down the hallway. In the cold air outside it seemed my blood flowed slower. I slammed the door behind me, twisting the key in the lock. We stood at the front gate exhaling steam.

"So he experimented on kids too?" my brother asked.

"That's what the pictures suggest."

He shook his head. I lit another cigarette, inhaling greedily so that it felt I'd overfilled my lungs. My brother looked off towards the wet shine of our cars under streetlights. He said it was incredible. Our grandfather had brought up two kids. Then we were born. We'd been told he read to us from picture books, his stumpy fingers pointing at pictures while he made exaggerated smiles to increase our excitement. He took us fishing, walked us through the insect exhibition at the museum, picked strawberries with us at Red Hill and swam with us in the still bay waters, showing us how to angle our elbows when stroking to go faster. How could he love us like that after what he'd done to other children? I asked again what we should do. My brother said he didn't want to think about it.

Rita met me at our front door. She pulled the coat off my back, saying it felt like I'd been trekking the steppes in Russia. Then she shadowed me past the smell of the clay pot chicken she loved to cook, through the rising currents of central heating and to the couch. She was asking what was wrong without speaking, her hand gliding up and down my arm.

"We found out our grandfather was a Nazi. He conducted medical experiments on people. Including kids. Jesus. You hear of people finding out their relatives cheated on tax, had affairs or gambled. But this?"

Rita asked how I knew. I told her quickly, wanting the recollection to be over with. When I finished she was silent. I picked up the remote, flicking on the television. We stared at late night news. I knew Rita was struggling with what to do, so I made it easy for her and lay down, propping my head in her lap. Her fingers traced gently along my scalp.

In the morning I rang in sick. I couldn't face pretending everything was fine during meetings. I lay in bed watching Rita dress. She drew on black stockings. Her bare back curved and strained as she twisted them into place. Leaned over her for a few seconds, kneading my fingers into her shoulder blades. She moaned softly and I felt the tingle of her nerves. She asked over her shoulder if I was sure I'd be all right. After she left the phone rang. It was my brother.

"Called you at work," he said. "How come you're at home? Decided the company coffee isn't to your standard anymore?"

"Was wondering how close Opa went to being caught," I said. "Maybe being arrested and appearing at the Nuremburg trials. He could still be charged. It wouldn't matter though. He wouldn't live long enough for any trial."

My brother said his blood also ran through our veins. We had the DNA of a murderer or sadist.

"I'm going to see him after work tomorrow," I said. My brother was silent. He breathed nasally through the phone.

"What're you going to do?" he said.

I said I wouldn't know until I looked into his eyes. Then neither of us talked. I sensed my brother's tension. The line was so quiet he could be holding his breath. I asked him not to do anything until we had agreed.

At work the next day I did nothing. I went to a bar at lunch, watching ice hockey from Canada. People mostly ignored it, standing in tight circles talking. I walked back to work the long way, past lattes being served to outside tables, cups and saucers ringing. After finishing the day I drove to the nursing home. I gripped the books and locked the car. As always it was quiet. It was possible at times to believe no one lived there. Glass sliding doors at the front of the building rumbled open. Reception always felt overheated, air stale as if breathed by other lungs before mine.

My grandfather was being fed. The nurse turned to me and asked if I would like to do it. I agreed to without enthusiasm and took the bowl from her. The food was pulped in a way that reminded me of baby food. As if you ate the same food at both ends of life. I displayed the bowl in front of his face. Without any expression he opened his mouth. Now and then I dabbed flecks of food from his lips. By the time we started on dessert the ice cream was melted. My brother came in to the room, crossing to the front of the bed.

"How is he?" he asked. "There's not much of him left. You'd find more body weight in a skin graft." He circled around behind me. "How goes it Opa? Anyone tried any unusual medical procedure on you today? See how you'd react to an injection of petrol? Infected you with typhoid to see what happens?"

I glanced around at my brother, trying to silence him with my eyes. Anger had welled up in him, his body bunched and hard. Our grandfather's mouth hung open but his eyes were sharp and staring. I set down the bowl, standing from the bed. I spoke to my brother while he bobbed in my corner vision. Asked him why he was bringing this up. I'd said we were meant to agree before saying anything. Why had he come here and just blurted it out? He stayed silent, slowly reaching inside a pocket. He took out a photograph. I saw it as he passed the picture across the front of me, dropping it on the bed. It was the one where our grandfather stood with children, handing them sweets. One of them looked adoringly up at him.

"Think of the care you have here," my brother said. "These nurses. The life you had. Married, children, then grandchildren. Driving the streets of this country freely to earn a living. Did you ever wonder whether you deserved any of it?"

My brother turned from us. At first he moved in a way where I thought he might shift the food tray. Move a chair into its right position. Go to a window and look out. But he kept going. His footsteps became silent so quickly I knew he had gone to that front door as fast as he could. From the room I heard the door tremble and slide as it opened. If I believed what I'd read about how thunderstorms were made I could have expected one right then as the cold air of the car park mingled with the stifling hot air of the nursing home.

I picked up my bag. Slowly I drew out the three books I had brought. I positioned them against each other on the bed head, so they tipped together at an angle. I waited for a few seconds to see if they would fall before I walked out.

Somewhere on a Dirt Road

Her fingers tugged the thread. She bowed her head and bit the end off. Then Bronwyn drew back to examine the stitches. She touched fingertips to the tip of her tongue, wetting them. Bronwyn dampened and twisted another thread before easing it through the end of a needle. Her needle glided in and out of material. When Bronwyn finished she passed a shirt hanging from fingertips.

"Thanks," Mark said. He kissed her cheek. Dabs of warmth from her fingers brushed his skin.

Downstairs their daughter Nicole slept. Mark eased into her room. He stood in gloom, eyes adjusting as her outline emerged. She lay on her side, breathing quietly. Mark stroked the halo of her hair. Earlier he cradled Nicole through rooms, speaking that dialect he kept for her. Honey, little one, my first born, he whispered. They were words he saved for the quiet moments when it was only them. When he carried her dozing across the floorboards his feet padded like muted heartbeats. Whenever she woke the space he picked her up from was warm with body heat.

The phone rang through the house. Nicole jolted in her sleep. Mark heard Bronwyn's single word answer, hushed and dry. Someone from the netball team he guessed. It could be her mother. But in a few seconds she was behind Mark, saying it was for him.

"Know you weren't expecting to hear from me." The call was six words in before Mark recognised the voice. "Didn't want to ring you. When did we last speak? About the time the Dead Sea scrolls were written?"

Mark looked around for Bronwyn. She was at the backdoor, staring into sunshine the seven day forecast had promised. He heard raspy, pack a day habit breathing on the phone. He blurted out what did he want? Why now after so long?

"This isn't a how's your wife, footy team or what's the weather like at your place call."

Mark never expected to hear from Joel again. He remembered lines like old surgery scars through his cheeks. Nails chewed down to dried blood. Soft, bloated veins lining backs of hands. Joel drawled they needed to meet. It was important and had to be today. There was no point in creating excuses about relatives visiting or everyone having the flu.

Bronwyn kneeled in the garden. She leaned over the vegetable patch she'd painstakingly built. Humps of dark earth rose from the ground with lines of tomatoes growing from them. Tangles of beans cluttered along the fence. She worked with gardening gloves with more soil ground into them than Mark had ever handled. He told her he was going out. Have a coffee with an old friend. No one she would remember. She squinted when looking back at him, shading a hand over eyes. Sometimes it was as if Bronwyn could see so far into him she could tell which knee would go first or what he'd say next.

Mark drove in stop start traffic.

"What? You demand to see me now? As far as I remember I don't owe you money. Didn't borrow anything of yours I never gave back. Didn't take your girlfriend. So what do you want?" Mark regretted not saying that now. He'd been ambushed. During Saturday afternoons he was usually in a daze. Still shedding his week of budget cuts and endless meetings. If Joel had rung on a Sunday he would've been clear headed enough to say to leave him alone.

Mark sat and wished for winter. His mind was more composed when it was cool. Some of that northern hemisphere December light would be ideal. Light that barely shifted above horizons uneven with low rise buildings and church spires. Mark was half way through a latte when Joel arrived. They sat opposite at an outside table. The years had been tough on Joel. As if erosion had worn his face back to eye sockets and hundreds of blackheads.

"They found the knife," Joel said.

"What? What knife?"

"Don't you remember? The knife we used. What do you think I meant? Something we once cut up a salad with?"

Joel said police had searched his house. He had a few stolen goods. Couple of televisions, some jewellery and a patterned plate he thought had gold embossing on it. The knife had been wrapped in an old Rolling Stones t-shirt. It'd been under a pile of boxes like a time capsule. Covered in dried blood.

"Why didn't you chuck it away?" Mark said. "Or better, become an accountant or tradie like the rest of civilisation."

A waitress came to the table. She had deep olive skin that seemed to run into her irises. Joel ordered a short black without looking up.

"Didn't want to throw it out. Thought it could turn up somewhere. Then I forgot about it."

Mark faintly remembered the knife. It was the type found next to Sunday roasts in hundreds of houses. Joel had held it under a shirt when they went to the service station. Mark was the driver. Ken accompanied Joel to the shop. Even then Joel was so skeleton-like security cameras would find him harder to recognise than a baby in an ultrasound picture. From the car Mark had seen Joel lunge forward with the knife. The shop assistant twisted away before collapsing. Joel leaned over the counter, grabbing money.

Joel said he had no idea where Ken was now. He'd always wanted to live in Laos and perhaps he was there. Probably chain smoking in a room thick with monsoon heat and a tribe of skin and bone kids.

Joel ran a hand through his jet black dyed hair. He said they would eventually find out the knife had been in a crime. That the blood on it was human. His fingerprints would be in it like little plaster casts of him. I'm rooted he said. He covered his face with hands. A coffee was placed in front of him. His face was blotched red when he reached for it.

"You and Ken. You just went your own ways. How much did we get? Forty bucks each? I saw you on the other side of the street one day. In your suit. Italian wool was it? That road I saw you across may as well have been a border between countries. And Ken. I hope he's shaking to death from malaria."

Mark sipped the coffee. It singed the roof of his mouth. People strolled by. Fragments of conversations blurred past. Joel wiped the corners of his mouth with a serviette.

"Don't mean to be a bastard," he said. "But I need money. I can get out of here, lie low. Know some people in northern New South Wales I can stay with. Who knows, country living might be like an organ transplant to my body. I'll have cleaner insides. But need money first. Need to get up there with enough to survive on." He rolled a cigarette. "You know what I'm saying? If they start charging me with this there's going to be a point that they offer some kind of deal if I name who else was in it. I might even say I snatched the knife to stop the stabbing. It was someone else who did it."

Mark said he had no money to give. That Joel would be better off looking for coins that slipped down the back of his couch. He shouldn't have used it up on becoming addicted to cough medicine and cask wine.

Joel finished his coffee. Mark heard him swallow its dregs and four heaped sugars.

"You don't know about jail," Joel said. "Watched 'The Shawshank Redemption' have we? Seen jail with a few ad breaks from the comfort of your two thousand dollar couch? Had two months there myself. Perhaps I'll be doing you a favour if I tell them. You could do with a little humility."

Mark pushed back sharply from the table. He felt like a swimmer tumble turning off a wall. He stood, glimpsing the grey roots of Joel's stringy hair. He balled up a ten dollar note and dropped it on the table.

Nicole was in a high chair eating. Late afternoon sun pooled along floorboards. Bronwyn sat back, letting their daughter put fistfuls of mashed pumpkin into her mouth. She smiled tiredly at Mark coming into the room. They kissed, her warmth whisking over his skin. He stood back. He almost told her about the afternoon, thankful that Nicole was too young to understand. He had the first word half out but Bronwyn stood, blowing air sideways so that a rat tail of hair lying across eyes puffed off her face. She went back and forth to the laundry. Through the thin walls he heard her rummaging. Clothes dropped dully into a washing machine. Water gushed. Mark went to the kitchen, twisting off the top of a beer. The moment was gone. A new life had started. A life of his body jumping whenever the doorbell rang. Imagining Joel on city corners on his way to the office. Being convinced someone followed him.

When was the last time he saw 3.30 AM? On his way back from a fortieth a few months ago as pea sized hail cracked over the windscreen? During the occasional sprint over cold tiles to the toilet? Now he lay there at that time, digital clock glowing red numbers. Mark turned over, dragging a sheet off his wife. He could explain it to her now. Rouse her gently, so that she would stretch, her back arching. He would wait up on an elbow while she asked what was wrong. Or he could tell her over breakfast so he would go to work and she had the day for it to sink in. He needed to say it in case Joel talked to the police. It was so long ago. He was someone else then. That person was no more him than all the dead skin cells he had shed since.

Mark showered, standing in thin streams of hot water, his skin patchy red. He dried. With a shirt on he went into their bedroom, standing over Bronwyn. She slept on her back, shoulders dipping and lifting in breath. Mark decided to write her a note. He normally avoided letters. He was more at ease with numbers. Share dividends, profit, loss and return on investment were his language. He could try to break it to her in that writing she often said a handwriting expert would say was an introvert trying to be flamboyant. Mark went downstairs and ate, biting toast down to crusts and throwing them away. "My Dear Bronwyn," he wrote on the note before screwing it up. He never spoke to her like that. "Bronwyn," he wrote and tore the paper into quarters. He would tell her tonight.

Bronwyn's eyes startled open when Mark bent to kiss her goodbye. He told her to go back to sleep. At work he drank milky coffees, keeping to himself. He cancelled appointments, closing the door to his office. From his sixteenth story window he watched the city bend under heatwaves.

Late in the day the drive home felt long. Mark kept trying to overtake someone driving too slowly. What he had rehearsed to say deserted him. He pulled into the driveway. Garden flowers slumped in the heat. He went inside. Bronwyn looked exhausted, eyelids half closed. They barely kissed. He knelt down next to Nicole kicking on the floor. Her eyes gleamed at him.

Mark told Bronwyn after they put Nicole to bed. Sat next to her on the couch before she picked up the remote. Her face creased with confusion at first. She asked if he was describing someone else. How could he keep this from her for so long? What else was there that she didn't know? She asked had she known a stranger all this time. Then Nicole started sobbing and Bronwyn rushed to her. Mark waited, sitting in half light, hearing occasional muffled sounds from Nicole's bedroom. Finally he went to the door and eased it open. Bronwyn slept in the chair she used to breast feed in. Her head sagged to one side. Mark went to wake her, even had a hand tentatively on her arm. But he left her there. Went to bed realising he wouldn't sleep. In the hours when the house cooled he felt Bronwyn come to bed, easing in like someone slowly entering a cold bath.

In the morning Mark lay in the twisted sheets. They'd been up to Nicole three times. He hovered around the door each time Bronwyn put her down. They were wordless, following routines, Mark picking Nicole up and changing a nappy, Bronwyn soothing and bottle feeding.

When Mark next woke he stood and remarked he might fall asleep driving. He went to the bathroom, lathering soap over his face then shaving with a blunt blade he couldn't be bothered changing. He scuffed quietly in socks between rooms. Then he paused over Nicole, shallow breathing as he looked at her.

By lunch Mark told his boss he had a headache. He packed up quickly before anyone had a chance to ask if he was fine to drive home. In a few moments he was in the cool of the underground car park.

He was home faster without the sluggish peak hour traffic. Flowers in the front yard were even more wilted. After last night he'd forgotten to water them. Inside was hot too, as if air conditioning was off. He announced himself as he loosened his tie, dragging the knot across his throat.

The silence stopped him. He listened to it, turning his head to hear anything through the open doorways down the hallway.

"Bronwyn," he called. Normally she told him if she was taking Nicole out.

In the kitchen he saw the note. Folded with the same precision Bronwyn arranged flowers, dressed Nicole or laid dinner on a plate. It was her voice when he read, as if she stood next to the angle of his elbow. She had taken Nicole. Don't look for us. Need time. How could you?

It was typical of Bronwyn's planning. Plenty of food. Bed made. Washing finished. Mark sat, staring outside at earth powdery from heat. A couple of times he heard something and went to the door. Neighbours slammed car doors and hauled in wheelie bins. There was no Bronwyn returning, telling him what he had done was terrible but she'd decided to come home.

A car door shut. The sound was right in their driveway. Mark set down a beer and hurried along the hallway. He threw open the door, half outside in frayed socks and unbuttoned shirt.

"Are you okay sir?" Two police walked towards him. One was a woman, carrying a folder. She asked if anything was wrong. Mark watched them cautiously. Ten years ago, he prepared to say. Wasn't I driving around Australia, somewhere on a dirt road up north? Don't know anything about a robbery. Think I was barramundi fishing. Maybe I have to confess to keeping a couple that were undersize. That's about it.

They stood opposite him. The policewoman asked if he knew Joel Storm. Mark said they met for a coffee recently. Were friends from a long time ago.

"He died from an overdose last night. It may have been a suicide. Neighbour found him. We came to see you because he had your name and phone number written on a piece of paper. We wanted to tell you personally." Mark nodded. "Do you know why he might have taken his own life?"

"Seemed happy when I saw him," Mark said. He was surprised at how easily that came out. He said it with exact eye contact, not a flinch or moving of feet that gave it away.

"Okay," the policewoman said. "We wanted to let you know. There will be an autopsy. Do you know if he had any relatives?"

Mark said he didn't know. They nodded and left, sitting in front seats and saying something that made them laugh. Mark never saw where Joel lived but guessed it to be a two rooms plus toilet above a shop somewhere. He probably woke rough from fidgety sleeps, shaving with dirty blades and drinking strong coffees that turned his teeth dark years ago. The police drove away, keeping to the fifty kilometre speed limit in the street.

He went inside. Cooled air enveloped him. He sat in a kitchen chair, angling it towards the front door. Twenty four hours. If Joel had taken his life twenty four hours earlier none of this would have happened. Bronwyn would be none the wiser. Mark would have told the police he hadn't seen Joel for years. Not since he left him half passed out at a pub that was demolished long ago. Bronwyn may have even come up behind him, giving the police that reassuring smile that nothing wrong could ever happen here.

Now Mark had to lie. He would in some ways have to go back to the person he was behind the steering wheel all those years ago. He raked over what he would say when Bronwyn and he finally spoke. They made him drive that night. Forced him. Joel had held the blade of that knife up to Mark's face. There was no choice. He would keep talking until Bronwyn's eyes closed so he saw spidery veins in her lids. She might cry and tip lightly against his chest. Within a few days they would again discuss whether Nicole's room was too bright in the morning, if they should try her on chicken or whether it was time to open a trust account.

My Mother's Wedding

I first smelt salt about half an hour from town. It gusted through car vents. I wound down the window and sea breeze skidded along my face. As the car slowed I heard waves collapsing behind pines lining the beach.

Two streets past the pub I turned off. On the dark road lay the gloomy outline of fences and front porches. Finally the hum of bitumen ended. I eased off the road, swinging into a driveway. A porch light came on.

The doormat was worn back to wires holding it together. There was a low throb of television voices. I knocked. Limping footsteps came to the door. Porch light fell across her face as the door opened.

"Oh thank God!" she called over a shoulder. "Let me look at you. You seem okay on the outside at least. Who knows what you're like on the inside from smoking. Come in, come in."

We hugged. Her hand patted my back. I asked if she would worry less if I brought along my latest blood test results.

She stood back and I looked at her. She was heavily lined around eyes. Under my breath I blamed the old man. She wound her arm around mine and led me into the lounge room decorated with dozens of photographs. I saw myself in black and whites of school uniform, sitting in my first car and smiling crookedly at a football club barbecue.

"It's how I stopped you moving out completely," she said.

"Well, well. Is he back for the real estate? Or to do his customary cameo appearance?"

"Good to see you too," I said to my brother. He breathed pub curry over me and shook my hand.

"Now, come on," our mother said. She looked at me and there was an old impulse to tuck in my shirt or wash hands. "I want you to meet my beau."

"Stop using those fifties expressions Mum," my brother said. "Do you want the National Trust to list you as a heritage site?"

A man stepped forward.

"Max. Max Barker. Knew you'd be Maggie's son. You've got her chin." He smiled nervously while my mother hovered. We shook hands.

She started explaining wedding arrangements. I would walk her down the aisle, being the older son. The ceremony held by the foreshore if weather permitted. My brother finished a scotch, swallowing deeply across the room.

"Keeping it small," Max added. "Strictly family. Give or take a seagull." She laughed, pirouetting around to him and kissing his cheek.

After a few moments I lit a cigarette and went outside. Waves thudded from distance. When I grew up here they sometimes kept me awake and at other times lulled me to sleep.

"Don't think Mum's garden approves of having to passively smoke," my brother said, coming from behind a bush and zipping up his fly.

"It'd rather passively smoke than be pissed on," I said.

"What do you think of old Max?" he said.

I told him he seemed okay. He stood around her as if he was a butler.

"Big bastard," my brother said. "He'd bump into something every time he breathes out."

I lit another cigarette with the old one and flicked the butt away. Orange embers popped in darkness.

"You'll be seeing Wren?" he asked.

I gulped cigarette smoke. Said I didn't know. His head hadn't turned towards me but I sensed him straining to look out corners of eyes, checking my expression. I took a long drag, trying to finish.

"Come on, you can tell me." I knew from the sound of his voice he was smiling. "It's the real reason you're here isn't it? Otherwise you'd just send dear old Mum a set of steak knives and say you were on another of your interstate trips. I see Wren from time to time you know. Wouldn't mind taking up where you left off."

"Why don't you ask all the men in town for permission? In case she's been promised in an arranged marriage. You could offer her father a dowry. Give him a couple of cows. Then have one of those week long receptions where everyone sings and throws rose petals over you." I walked off, pausing to step on the cigarette.

Inside my mother insisted I eat. Food was not just to fill a space she lectured. Eating wasn't a chore, not another thing to be rushed the way cities make you hurry meals and telephone calls to your family. I asked if she'd like to start packing my lunches again. Max lumbered in and said if only we had a fifth of her wisdom. She ran a hand through his hair and dandruff flaked away.

I picked through dinner and went to the lounge room. Max and my mother crushed together on the couch watching television. When she laughed her head tipped against his shoulder. I went to the car and peeled a coat off the driver's seat. Drew it around me, squeezing hands deep into pockets where they touched clods of lint. Then I walked to the pub. The sea breeze blew old decades past me; stomping through puddles on the way to school, being sea sick on the trawler in my first job, hanging around billiard tables and my milk teeth smashed in by the old man.

I stood outside the pub, smoking and blowing circles of smoke that bent and faded away. Inside it was hot, as if they'd trapped a little of last summer in there. I ordered a scotch to wash down the nicotine. A few people who remembered me came and went.

"Here he is. How yer been? Hear your mum's getting married. To Max from the bowl's club? That's where they met isn't it? They say he was always peeping through the fence when it was ladies day. What about you? Heard you're a real success in the city. No wife or kids, just sitting in an office and travelling around. Sounds like the life to me."

I was quickly bored with the conversations. Perhaps that's the effect small towns had on me now. I ordered a last scotch as I couldn't rely on body fat to keep me warm for the walk home. Right then I knew she was there. Turned around and she looked hard and unsmiling back at me.

"Heard you'd be back. Didn't believe it though," Wren said. "You're not one for visiting." She slouched on the bar and rolled up sleeves on a man's flannelette shirt.

"How are you?" I said.

"Let me think." She shrugged. "During the past three years? Well, I've had eleven colds, fourteen mosquito bites, one sprain. And a breakdown because of some guy who suddenly left that I had to get over."

I looked away to the rows of labels on bottles. Conversations lifted and fell dully around me.

"Wren..."

"Scotch and ice Mannie," she interrupted, calling across the bar. "Wren. You remember why you called me that? Because I was thin and jumpy like those little birds that can't keep still."

I went to mutter had I arrived in a time warp? Had nothing moved on from three years ago? I put a cigarette in my mouth and let it hang there unlit. Mannie looked at me, trying to catch my eye so he could tell me not to light it.

"So what're you doing?" I asked.

Wren snatched the cigarette out of my mouth. Backs of fingers grazed my lips.

"I'm with Steveo. Remember him? Works on the trawlers. Never bought his own boat. Gets his wages on a Friday, spends all day Saturday pissing them out. Still, if I get sick of him there's always your brother. He's made more passes at me than times Steveo's nodded off during foreplay."

Wren laughed and sat on the stool next to me. That was the Wren I knew for a split second, rush of shoulder along mine and that easy laugh. Her drink arrived. She tilted it to her mouth and half-finished it.

"Do you ever wish you stayed?" Her voice was hushed, coming under the blur of conversation close to us.

"Sometimes." Shook my head and smiled. "Imagine if I stayed. Be living in a caravan up in the hills, scratching a few dollars from making organic soap and flogging it at the markets."

Wren stirred her drink with a finger and looked at me. We'd gazed at each other like that across pillows, coffees, my bad cooking and bench seats in an old Holden.

"You left me," she said. "You just went. You were gone before my smell would've faded off you." I pulled away from her gaze, staring into my glass before swigging.

"You know what happened," I said. "Couldn't stay in a place where the biggest event of the year was a thunderstorm. Had to get out. And you wanted to stay. That's all there was to it."

"Then take me with you this time." My glass grated against teeth when she said that. I closed eyes, safe in that darkness, like replaying a recording of the last few seconds of my life and erasing it. Then my back was slapped, the same sound against Wren's, as if there'd been an echo.

"Nothing like a little kissing and making up!" Steveo said, pushing between us. "Hey Mannie!" he called. "These two lovebirds try to drag you down to the registry office as a witness? Or maybe we'll have a double celebration tomorrow. Mother as well as son tie the knot."

Wren hung her head.

"Stop it," she hissed.

I drained my glass and stood eye to eye with Steveo. His cheeks were ruddy red from windburn and alcohol. He smiled lopsided, as if there was too much weight on one side of his face.

"Been great seeing you," Steveo slurred. He slithered an arm around the back of Wren's neck, pulling her towards him. She tipped heavily against his beanpole physique. "See that? She swoons into a coma at the sight of me."

I shrugged into my coat.

"You could get work in one of those animal research places," I said. "All the lab rats would pass out at the sight of you. They wouldn't need anaesthetic." For a second his eyes went sharp and beady, then the drunkenness seeped back in. I left, walking home and checking over my shoulder every few paces.

I was up early the next morning despite a headache above my eyes. The house was still and quiet. I went outside, climbing inside my car and driving into the nearby hills. Tourists often went up there to admire the views. They looked out over the ocean at furrows of water drifting closer and in formation like the rounded bones of a ribcage. They could look along the coast at long strips of sand and horse shoe shaped bays. Some of them would gaze back towards the hills, deeply forested with crevasses shadowing through them. I sometimes went there when I lived in the town. From the cliff, slightly back from the white poles of a safety fence I now stared back over glaring metal roofs. That's when I remembered how much I hated that place. How Sundays were slept away by the trawler crews on their only day off. Tuesdays people milled around the school fund raising stalls, buying scones and apple strudels so fresh farmers said the pieces of apple were still growing. Wednesdays were who would be the goal umpire for the away game and Thursdays was the pub's weekly snooker tournament. Then Fridays were a counter meal at the pub with the family, eating together in silence. Around the third time I was beaten up in Year Seven high school I realised there was nothing for me there.

By the time I arrived back it was still early. I dozed on the couch. My mother's voice brought me awake. She called my name shyly through the blanket I'd pulled over myself.

"You want your old mum to make you breakfast? I'll make you a logger's special. Bacon, eggs, toast, tomatoes, coffee so strong it'll snap the elastic in your undies. Have you looked outside? It's going to be a beautiful day for a wedding. We're so lucky."

I sat up, massaging temples with thumbs. The thought of breakfast made me sick. I stood next to the window and pulled back curtains. Rain long gone had left dirty streaks on the window. I went to the kitchen.

"Got a real artery cloggier for you," my brother said, sliding a plate across the table. "Mum's triple cholesterol special."

"Where's Max?" I asked.

My mother smiled as she sat down with us.

"Bad luck to see the groom before the ceremony on your wedding day," she said.

"Is that what went wrong last time? The match made in hell wasn't it?" my brother said.

"Let's hope all that bacon gives you a blood clot in the tongue so you can't talk," I said to him.

My brother cut hard into the food so that his knife screeched across the plate.

"Surprised you could make it," he said sullenly. "Heard you couldn't decide between necking a scotch bottle or pashing Wren last night."

"I gave her that name," I muttered. "From now on you can't use it. Make up your own if she lets you into her life enough for you to use one."

Our mother dropped her knife and fork. They clanged on the plate, chipping an edge. Her head dropped into hands. We watched her sobbing behind grey ropey veins. I stood, cupping hands over her jerking shoulders.

"Can't you two ever get along? Even on my wedding day?" she said, sniffing and dabbing a handkerchief to eyes. She folded it and stood, shaking me off. "I have to get ready."

My brother and I cleaned up without speaking, swerving around each other as we carried plates. When we finished I went outside for a smoke. To my surprise he followed. He stepped back from where my smoke blew past him. I asked if he ever heard from the old man.

"Not a word. He could be dead, at sea, suffering amnesia or just out there not giving a stuff. I don't care as long as he doesn't show his face here. You're marginally more welcome."

The cigarette trembled between my fingers as I put it in my mouth.

"What's your problem?" I asked.

"You'd never think the same blood flowed through our veins," he said. "Sometimes I'm not sure if I'm just a house servant."

"What do you mean?" He stared towards the sea, biting his bottom lip.

"Three years ago you left. The old man hadn't been long gone. Whilst you swanned around the country, I'm stuck at home looking after our mother. You visit at Christmas and get fussed over. Meanwhile I'm just a household appliance doing domestics. Now you're asked to walk her down the aisle. I mean, what am I besides taken for granted?"

I watched him grimly.

"Probably be cut out of the will for farting at the dining table," he added. "Find one of those gutless letters with the will they write before dying, saying what a disappointment you've been."

We walked inside in silence, going to our separate rooms. Heard my mother humming, voice trailing off at parts she couldn't remember.

After we were ready my brother drove us to the foreshore. People had gathered, even a few tourists expecting a market. Max faced the sea stiffly, gusts of breeze flattening clothes against him. I nodded at a few people as I slid out of the car and opened a door for my mother.

"It's chilly," she said. I hadn't noticed but agreed anyway. My brother hurried ahead, detouring around the aisle marked out with lines of pegs with little ribbons trailing from the tops. The celebrant signalled us forward. I noticed Max mumbling to him, probably about bowls to ease his nerves. I fell into step with my mother's limp. Her fingers nestled over my arm. Off to one side I saw Wren, a couple of rows back but moving slowly in time with us. Our eyes met and held, finding each other again and again between the bobbing heads lining the aisle. My mother squeezed my arm.

"Remember your brother." Her lips never moved and I thought it was telepathy. Her smile glided along the rows of faces and settled on Max. He looked around to her at the same time, nervous but happy. Her hand lifted off my arm, leaving a palm print of warmth through my sleeve. I veered off, going to stand next to my brother.

When it was over the celebrant came over to us.

"You know a lot of young couples don't look happy as those two."

"Thanks," my brother said. "But don't expect a tip for telling us."

People mingled, slapping our backs and shaking hands. As the crowd drifted away Wren came up to me.

"Stay right there you two," my brother said. "I'll see if this celebrant guy offers bulk discounts." He walked off to where my mother was being photographed.

"Wren," I said. "I've been thinking."

She turned me as if I was swung gently through a step from a slow dance. When her back was to the crowd she pulled me by the shirt front to her, kissing me hard on the mouth. Just as my eyes closed she swayed back.

"In case anyone gossips that's for congratulations," Wren said.

"Look," I blurted out. "You could come with me. It wouldn't be that hard. Get away from here and leave bloody Steveo." She stood in front of me, squinting into glare off water.

"Forget what I said at the pub," she said. "I don't know what it was. A rush of blood from seeing you, mixed with a couple of scotches. You know I can't."

I went to speak again but she covered my mouth. Warm breath blew back into me off her hand. She tried to smile and backed away. I took a step after her but Max intercepted me.

"What're you doing? Finding out where the fish are biting? Come over and be photographed with your mother."

At home my brother was packing his car. He thrust a saucepan into the boot and clumps of hair fell into his eyes. He wiped it out with the back of a hand.

"Off again are we?" he said. "See you at Christmas? Or will I just snap freeze your Christmas dinner and post it so you can microwave your helping. Maybe send us a DVD of you eating it."

I asked where he'd be living. He dropped a box into the last space in the boot, forcing it so that the cardboard sides split.

"Found a bungalow. It's out the back of a collapsing old place. Will be rent free if I help fix the house up. Reckon where I'll be sleeping has been a shed, stable and garage.

Long as I can get a TV reception and find my way home from the pub I'll be right."

"Send me the address," I said.

He nodded.

"I'll keep an eye on the honeymooners," he said. "Don't worry about them."

For a few seconds we stood in silence, staring into distance. Then we nodded goodbye in such a similar way it would have been the only time we looked like brothers.

Just before I opened the car I turned my head into the breeze, breathing deeply to find that smell of salt I'd noticed on arriving. It was still there, only something a stranger would notice.

Drowning

Sea breezes shift. Surface of water wrinkles and froths under skidding wind. Back from the quiet lapping of small waves I sit in the park, sheltering from the churning shocks of heat accompanying wind squalls. At times I squint from sharp glints of light. Scrub fires mist distance across the bay. Tourists walk the pier, looking tentatively over sides. Halfway along someone casts out. A father holds a child by shoulders as he points at schools of fish swimming by. Scratchy voices float across water.

I am alone at the picnic table. Everyone stays away when I kick at seagulls. People hurry past when I lob a beer can at the bin. I don't fit with the mood day trippers expect to find here on Sundays. My face has lines as if drawn by someone who pushed too hard on a pen.

Last Sunday someone called the police again. I'd finished a half flagon of port and been sick. Threw up over the wooden picnic table bolted down by Rotary, scalding my throat and nasal passages. Was bending over a bubbler washing the front of my shirt and swishing water around inside my mouth when they came.

"My son died. Don't you remember? Washed up near the outfall. Drifted in like a log. Leave me alone. I've bloody been through enough. All I need is a drink when I'm near the sea."

Sometimes they ask if I'm okay. Offer to drop me somewhere. At times they tell me to move on. I stand emptily in front of them. Over their shoulders grey heat haze and the faint lines of trees shimmer on the horizon.

I haven't walked that pier for years. Not since those king tides, shark caught where people dive and the mine that floated in, bumping menacingly against timbers. Remember how the pier looked under feet back then. Blackened pieces of old chewing gum spotted the planks. Swell sloshed against posts, thudding like the kicking of a football. When leaning on the safety rails I could see rippled sand, the whisking by of a porcupine fish and shards of light in water like torch beams.

I'm not sure where he drowned. It's somewhere past where the pier ends. Where waters turn blue or green, depending on the light. It should be burned into my memory. I'd stared at it so long, willing him to come up. Would think I'd have every detail of it. How the water creased and broke, tug of sea grass in a particular direction, how the exact place would line up against a jut of land or a Banksia tree.

The park empties. Traffic is like tide, coming in through mornings, receding away during afternoons. Light softens. Warmth no longer goes down three layers of skin. I throw a can at seagulls. They lift, swirling around the park, screeching with wings beating. Then they land on an abandoned picnic table.

Our home is two streets from the beach.

"Get you a fortune for this," the real estate agent once told us. "Renovate or incinerate, whoever buys this can't go wrong. Put it on the market and you can buy the whole retirement village. Shout yourself a couple of heart lung machines for when you need them."

My wife Dawn and I eat with the television on. Some nights we hear the neighbour's television too, mounted on a wall in their theatre room, its silvery light glints in our windows. We sit with trays in our laps. Afterwards we have ice cream and a scotch.

"Why? Why now?" Dawn says. "It was thirty three years ago."

I wait for the ads to come on to reply.

"I'm only walking out there. Might try to swim if I make it to the end of the pier."

Dawn wants to know what's the point. Why dwell on it? She's learned to live with a hip replacement, chipped tooth and loss of a son. Why can't I learn to live with our loss? She pushes back in the chair. It screeches over floorboards. She stands. Behind me her plate crashes into the sink. Knives and forks ricochet around.

"Jesus!" I say, but not loudly as it will only make matters worse. Dawn scuffs away. Loose slippers slap along the hallway towards our bedroom.

I swallow some food. It goes down whole, lumpy as a sob coming up. I set the tray on the bench next to the flints of Dawn's broken plate. I follow her path to our room. The door is half closed. There's a familiar smell of lavender soap. Dawn lies across the bed. Her feet hang over the side. From the doorway her soles are brown and cracked around the heels like loaves baked too long. Her top twists half way up her back. There's the bent cleft of her spine and sunspots.

I go to call to her. Feel a whisk of dry breath as I inhale and her name forms in my throat. But her crying stops me. It turns me back so that I slink out of the dull light shining from the room. Even though I retreat through the house I hear her crying from every room.

Without the television on our house is silent. I wonder if Dawn pulled a blanket over herself, burrowed into the bunched sheets of our unmade bed and fell asleep. Perhaps with the faint odours of my perspiration to comfort her.

The warm air of our house bristles along my forehead as I pad towards the second bedroom. Quietly I stand on a chair, reaching through dust and strands of cobwebs into storage space above the wardrobe. Feel around for my old swimming trunks. Smell salt as they tumble out. Colours have leached out from washing machine cycles and diving under waves billowing sand. But my name is still written in slow, careful capital letters on the label.

People say there's a smell with storms. Cool changes blow in the scent of downpours, overflowing gutters and damp earth. In our front yard I notice it when I turn a particular way. When I face the puffed grey cloudbank. Where I feel breeze soft as a secret whispered to my skin. When I return inside Dawn stands from bed. Her skin hangs loosely when she stoops like clothes two sizes too large. In front of her I pull on swimming trunks. She steps into a dress and stands wobbling as she pushes the other leg through. Half way through she looks at me.

"What're you doing?" she asks.

I'm in front of the mirror. Perhaps my body shape when I last wore these was only a moult. It was shed down plug holes, between sheets. The swimmers feel stiff and graze along my skin.

"What're you doing?" Dawn asks again.

"Going to the beach," I tell her. Side on I look like what my son was becoming. Hair wispy on temples. Bony shoulders. Dark creases under eyes that people said made him seem mysterious and me alcoholic. Dawn walks up behind me, holding my gaze in the mirror.

"It won't change anything," she says. Dawn has also been through moults but not her voice. It's still young.

When we speak with lights out it's as if I could touch her skin and it'd be young and taunt again.

"Would he want us to be so timid? That we couldn't go near where it happened? That we can't even look at the place?" I'm speaking louder than I need to. I hang my head as the last word echoes off a window.

Dawn stares at my swimmers. I taught our son to swim while wearing them. Stood by while he furiously dog paddled, his matchstick arms thrashing through water, slapping through the choppy surface. He'd pull up coughing and proud, wiping water from eyes. At the funeral I thought people glared at me, as if I hadn't taught him enough. Perhaps I stopped too early, the way I might have with driving lessons once he could change gears and reverse park.

"They look ridiculous," Dawn says. "They'll fray to nothing if you swim in them."

"You have to come with me," I say.

Across the bay there's lightning. Wads of black clouds scud by. At times thunder throbs. People still swim in the dimming light. Dawn's dress billows in the breeze. She walks with uncertainty on the sand like someone without shoes for the first time.

People stare. My shorts chafe against the insides of legs. From the start of the pier there are small groups of people here and there. They look out over water or point back to shore. That was the place I couldn't go further than after it happened.

"I can't," Dawn says. She falls away from corners of my eyes. I keep walking, even as slow rain falls, coldly prickling my shoulders. The pier is concrete now. There's no slats against arches of feet, no splinters nicking heels. Now and then a cigarette butt sticks to the soul of my foot before it flicks off. People look at me curiously as they hurry the other way, holding newspapers or towels over heads.

I stand at the end of the pier. Thirty three years ago I passed through this space. Left twirls of breath, perspiration, dabs of warmth from the touch of Dawn's toes behind my knees or squash of her ribs to mine when we slept. Can guess now where he slipped under for the last time. Where I shoved past others, shouting "Help me!" Where I finally dived in to the fizz of bubbles where he'd thrashed.

"Mate, there's a storm coming," a fisherman says, folding up his chair. "You know if lightning hits the water around here anyone swimming will be electrocuted?"

At the edge of the pier I stand as my son used to. Toes fold over the edge and arms stretch out. Dawn's voice reaches me, feeble but still that young voice that used to call to me. My dive isn't perfect. One leg is bent and I fall crookedly. Water is like a single slap from an open hand. Underwater I open eyes. Shadows turn. Clumsily I swim up, my head bursting out into rain that swirls and rings across the bay.

I lie flat, bobbing there, eyes half closed against driving rain. If things were different, he may have trod water next to me, before rolling onto his belly to stroke back towards shore. I probably would have followed him, swimming through eddies spinning from his feet.

The salt water holds me up. The beach mists over with slanting rain. Seawater slops into my mouth. I glance towards sand and the last beach umbrellas folding down. On the sand I see Dawn and swim towards her. With each pull of an arm the shoreline bobs into view. Sun breaks through and I glimpse Dawn shielding eyes against glistening columns of rain. I push on, breaths swelling hard in my chest. At last ridges of sand scrape along my skin and I stop. Dawn runs awkwardly to where I finally stand from the water, bent over and gasping. She slaps cold arms around me, her head settling against the hard edge of my shoulder. I know she cries from the small heaves of her chest. I do my best to comfort her, stroking ringlets of hair and patting the skin across the back of her neck.

We stand still, clasping each other. It's something we haven't done for a long time.

The Holiday House

The house nestled between peeling bark on tea tree trunks. Behind it glaring light hung over the bay. In the evenings mosquitoes twirled against sunsets. We sat outside, slapping at bites on skin blotchy with sunburn. My arm hung loosely around Lana's neck. We read books. On slow afternoons we sat in cafes drinking weak coffee, watching light change through bloated clouds. One night I asked Lana whether we still needed a holiday house.

She flexed in a way that reminded me of her ballet. I used to love her dancing. Arms unravelled from sides like long ribbons as she turned across stages. I'd shiver outside a stage door at the Nunawading Theatre on June nights waiting for her, currents of dew oozing through car park lights.

"We found our place," she said. "Somewhere to take long walks. Where we'll talk about things besides whether the car has petrol and if we've run out of toilet paper."

We had little money for furniture. Her father gave us a ripped couch dogs slept on. I took a couple of broken chairs from work to fix. We scattered cushions everywhere. Bought saucepans and cutlery from garage sales.

On Friday nights we drove to the holiday house. In the evenings long necklaces of headlights curled along the roads in front of us. Uneven hedges of dark scrub blurred by. Lana rested a hand on my leg, drawing circles with the hollow of her palm. I kept glancing at her, catching smiles that waxed and waned.

All our decisions were made on those trips. That's where our dreams formed too. Dreams of better jobs, adding a room, trips to Kakadu and having kids. We ate potato cakes on a tree stump. Lana raced me along the beach, cold air cutting over my cheeks like a blunt knife. I lost to her ballet strengthened legs. She ran up on toes along firm sand beside the water's edge. We dashed to the pier, leaning on its flaking paint, gulping breath. We walked into sunsets on that pier.

Lana saved her news about the baby until we were at the holiday house. She told me during the third quarter as I listened to the Bulldogs lose a football match.

"Most of the games were one sided and over by quarter time. So we had time to work on starting a family," Lana said. "Now we have to set up where the baby will sleep." I smiled and glided fingers across her belly like brushstrokes.

Lana slept against my back. Her tummy grew into the hollow between my hips. I felt the kicks. Tiny feet or arms pushed into me. Lana asked if she would have stretch marks. She worried if she'd be able to breastfeed. I asked her if she thought our child would fail university too. Her laughter trembled into me.

I was there when Emma was born. Cradled her head so softly she would barely have felt the outlines of my fingers. Missed the opening of her eyes because of the tears in mine. Walked circuits around the room, holding her swaddling and murmurs to my heartbeat. Lay her on Lana's exhausted body, her mother's pale face smiling easily. Stroked back spikes of hair off Lana's forehead. She turned her head to look at Emma.

We left hospital after a couple of days. Lana felt flat. Blame the epidural and hormones the nurse told me.

"Take me to the holiday house," Lana said when we were in the car.

We drove slowly by the bay. Water was flat enough to skim stones on. Lana sat in the back, stroking our baby's face. We stopped where the semi drivers pulled off the road to drink service station coffee. Lana eased a breast into Emma's mouth and struggled to position her.

"Why won't she take it?" she snapped. Emma cried. I reached across Lana and lifted Emma against my shoulder. Lana slumped back.

We reached the house at dusk. They both slept on the way. Watched them in the car's dim light. Leaned around to search Emma's face for Lana's small nose, curve of cheekbones or my forehead.

I took them inside. Emma slept, her breathing slow. Lana was so tired I saw shades of her mother's face like an old coat of paint coming through.

We stayed at the holiday house. Cool changes swerved rain along weatherboards. Rain tinkled against windows. Days became shorter. Lana's pallid face lay barely awake. I rested in front of her. Dust drifted through a column of light. Cold air bent through the room from under the door. Told her I knew it was difficult.

I returned to work. Lana pleaded to stay at the holiday house, clutching my arm so her fingers jammed into me. Looked into her eyes, purple quarter moons circling under them. I agreed to commute to work for a few weeks.

Weekends later we prepared to run a race. Lana told me she felt stronger. We left the holiday house, walking through cool sand dunes. I carved a crib out of sand and lay down a towel, then a blanket. Eased Emma into the space and she smiled for the first time. Lana said it was wind.

"Are you sure about running?" I asked. "If you're tired we can leave it."

"What's the worst that can happen?" she said. "Find out having a baby makes you run slower as well as all the other ruin it puts you through?"

"I just thought..."

"Come on!" Lana said. We lined up. I thrust feet into fine sand. "Go!" she shouted. She ran ahead before I was ready. I lurched after her. Lana crossed in front of me, so close I heard the hard grunting of her breath. She was up on toes, beating me easily, looking back with streaks of hair layering her face. Bowed my head and pumped arms after her, sensing the gap closing from the sound of her padding feet. Glimpsed blurred pink soles. We drew level, going stride for stride.

We rounded a tree and started back towards Emma. Each step thudded through me. I started dropping back and running crookedly, finally stopping, holding sides and breathing salty chunks of air.

"Look at Daddy," Lana said, on one knee beside Emma. "He was a bit like that after we made you."

The weeks felt longer. By Friday night I fell asleep listening to the football I used to stay up for. There were only feeds, sponging away thrown up milk, sleep walking through the house patting Emma down and sterilising bottles. Otherwise I just commuted. My life was peak hour drives with golden oldies on the radio. Some nights I stayed at our house in Syndal, dead heading roses just to think of something else.

The following Saturday we sat on thin grass rolling down in clumps towards the sand. The bay lapped along the shoreline. Lana handed Emma to me, buttoning her blouse closed. I tasted lipstick on our shared coffee cup. Sunlight sparked on the water. The Queenscliff ferry glided into distance. Lana told me she was struggling. Bored and exhausted. I'd kept my life, mixing with people at work, occasional Friday night house reds at the Geebung Hotel and golf once a month. Her life was nothing but supermarket aisles and watching what she ate. I asked what she wanted me to do. Just understand me she said.

The next day we returned to Syndal. I surface sprayed around holiday house doors to keep out spiders.

When we arrived neighbours crowded around us. They paraded Emma around while her plump arms bobbed at sides.

Under my drifts of sheets and blankets I sensed Emma move. I always came awake with her sounds. Lifted my head in the gloom to see her puffed cheeks. Rested my hand in the small of Lana's back.

When Friday came people said how tired I looked. They asked if our baby kept me up. You find your dreaming when you have a child I explained. Your place is the ground under wherever they are.

After work we went to the hotel. I talked to Wendy with the pile of red hair that made her seem taller. She spoke so closely her whispers touched me like lips. She drew back to laugh and leaned in to speak again. Her voice was warm, breath a vapour against my bristling skin. Her chin tilted upwards when she laughed. I smiled with her, even when she spoke so closely it was like listening to static. Felt her words brushing my face in different shapes as if her mouth slid over me.

I put down the wine that had turned hot in my hand. Looked at her and kept staring as I walked away, my eyes dragging her after me. Through the crowd her heels clicked and I felt it in my skin.

Standing in the car park I rang home. In the background Emma cried like holding music played at the wrong speed. Stood away from Wendy. Lied with ease. Comforted myself by deciding I could blame the alcohol or that it only happened because of how much I missed the intimacy Lana and I used to have. Slipped the mobile into a pocket and opened the car door for Wendy.

It was one hour's drive. Moments of flirting followed by moments of wondering what I was doing. When we arrived the holiday house was set back in thick darkness. I led Wendy in. We smelt the heavy sea air. She was so out of place. Asked where the toilet was, where could she freshen up, where exactly was the house anyway? When she returned from the bathroom I smelt Lana's perfume on her.

I brushed the grooves of Wendy's ribs. She pressed fingers fiercely into my shoulders and my body juddered like pipes. Jammed my head back into the pillow and everything streaked, shapes running in a child's water colour. I cried out loudly, my throat burning with salt and rawness. Her eyes lay close to mine and I saw the flinting of overhead lights in her irises.

I sped on the drive home. We slumped into our corners in the front seat. Wendy propped her face to the window, staring into gloom broken occasionally by the surface of a dam like dirty glass. With clothes on and alcohol faded we were strangers again.

She gave me directions. Outside her flat she asked lamely if I wanted a coffee. I said no, watching her gather up handbag and slide over the seat. She stood motionless outside the side window like one of those photographs where the head's been cut off.

I drove home. In the rear vision wiped around my mouth. At the door took off shoes to tip toe down the hallway. Looked in on Emma. She slept deeply on her side. Lana was asleep too, only a ruffle of hair showing above sheets. I showered, coming out pink and hot. Then I crept to our bed, easing in beside Lana but sleeping on the edge, so that all I could feel was the faint rising and falling of her breath.

In the morning Lana shook me awake. I moaned into the pillow. She leaned over me so that her shoulder cut into my back. Lana said she needed a weekend at the holiday house. We would come back Sunday so there was no long drive to work for me. She just needed to be near the sea, stand in it up to her ankles.

I swung out of bed. We packed a few clothes. Lana fed Emma. Carried our baby out to the car, strapping her in.

Roads lay empty. Damp air blew. Lana slid down in her seat, resting where Wendy had been.

When we arrived I went in and turned on heaters. Rain slapped across windows. It lifted and fell as if a sprinkler turned loops of water over the house. As the downpour faded I heard quiet sobbing at the end of the house. Followed it, the sound muffled as if breathed out into folds of a pillow. From the bed Lana turned her face to me. She said I was a bastard. How could I, in our own bed. My shoulder blades ground against the wall behind me.

Lana dashed past me. The down draught of her rush grazed me. She went to Emma, scooping her up. I called after her. The front door slammed. I ran up the hallway and outside to the car. Expected to see it reversing back, spinning dirt and mud. Instead it was motionless in shadows. The rain sprayed down again, tasting of the tea tree it dripped through. Found Lana's shoes on the edge of the sand. Jumped over them, knees jolting as feet hit sand. Ran through the rain and haze, heading for where the sand would be harder, where her ballet muscles would be leaping. I sped up; water rushing up sand and filling my shoes. Lifted a leg to wrench a sandshoe off, then the other.

Around me water drained back. Rain hit the skin of my neck. The next wave broke and rushed towards me, sucking around my feet. In the split second of silence with eddies of grey water spinning next to my ankles, Emma's cries become fainter as her mother out ran me and carried her further up the beach.

Wet clothes draped heavily off me, dripping on carpet. Through the window it was dark, broken by the white of breaking waves. At times thought I saw someone and leapt up to watch for them. They couldn't be much longer. It was colder and the rain heavier. Turned up heaters, left food in the microwave and turned back the beds. Then I went out, walking over wet sand pocked with old footprints, heading straight towards the sea. The first wave knocked me down and I tried to breathe in the grit and water but it was only enough to start me coughing. I waded in further. Even the next slamming me in the chest didn't snap me out of what I was doing.

When the Crickets fall Silent

The last cricket falling silent meant winter approached. I understood the cycles after one year of living on that hill. Every one hundred steps of climbing the temperature fell a degree. In August winds tore through like shock waves from an explosion. During October rains approached from distance like grey beams of light. January brought sunshine and searing heat. Along the avenues passing the cafe strip and caravan park below I knew which trees would lose their leaves first when the El Niño weather patterns set in.

Last week a dog barked at night. It was a long way off, out past forest canopies and hills. So far it hadn't picked up the scent of the used cans of braised stew I'd strewn around. The dog was probably abandoned by campers. Now I listened to mountain bikes jolting along trails. I'd willed the bikers away, closing eyes and wishing them accidents, concentrating so hard that when I looked out again my short sightedness turned the landscape watery. Wishing mishaps on them never worked. I should've hidden behind trees and lobbed stones in the direction of their sputtering engines.

In winter I had the bush to myself. If I washed in those waters from melted snow my skin greyed. Dew lay thickly on the ground as if it'd rained. In shade frost crackled under my footsteps. If sun broke through I hung old clothes and blankets over tree branches.

Over a year ago I worked back on Thursday nights. Rang people during that time dinner was prepared. They rushed through my questions about how they were. Kept asking what I wanted. Some people I rang caught their breath when I started, as if holding it before diving into a pool.

That's where I spoke louder about investment options, negative gearing and shareholder returns. Talked over the top of their voices and the spaces between attempts to blunt me. I calmed them with my title. "Strategic Investments Advisor," spoken with hushed seduction.

"How about Wednesday night? Say 7 PM? That'll give you time for dinner. Good decisions are made on full stomachs. One of our consultants can call on you. There's no obligation. They'll take you through a few choices. I'm sure there's a day out there where you'll be able to say your life changed with this phone call."

No qualifications were needed for the work. I just followed the script. After a few calls I recited it as easily as the stories I used to tell women to attract them. If they didn't hang up in the first minute I knew I had them.

I never enjoyed the walks into town. It was steep at first, down a hillside loose with rotted leaves and damp soil. In summer my breath grunted with every step and at times I rested, leaning into the wafer thin bark of gum trees. Above the lake I watched people wiping bread around the bottom of fishing nets and hurling them into water. During summer people swam out to the partly submerged trunks of long dead trees, sometimes draping themselves over them, sun baking in the heat. Where the track flattened out I reached a path that passed a barbecue I occasionally found leftovers at. I wasn't beyond chewing on chicken bones if flesh still stuck to them. I had to find them before the crows. From there the path weaved into town. After the moment I crossed into the main street I realised what it was like to be an outsider.

The town convinced me to stay in those hills. Kept me out the way they tried to fence out rabbits and foxes.

Resentment wafted off people the way smells of soil and campfire smoke lifted from me. It would be easier to be homeless in the city. There'd be someone to share a bottle with. An occasional stranger offering a few coins. A place to receive a bread roll, cup of soup and a blanket. This place offered nothing but distrust. The shop keepers watched me as if I'd steal their matured cheese and marinated olives. It crossed my mind enough times to scoop whatever gourmet foods I could lay my hands on into pockets. But as always I went to the budget section. Carefully spent what was left of the money I'd emptied from bank accounts before coming here. How long would it be before I'd buy cat food instead of bacon, eggs and milk? Perhaps cat food was more expensive.

I had my own seat in the hotel. It wasn't really mine but no one came near me when I sat there. It looked out across a street facing straight out of town as if a line marking the Equator was drawn through there.

It was the weight of another person's touch. I hadn't felt it for so long I may have jumped slightly. What was there to feel in my life? Heat, cold, a mangy shirt worn back to material thin as breath or a twig scraping my face when I didn't watch where I was going. The inside of a palm balanced on my shoulder, cupping over where there used to be a muscle in my javelin throwing days.

"Mate, I'm sorry. You can't keep drinking in here. I have families coming in. You know? They don't know what to make of you. Think you're a yeti. Or a close relative of the Loch Ness monster. Can you finish up your drink? I'll let you go after that."

Along with a couple of shop owners the publican was one of the few people I spoke to. Usually it was only to order something. But it was conversation at least. I looked around at him.

"I haven't harmed anyone. It was fine when I first started coming here. You couldn't wait to put a beer under my nose then," I said.

"Sure," the publican said. "You're just…a bit whiffy. Anyway I don't want to offend you. Please have your beer. You're welcome to buy any more drinks you need from the bottle shop."

The end of the street was glazed in mist. I stared at it, drinking down to slops of foam. Grey fog began swirling in, the old weatherboards twenty or so doors down disappearing behind it. Past me the publican veered away to pick up empty glasses, clinking as he walked.

There was silence. That's how the Global Financial Crisis arrived. The phones stopped. A few people stood from their booths. Our supervisor came in, setting coffee down on a table. Sensed what was coming as his eyes looked down. I could've left right then. His body language told me everything. I only needed to decide whether to stay and be pissed off like everyone else or make my way to the door and hope a final wages payment reached my account. I yanked off the headset and filled a pocket with a few pens. As I made my way to an exit I heard the supervisor speaking.

"Try not to damage the furniture," he said. "We might need it for a garage sale."

Clare had already left the house. I only lived in the bedroom and bathroom anyway. Didn't take out the pizza boxes so I could erase the fastidious cleanliness she used to maintain. It was three weeks before they came looking for the rent. Explained I was between jobs and I'd pay soon. One of them craned his neck slightly, looking over my shoulder into spaces behind me.

"Two days," he said. "If you haven't paid in that time, we'll have to proceed with an eviction. Sorry."

I rang Clare. Didn't even know what I wanted. Threaten her with taking any other money perhaps. Then in the next breath offer reconciliation. I'd kept leaving messages, reasoning with her, then pleading, finally ranting. I hadn't changed the sheets since she left. Couldn't bring myself to shake out her threads of hair. The next day I called one of her friends. Told them there'd been a death and I needed to see Clare. They blurted out her address. In the evening I drove there. An outside light lit up pot plants. Leaves dried and curled lay on a square of porch. I knocked, standing back. She came out, pulling the sides of cardigan together across her chest. Clare asked what I was doing there.

"Why'd you leave?" I said loudly. From the corner of eyes I saw two men approach cautiously from a neighbour's house. "Who're they? Have you organised your own vigilante squad?"

Clare called to her neighbours, assuring them everything was fine. Her voice wavered like a singer struggling to reach a note.

"We'll just stay here," one of them said.

"What're you going to do?" I said to him. "Run a conflict resolution workshop?"

Clare stepped off the porch. It was impossible that I used to undress her down to suntans and that dip in her back. That we'd travelled through the smoky heat of Malaysia together. Slow cooked roasts in our matching aprons. Looked for an apartment that let in winter sun and nursed each other through tonsillitis and sprains.

"Please go," she called to me in that husky, breaking voice I used to love. Her neighbours looked away, as if they'd barged in on us naked together.

I just nodded. Turned back to the car. Saw the front porch's light reflection in the passenger's window go dark as it flicked off.

I never answered the door when they knocked. Watched the eviction notice slide under it, envelope bunching and creasing. That same day I left the apartment with a backpack stuffed with clothes. I threw away anything that went with my previous life, determined never to return to the suits and pin stripe shirts that'd ruined me. After that I drove to a car auction outlet and allowed them to cheat me out of most of what the vehicle was worth. Then I caught a tram to Southern Cross Station. Followed signs to listings of country destinations. I'd made my decision by the time I'd moved two places up the queue. It'd been a gold rush town that now featured rows of olive trees alongside the approaching road. There was a red brick church that barely fitted in the guests when there was a wedding. A pub with a view sweeping up into hills. A town to disappear in.

At first I stayed in a motel on the main road. It smelt of diesel when log trucks shook past at dawn. Tiny rooms jammed together. Through walls I heard murmured conversations and people turn over in bed as if they slept with me. When money started running low I rented a room out the back of a single mother's home. There was little to do. I explored the hills and around the lake. At the pub someone warned me to be careful of abandoned mine shafts.

I found the old shack on one of those walks. So tucked away behind blackberry vines I only noticed it because of light sparking on a window. I'd tentatively gone to the door, pushing so hard it opened, scraping loudly away from a swollen doorframe. There were a few tin plates and cups stacked in a corner. I noticed an old bed without a mattress. In the hotel I asked about it. Someone looked up from a newspaper.

"The last of the miners from around here lived there," he said. "Would come across him panning for gold when the creeks were running. Or hear him chipping away down one of the shafts. Stunk like he was part compost. There was this day when we realised no one had seen him in weeks. He disappeared. Probably lying at the bottom of a mineshaft somewhere. Was harmless enough although everyone avoided him. There were no search parties. Maybe he went bush somewhere else."

One evening the single mother knocked. Her son stood next to her, smiling his crinkly two teeth smile. I'd read to him a couple of times although I sensed his mother was unsure about it. I'd often wondered what she would be like under her clothes stained by toddler food.

"I'm sorry but I need the room back," she said. "My sister is moving home. She's going to stay in the room you're using."

I was motionless, looking at her. She took a step back.

"You're throwing me out?" I said. "Can't your sister stay in the house with you? Not like I had the music up too loud or dealt drugs. Even put your bloody bins out every week. Why?"

She looked away, ushering her son behind legs. Side on and under the hard light shining above the door clefts of shadows bobbed on her face. Her tone became hushed, barely audible. It could've been one of those voices I'd heard through motel walls.

"His dad is going to be living with us. Okay? We split up a year ago. He's sorted out his problems and wants to come back. His son needs him. But I can't have you here. Another male around will set him off. He's jealous. I didn't want to tell you because I'm tired of men telling me all their solutions that never work. I'm doing this for our son. So you have to go. I'm sorry." She turned, picking up her son, hoisting him onto a hip. "Next couple of days. Please."

There was a point where Clare stopped talking to me. She blamed me for being bitter and angry before she fell silent. It was true work stressed me. Business was weakening. Without sales we're fails the supervisor said. They kept demanding we work harder. Some of the employees saw the collapse coming, others stayed in denial.

"How we react to this depends on whether we believe we are in control of our own destiny" the supervisor told me in the coffee line one morning, his voice loud and wooden.

I told him I'd be interested to hear any of his other homespun philosophies. Did peroxide remove stains? Do carrots improve eyesight? If you swallowed popcorn while suffering a temperature would it explode?

I brought my problems home. My anger made Clare stop loving me. One night she showered, water shrilling down pipes. After she stepped out she padded past me. I followed, her skin polished under light reflecting off white walls. I came up behind her, kissing where she was still damp under the hairline. Clare writhed away from me.

"Don't," she said. It was her first word to me in days. And her last in that apartment. By the time I was home the following day she was gone.

It was a long walk to that shack with a backpack the first time. Just stay for a few days I thought. Listen to the breezes, remember how to light a campfire, smell the gum trees. Sweat poured off me with the effort of climbing the hill, chilling as soon as the breezes gusted. Outside the shack I gulped air, lungs hard and heavy. Threaded the blackberries away from the door, some dangling mid-air. I scattered the clothes I'd brought over the bed frame. Then I curled into their shallow warmth and the shack's mustiness with its creaking walls and wind cooing through gaps.

I've come to know the bush now. Familiar as a room with juts of furniture, splotch of mildew, chipped tile or loose doorknob. I know where the warm currents of air turn up here. The smells following rain. The scratching of grass seeds in socks. How water tastes as it trickles past the fibrous roots of gum trees. I notice seasons by the arrival of birds. By the building hum of insects in treetops and slow whirling of stars. By the changing sound of footsteps as ground dries. I track campers without their knowing. Sometimes so closely they spin around, sensing someone there. I'm as silent as light. During nights I enter their camps. When cinders from campfires twinkle. Eat their leftovers. Steal cereal boxes left out for breakfast. Imagine their blaming dingoes or feral cats. Sometimes I linger by the radiating heat of their dulling fires. Listen to their snuffling breath inside tents. At times I sit slightly outside the waterproof plastic of their tents, hearing them grope and kiss. Last night I entered where hunters had set up. They'd butchered a deer. I picked up a camera sitting on a backpack. Tilted it towards them as they slept, angling my face into the shot. I smiled over their bulges through sleeping bags. I'd love to watch their shocked faces when seeing those pictures. The idea swelled through me.

Wished I'd said goodbye to Clare. Nuzzled into her through a threadbare t-shirt. So close that her breath and warmth glazed my skin. Would liked to have said goodbye to that single mother where I lived out the back too. Probably nothing more than a handshake, a clasp of her thin fingers and still bones inside my hand. I thought about it during setting sun and warmth draining out of air.

Further down in the valley, towards the creek and clumps of ferns I heard a gunshot. The sound rolled past, pitching then falling. For a second, the forest was still, as if air was sucked out of everything.

Five Decades

We stored junk in our son's room. A broken desk with his initials splintered into its timber pushed against a wall. Old year 12 textbooks piled in a corner. A telescope with a cracked lens lay half dismantled on top of a cupboard. I used to stand in the doorway watching him push out from under blankets as he woke. Matt used to sit on his mattress, grinding knuckles into eyes. Sometimes he brushed past me so closely I smelt stale take-away on his breath. Now I sat on his bed in the silent room, stroking a hand down sheets that once bulged to his shape.

I walked in socks through the house. Then I sat outside with scalding coffee and the day's first cigarette. Only ever tasted the first. The second cigarette was nothing more than heat. After that I couldn't taste anything through nicotine and scum on my teeth.

The backyard was a tangle of vines plaited and twined together. I'd started painting the house seven times. There were half finished walls and window sills touched up in faded undercoats. For years I sat at an iron table sticky with spilled drinks. Grinded cigarette after cigarette into a clay pottery ash tray my son made me at primary school.

Jenny my wife left two years ago. She still lived in the house but it was no longer her. Jenny once loved wearing necklines that showed her summer skin. She spun a few steps of the rumba down our narrow hallway and read books cover to cover in a day. Jenny enjoyed making sauces that lingered aromas between rooms. That Jenny was gone. The Jenny I lived with was tired, drooping over tables and sipping scotches that tasted of smoke. She spent hours on the couch playing games on her iPad, silver light shining into transfixed eyes.

Wheelie bin washer, bricklayer, taxi driver, cashier and security guard. Those jobs were just the last two years. I often bent over newspapers circling vacancies that would never last. Drew rings around jobs so hard the pen left lines on the table like worm trails. I wanted to drive trucks next, taking them on long interstate hauls under clear skies bleached with glare, through mirages and plains of blue heat haze.

Deep down I didn't mind unemployment. There was no one looking over my shoulder at work with start times so early I woke in a semi coma. Most people in workplaces I disliked. I had no interest in their conversations about football, what they saw on television last night or would it ever cool down.

It was over five decades ago I came home. Afterwards I spent days on my parent's porch. It angled grandly into the garden. Stared vacantly for hours at cars and people passing. My parents came out, urging me to join the local football team. My father joked about how I was tall enough to take a screamer, leap so high I'd have altitude sickness. He said the team trained two evenings a week. On a still night if you turned down the television and stopped chewing you'd hear their coach shouting. My father told me to go down and show them one of my torpedo punts that sent the football straight into the spreading hands of a full forward. Slightly behind his shoulder my mother pleaded with her eyes. What happened to you? I should have stopped you going. Are you ever going to be the son I kissed goodbye? When will he come home?

Now there was a different porch under my feet. In certain sections it creaked, timbers straining. Sap leaked from cuts in the wood. Jenny used to come out, layering hands over my shoulders as I sat facing the street, whispering close to me so her breath whisked over the undulations of my cheek. She asked what's wrong. I sat in silence, sometimes shrugging. There was no one to confide in. People who'd been through it would be the only ones to understand, even though it was decades ago. I often woke confused when disturbed during sleep. Frightened if I heard another language. Suspicious if someone stared at me.

Eventually Jenny stopped coming out. She called me in for dinners or because the leg on the coffee table was loose. I paced the porch otherwise with wide, measured strides up to the peeling paint handrail and then swivelled back the other way. I saw seasons change from that front porch. Horizontal rain, thunder so close I was looking for a flesh wound and yard turned into streaky currents of brown topsoil under downpours.

Skateboards often grinded and crunched down the street. The riders had futures. The one out front tilting into corners would be on the board of a bank. The second with his arms out would work in engineering. The bony looking kid following them might be a surgeon. At their age I had war. It was on the black and white television news every night until I was called up to it. My life became a haircut, uniform and basic training.

I heard the doorbell from the backyard. Waited for Jenny to answer. She would be by the front window, parting the curtain to peer out. She may not have recognised Rick at first. He had a grey beard with dabs of nicotine stains. He'd become round shouldered. His limp more noticeable. His left shoe would always wear out before the right.

We hugged, slapping each other's back. Rick's spine was cobbled and hard against the palm of my hand. We discussed our boredom and restlessness. He said he'd given up on employment and marriage. His last job had been mining. After six months he suffered arthritis and migraines. His wife walked out around the time he resigned. Rick's moods always swung she said. For a while he stayed in caravan parks on the north coast, fishing for bream and blackfish, cooking them on open fires before nights of losing billiards games in the pub.

"My first kill was strange," Rick said hours later. "I was empty until the next patrol. Kept thinking about whether the guy had a wife, kids. What did he do when not hiding in the bush shooting at us? Where did he live? How big was his family? But from there it started feeling good. Each time, you know. I was really into it. It became exciting."

I lay back on the chair. I wouldn't want to close my eyes tonight. There was the risk of being there again. Those smells back in my shirt. Mud sucking at feet. The thudding of helicopters skimming treetops. Being unable to find the top half of a man's body who'd panicked and run into our line of fire. Hearing something that stopped our patrol so still that there was nothing but the rhythm of the next man's breathing.

"They trained me to be a killer," Rick continued. "You don't unlearn that. And you don't come home and calmly start planting a new garden bed or taking your favourite book off the shelf. Killing is with you all the time. Nothing you ever do is the same after you've killed someone. It's a secret you walk around with. Even now, all these years later. People used to ask what it was like over there. Was it scary? Were you afraid? I never know how to answer."

In the light thrown by a bare bulb above the back door Jenny came out. Her shoulders gleamed as she peered down the backyard at us. Our cynical laughter must have unwound into the house. Her dress lay misshapen along the lines of her body. She called out and I heard my name at the start of other words. I shouted back to come down and have a beer with us. The door cracked shut.

"When I talk about a pack a day habit it's not only cigarettes," I said. "It's pills. Stop a headache, manage depression, lower blood pressure, clear up rashes. They should coat those little bastards in scotch instead of sugar." We laughed again. Eventually Rick stood, offering his hand. I said it was only early. There was still a lot to talk about. But he shook my hand so hard circulation to my fingers stopped. He weaved up the backyard. I told him not to drive. I could throw down a mattress and make a coffee so hot he'd feel he was back there. But he only half turned and waved. I heard his crooked steps up the side of the house.

Most people stopped visiting years ago. Even Jenny's sister rarely came. She was guarded around me. Her greeting kiss had as much feeling as if she spat on me. Jenny once told me her sister disapproved of her marrying me. Despite that she stood in our wedding party and smiled through all the photographs. It was a lie dressed up in a bridesmaid's outfit.

Last year Christmas was at our place. Our son sat down the other end of the table, retreating there with a pile of food that would sustain me for a week. Jenny's sister and her real estate husband joined us. He talked over the top of everyone.

"They should crush hoon cars with the hoons still in them. If there's global warming how come the windscreen of my car was frozen last winter? Nuclear weapons have brought more peace to this planet than the Dalai Lama."

Jenny said how hot it was. Trees in parks died, as if losing leaves for winter. It took two days for the house to lose heat after a cool change. Possums had started coming out in the daytime to find air.

"You wouldn't believe how much I hate Christmas," I murmured to Jenny's sister before dessert. I leaned well into her personal space to speak, spraying cranberry sauce and saliva into her hair. "Every year I'm asked what I want. If ever you hear they are buying me a gun, you'd better ring up that day and say you're too sick to visit."

They left soon afterwards. As they went out the door Jenny trailed them up the footpath. I lip read her sister saying I was a pig. Down the other end of the table Matt picked his way through plum pudding. I told him he'd eaten so much he'd better floss his teeth with razor wire.

Back inside Jenny was silent. She circled the table, collecting screwed up serviettes and a party hat still damp from my sweat. I told Matt to help his mother. His chewing stopped briefly, his lips thin as a ruled line.

"Sure. I'll just get my breath back from the excitement of my father saying two things to me today," he said.

Later I would sit in a corner, sullenly admitting I over reacted. I'd gripped him around the front of his collar, swinging him so his head butted dully into the wall. Through my fingers I felt him go limp as if he'd died. Jenny shouted from behind me, pushing between us. He fell back, hand grabbing and pulling over a chair. Jenny kept yelling so that I put hands over my ears to block her out. Air whispered in that space the way it sounds when listening into a sea shell. I kept my hands there until her mouth was still, until her muted voice stopped sounding as if she was talking underwater. Then I pulled hands away, the mild suction popping against ears.

Matt and I hardly spoke after that. Sometimes I called down the hallway to tell him dinner was ready. My voice hummed down corners and walls. Occasionally I asked him about a new job, girlfriend, his cricket training or a couple of his mates who stopped dropping in after that Christmas.

"Okay." He always replied with that. There were flat okays and barely spoken okays. Okays that I thought might continue into something else and impatient okays. I knew them all as if they were part of a dialect.

Matt moved out a few months later. He trooped out our front door with clothes laid over arms like carrying a bride across a threshold. Jenny blamed me. She said I should've concentrated on being a father rather than living in 1969. She told me to go back to Vietnam and find a way to leach it out of my system. I told her I wasn't interested and it was as impossible as booking a flight in a time machine that would land me into fifty years ago. But the next day I was half asleep on the porch before stirring awake and finding a ticket in my lap. I went inside and found her leaning over the kitchen bench, jerkily peeling carrots. I said we can't afford this. The Vietnam I knew was long gone anyway. But she half turned, telling me to go. Sort myself out.

The following week Jenny drove me to the airport. Cold fronts blew through on the freeway. Ridges of grey cloud slanted heavy rain into the windscreen. It was nine hours flying and at Ho Chi Minh City I breathed heavy heat while waiting for a taxi. I checked in at an old colonial hotel with high ceilings and fans turning drowsily. The next day I took a taxi out to where the battlefield used to be. Over there, no wait, there, down that track. But I was never sure. In the end I sat on crumbling dirt at the edge of a rubber plantation. The taxi driver read a newspaper. Finally he drove me back to the city. Along the way we passed waving kids and motionless men lying in hammocks. For the next four days I never left the hotel room.

Jenny met me as I returned through customs. She kissed my stubble. Asked how the trip was. Did I feel better? Had it given me a chance to make any kind of peace?

"Yes, you were right," I said exactly as I rehearsed it. "Going back helped me a lot."

We threaded through huddled families and couples colliding into hugs. We walked with the bag I lugged between us. I listened to people following, talking about how hot it was over there, that clothes were cheap and how the food never made you full.

On my last day in Vietnam I'd sat by the window in my room. It looked out over brown haze and I could make out a murky bend in a river. In the past, whenever I'd been away, I used to be able to close my eyes and imagine I was home. But at that moment it was gone.

Rope Walking

I swallowed dryly whenever thinking about it. Couldn't put that picture out of my mind. Feet skidding off the wire. Writhing through layers of pollen as fine as sand between toes. Dropping silently through wafts of warm breeze. Then shallow, whispery breath before thudding into asphalt.

My trainer used to lecture that the minute you believe you cannot do it anymore is when you stop. It's not like losing a tennis match he liked to say. You can be back on court the next day, shirtless and barefoot if you want, fixing your technique, perfecting your grip, adjusting to a grass surface. Even boxing is a sport where you can come back from a split lip and black eye. But not rope walking. If you want the big crowds there can be no safety nets. People want death defying in its quadriplegic, bleed to death glory.

Recently Rhonda asked me to stop. She said it was the rope or her. In sleep I draped over the joins and turns of her body. Told her it was like sleeping against dislocated joints. Her skin was so unblemished it seemed barely lived in. The only time it marked was from the welts of wearing something too tight. Across the table in the mornings we drank burning instant coffee and she gathered up my hands. Rhonda said she preferred I left her than lose me to a fall.

At times I felt doubts. Kept them private and never told my trainer. Hid them so he wouldn't notice any uncertainty. What if a knee dislocated or there was a wind gust as powerful as a push in the back? Could my concentration fail me? To remind myself I'd made the right choice I sometimes drove to the local railway station.

Office workers plodded up the grey walk way to the platform, waiting in clumps of suits and overcoats. The train curved in, clacking and swaying. My father used to bring me to the side of the platform when I was young. Originally I thought it was because he loved trains, especially the diesels with their deep thrumming and horns that vibrated behind ribs. His giant hands rested on my shoulders. His skin was calloused and spiked by splinters from his gardening work. Often his hands snagged in the material of my shirts as they lifted off me.

"See?" he said. His mouth positioned close to my ear and he exhaled smells of melted cheese on toast. "You don't want to end up like them. Every day is the same. Sit at desks. Do what they're told. The only time anything changes is whether they take an umbrella. Live in your own true skin, not someone else's."

The trick was to move with the rope. Like breathing in time with another person so they exhaled as you inhaled. The trainer told me I couldn't be rigid. Limbs must be loose and flexible, how they were when floating in water. During my first walk the rope extended across a court normally used for basketball. I balanced barely half a metre off the ground. The trainer told me it was one of the few times mistakes were okay. The worst that could happen was straining a ligament. In the weeks ahead I'd have the risk of serious injury.

Rhonda refused to come to my practice sessions. She said if I became a famous soccer player or a busker she'd watch. But not rope walking. At times she sat in the car, windows down and reading Emily Bronte books. Eventually someone would go out and tell her I'd finished. She always asked if I was all right. Once one of the cleaners told her I'd fallen and had a nose bleed so serious the Blood Bank should visit and bring a couple of buckets. She rushed in hysterically. I was unlacing shoes and she toppled into me sobbing. When she realised the cleaner had been joking, she hunted him down in the car park, slapping him so hard he fell across a car bonnet. The sound came through the door like the crack of a starter's pistol.

"I understand your choice," my father said to me after I failed Year 12 exams. "Better something you love than a life stuck at a desk. But I hardly have any money left to help you." He spread hands. There was so much dirt ground into them I once told him to plant potatoes in his skin rather than wash. "Your inheritance won't be much more than a packet of tomato seeds and a few spades. So you will need money. Where will you work to walk ropes? In a circus?"

I told him I hated circuses. Couldn't stand animals held captive and performing mindless tricks. I intended to appear at festivals and make my own name, eventually starting my own show with costumes and assistants.

He examined me with his diluted brown eyes. To him it was just another stage of my life. There was that time I considered being an artist, taking a portfolio around galleries where they either refused to see me or said I should enrol in art school. Their voices were strained and impatient. As soon as the first page fell open I knew from their faces they'd dismissed me. I considered stunt driving, persuading my father to give me a few hundred dollars he couldn't really spare. I drove an old Commodore with bald tyres around hairpin bends, trailing acrid smoke I kept smelling long after parking the car. Later I decided on wrestling, running hard and panting through the mist on cold mornings for fitness. My first opponent clasped me in a full nelson, his chest hair grazing my back like a brush used to scrub out bottles. He pinned me and off to one side I saw the coach shake his head. Later I still stunk of my opponent's aftershave.

My father told me I needed to earn a wage. He no longer wanted to hear me asking for money for a car to drive stunts with, to pay a wrestling coach or buy all the protein powders to build myself up. It was time to bring money home and pay for my own coaching for the rope walking. So I started cutting lawns. I cut sidewalks back to grass that glistened with bleeding sap. I cut around manicured front yards crowded with flowers. At times people leaned from front doors, offering lemonade or bringing out tasteless coffees. Otherwise the suburbs were empty when I worked. The only other people were like me, towing old trailers filled with plastic bags of grass and cuttings. Suburbs were just well kept ghost towns that occasionally flickered with anaesthetised life when the mortgagees came home.

I practised in my backyard. Strung a wire between two old elm trees. When wind storms blew it looped around like a skipping rope with no one jumping. I put on shoes that looked like they were meant for ballet. Soon I walked between those trees smoothly, crossing above the vegetable patch with tomatoes blushing orange, the aviary we gave up on when the last canary died and the thickets of weeds. The rope dipped gently, yielding to each step before tightening. Sometimes my father came out, standing with arms folded but his face in wonder. At the end I often turned into his faint smile and muted clapping.

"You are ready for the big time," my trainer said one day at the basketball courts. It was my first walk at the highest level, wire strung across the courts. Half way along my heart beat so hard it nearly upset my balance.

I was going to perform at a show in the country. It involved a rodeo, an attempt to set a record for the largest number of people performing "Nutbush City Limits," a bake off and watercolour painting demonstrations. The trainer said my performance would fit right in. They had safety nets and I was quietly relieved. That night I told Rhonda. She sat with her head in hands. Rhonda had spent the previous night twisting her hair in a curling wand and now it fell in rivulets down the sides of her face. She asked why. Why all the danger? How long would it be before we had normal conversations about steady jobs and buying our own home? When she pictured us we bent over in the sun with trays of plants, creating gardens bobbing with colour in spring. She saw us being serious over newspapers and espresso coffees at a cafe, talking about growing vegetables, what car we wanted to buy and should we have a television in the bedroom. Give her a canvas and she would pencil sketch us on a typical Sunday morning strewn over a bed we were too lazy to make, our chests lying together, talking so that we felt the rush of each other's breath. Rhonda accused me of expecting her to live every day of her life with fear.

Each day I continued mowing grass. At night I walked the wire, sometimes with eyes closed. My father asked had I looked at Rhonda lately. I told him I saw her every day. He said no, not the way you look at someone when leaving for work or discussing a household budget. Had I looked into her? Had something changed? I said he needed to let me concentrate on my performance. It was my first time in front of a crowd and I wanted my mind clear.

That night Rhonda said she wouldn't come to the event. She refused to watch me risking my life. I leaned against a wall as she spoke, looking out at night time horizons flickering and winking. I told her this time there'd be safety nets. Weakly I added it'd be fun. We could stay overnight and go to as many events as we wanted. We'd probably end up at a hotel, stuffing ourselves with the fish of the day. We might be able to spoil ourselves with a decent local wine. Not one of those wines that burn your gullet.

It seemed I had to roll further to find her that night. Usually I could hook my arms around her and smell her hair. Rhonda's bony shoulders often pressed sharply into my hollows.

The next morning I jogged. Felt each footfall, its soft thud like an extra pulse beat. It was already warm. A northerly that would bring rain in a couple of days gusted now and then. I accelerated where the paths were wide. Past some houses dogs barked, toe nails scabbing as they rushed the gate. I returned inside quietly, not wanting to wake Rhonda. She slept diagonally on the bed. On any other day I would've eased down next to her, draped an arm over her belly and felt the quiet pitching of her breath.

I slid clothes out of a drawer, packing shoes, costume and antiseptic cream in case I grazed myself.

My trainer pulled up outside. His car idled. Through a gap in the curtain I saw the exhaust trailing thin steam. I kissed Rhonda on the mouth, lingering long enough to rest our foreheads together. She stirred, eyes opening. Her hands went around my face. The room darkened slightly as her fingers glided tentatively over my eyes. I lifted from her.

"I cannot be with you like this," she said. "I can't live wondering if you are going to come home or be injured. I'm sorry."

"What do you want me to do? Sell real estate? Knock on doors and flog mobile phone packages?" She looked away. I nearly continued, almost accusing her that now when I really needed her she was giving up on me. But I couldn't. Her cheeks were an angry red. Outside a horn blew. I lightly kissed her bare arm. Then I left. My trainer already had the boot open and I speared the bag in.

We left the city. My trainer said to smell the difference in the countryside. We drove up the freeway, four lanes with curves so gentle they could rock you to sleep. After a couple of hours I offered to drive.

"No stunt driving!" he said.

We arrived in the heat of the afternoon. The oval was being set up. There was a shooting gallery off to one side and a merry go round partly unloaded. They said I was booked for two shows the next day. One at 11 AM, another at 3 PM.

I would've drunk the murky brown beer in plastic cups at the hotel. Would have sat there alone, tipping packets of nuts into my mouth and drinking until the moment when I looked at something it took three seconds for the focus in my eyes to catch up. But at the end of dinner my trainer steered me out of the seat and into my room.

"An early night for you. Count broken lines on the road instead of sheep."

The bed was uncomfortable. Heat seemed to radiate into the room from ovens, dishwashers and the bitumen outside. I tossed and turned, facing the window and the black crayon darkness. Eventually I woke to the sound of knives and forks clinking as tables were set downstairs. I dressed hurriedly, rushing down. Went out the side door to the car park. Then I looked around for Rhonda's car. Heatwaves radiated off concrete. My father's car was parked crookedly. I went back inside, finding him by the window, having breakfast with my trainer.

"Today's the day," my trainer said. "Try not to slip over when you're having a shower. It'd be a bad omen."

"Did Rhonda come?" I asked my father. He glanced from his cereal to me, then out the window. Milk tipped off his spoon. He shook his head. I leaned back in the chair.

"I'm sorry," he said softly, almost under his breath. "Called by late yesterday to see if she wanted me to pick her up on the way through. She wasn't there. Car was out. I thought maybe she'd driven up herself. Perhaps she'll be at the carnival."

They had their coffee and we stood to leave. My trainer paid, meticulously counting out notes and lying them down. I went to my room, changing and adjusting the costume in front of the window. It was so tight even my modest muscles bulged through. My trainer called through the door.

"Better go. Unless you'd prefer to practice by walking there along the telegraph wires. Might be a few dead possums and crow's nests to step over."

I threw a coat around shoulders. It made me hot but no one was meant to see the costume until the performance began. We crossed the car park. Again I looked for Rhonda's old car with dulling red paint. At the oval an official greeted us. He said he was going to announce me. A decision had been made to tell the audience I had walked a high wire in St Petersburg, Chicago, Mexico City and now here I was in Red Hills. My trainer peeled off the coat. I flexed my neck and people started to stop and watch as if that was the act. Then I climbed the pole, moving smoothly, my feet scratching faintly on the metal steps. As I climbed I saw iron roofs, a dry creek bed snaking into distance and the flat tops of eroded hills. Below me upturned faces shielded eyes from the glare. A voice boomed from speakers, announcing my performance.

On the tiny platform in front of the wire I stood dead still. A light wind fanned into my face. It blew smells of fertilizer and semi-trailers billowing exhaust as they changed down gears. I glanced at where I knew my trainer and father would be, alongside a space where I pencilled Rhonda in, her cheers winding their way up to me through the heating air. I held out arms, lifting my chin and finding balance. Then, trembling through the joints in my legs, I stepped out.

Foreclosure

Only two of us in town wore ties. The real estate agent always wore the same one. It was covered in logos of a football team he played in before he had a weight problem. I owned six. One for each working day and a spare for a wedding or funeral. As the bank manager I needed to wear ties. The two customer service officers were provided uniforms. Last week there was a memo announcing management decided to call them financial services officers.

Working inside meant my complexion was one of the few in town not ravaged by sun or windstorms of topsoil. People said dust churned in from half dead wheat crops ten pub crawls away. Some nights I was sure I flossed brown volcanic soil from between teeth. One of the truck drivers said if I stayed long enough my ligaments would ache before cool changes. I could save money on barometers.

People in the street used to say hello. Even grade three kids queuing for the bus to take them to Shepparton Primary.

"Must catch up for that beer," the farmers often said. Their sons who'd turned eighteen and decided on a life on the land shook my hand. I was brought armfuls of silver beet and sacks of potatoes with deep brown earth still caked on. They gave me cobs of corn so precisely enclosed in leaves they seemed gift wrapped.

It started to change during the drought.

"Sorry Mate." Jeff who ran four hundred hectares was the first to say it. When the wind blew from the east the sound of his cows drifted through town the way hymns could on Sundays. "Have to have that drink when things aren't so tough. No more parmigiana and a pot of beer on Friday night."

I noticed repayments being missed as the drought went on. Management said to start making telephone calls.

"Carol? How's Steve? And the kids? Well, I reckon that if they've been able to invent a snow making machine, why not one that makes rain? Anyway, only a courtesy call. You may have overlooked this month's repayment? Know it's easy to do. I'm sure you'll organise it. Just a reminder."

On Saturdays we played cricket. I wore a hat with a wide brim. It was like an eclipse of the sun every time I looked up. The ground was immaculate, a sweep of tightly woven grass that ran close cropped down past the boundary. It was so thick I liked falling on it. Last week I intercepted a boundary. As I rolled over on that grass it was like turning over in bed. The team applauded crisply, a couple of players jogging over to me and shaking my hand. The captain slapped me heartily on the back.

I bowled off spin. Felt the ball's stitching inside my palm like the outline of an old appendix scar. The captain signalled me into the attack. The ball was rough on one side and I turned it inside my hand. Then I loped in, pitching the ball up so it spun through the dry heat. The ball dropped dully on the pitch. From my end small cracks ran through ground like capillary veins.

They congratulated me at the end of the over. It was a wicket maiden and I saw my name being added to the scoreboard, letter by letter.

The bank told me to build up the business. They told me to join the small trader's association, Rotary and the cricket club. They said to join the supermarket queue if it meant I could talk to customers.

A month ago the bank told me a property had to be foreclosed. I knew this had already happened along the Murray River. Orchards were bulldozed and piled up trees burnt so that the sweet smell of sap floated down river. It was Gary and Heather's property. Their family was third generation on the land. Gary said he walked paths worn into earth by his grandfather and father.

Heather was on the porch. My trip left an airborne line of dust so thick I could have found my way back by following it. I parked and called up to her quietly. My voice barely crossed the space between us. The sound of her name must've been smaller by the time it reached her, the way a raindrop decreases as it falls to earth. She looked up. I always thought she was wrong for this town. Once Heather told me she loved it here. That she sat outside on still nights watching lines of heat lightning flickering and trembling along horizons. But I'd seen her uneasily standing in groups where she never said a word after the niceties were over.

"I'll get Gary," Heather said. She went inside the house. Gary came out, Heather slightly behind.

"You've come out to tell me I'm dropped down the batting order?" He laughed and played an air hook shot, wrists rolling over, technique perfect.

"Gary," I began. "Have you seen the letters from the bank?"

"I've seen one or two."

"I'm sorry," I said. "The bank has instructed that your property be foreclosed." I stepped up to him, handing over a sheaf of documents. "It's because of the non-payment of loan instalments. The terms and conditions are that the loan defaults after six months of missed payments."

Gary thumbed blankly through the papers. His face was hard, mouth clenched in that way when he drew on a cigarette.

"You have two weeks. The date is on there. I'm very sorry. Please move your belongings out by then."

I hung there briefly, not wanting to look at Heather. The bank had told me people were usually stoic. They take the news in the same way they handle a flood or drought. I turned back to the car, pacing out the steps, waiting for abuse or for him to run up and hit me with a rabbit killer punch. But there was only one sound and I didn't recognise it at first. It was so quiet I couldn't be sure it was even behind me. But as the angle of it changed, I realised it was Heather sobbing as she turned back into the house.

I had three wickets for ten runs. They were mostly teenagers, their only technique to swing at every ball as wildly as possible. I saw in their faces they'd already lost. Their minds were in the change room, sneaking an underage beer and discussing the next ute muster.

"It's okay mate," Gary said to me afterwards. My fingers squished in his handshake. "Decided what I'm going to do. Not your fault. At least you weren't coming to tell me I was twelfth man."

There was nothing to do Saturday nights. The choices were pizzas or whatever the Graceful Swan cooked without the risk of salmonella poisoning. I lived above the bank. It was possible to see to the next town at night, an aura of light barely brighter than what some people saw before a migraine.

Gail and I had been together three months. She was thin. Gail loved foot massages and sometimes dropped feet bony and hard into my lap. Her heels were cracked like the bottom of a dried up dam. She liked that I cooked, slapping down chicken in white wine and mushroom sauce, or salmon in that lumpy hollandaise I could never perfect. We had nothing in common so the television mumbled conversations for us. She stayed over on Saturday and Wednesday nights.

On Sunday morning I woke to knocking. It lifted through the floor from downstairs, so loud it tapped inside me. I undid myself from Gail like taking off an outfit. People rarely knocked on Sunday mornings. Occasionally there was a form dropped in or someone leaving a bag of vegetables. I pulled clothes over myself and went down stairs.

It was the real estate agent. I barely recognised him without a tie.

"So what's this about?" I said. "Got a bargain basement wheat belt property with a three bedroom California Bungalow going for a song?"

He glanced sideways at a truck heaving through a gear change.

"You remember that time you told me over a few beers about business opportunities? That properties would be foreclosed and there was the chance to sell them cheaply or even subdivide?"

I nodded vaguely. I'd been big noting myself at the time. Could have been the beer talking. Once I had that first drink after a day of hearing about water tables and waiting for tractor parts I could say anything. Blurt out I was standing for mayor, coaching the under elevens or building a solar panel so large it would power reopening the cinema.

"Well, that property you were foreclosing. Gary and Heather's? Gary committed suicide last night. Was that going to be one of those opportunities?"

I went to say how. Where did it happen? What about Heather? He jerked away from me. Then he walked up the empty street and I stood in the aftermath of his contempt.

Gail slept. A sheet lay diagonally across her chest, baring a shoulder. At times the softening muscles of my chest pushed into the spaces of her back like putty pressed into gaps. Outside the street would fill with cars returning from church soon. I'd been there on Sundays occasionally. People stood shoulder to shoulder as lifting organ notes vibrated through the pews.

I heard Gail come awake. She said I'd better cook eggs because I was going to need the protein if I went back to bed with her. I sat on the edge of the twisted sheets. She asked if anything was wrong.

I explained Gary was dead by suicide. She gasped, leaping up, ribs thudding into my back.

"Oh no," she said into my neck. Her mouth opened and closed on my skin and I felt her spittle and the shape of each word. Then slowly I told her I blamed myself. Maybe even that bloody bank with their three billion dollar quarterly profit. Gary had to take some responsibility too; he shouldn't have let the problem go so long.

Gail tore off me like a Band-Aid ripped off a scab. My skin cooled where I'd felt the slats of her ribs along my back. She hurried around the room, scooping up clothes and dragging them on roughly. Her top stretched out of shape as it squeezed over her head.

"Gail, I had to. Was just my job. There was no choice. Please understand."

She didn't bother with her shoes. They're probably still under the bed with dust thick as fairy floss and socks I gave up trying to find. She left me barefoot and I heard each step sticking to the floorboards as she walked out.

You had to be born in this town to ever be a local. There must be a headstone dated 1890 with your family name on it. Your DNA from three generations ago had to be sweated into the ploughed soil. It helped if there was a rumour your great aunt slept with Captain Midnight after he robbed the post office. I leaned against the cold of the driver's side window as they filed into the church. Past the smears of squashed insects on my windscreen I glimpsed the back of Heather's head and Gary's family trooping inside.

I probably wasn't going to be welcome. But I expected to be safe in church. No one would put their face up to mine and demand I leave. There was unlikely to be a dozen strapping sons of farmers marching me to the door and throwing me into a week of recovering from gravel rash and a cracked rib.

When the last person was inside I snuck in. There was nowhere to sit so I stood behind everyone. They glanced at me, expressionless I thought until I saw their eyes. Someone muttered what's he doing here? Then it ended and the casket was hauled up onto the shoulders of men in suits not worn since their wedding day. They trudged past us. Gary's round-shouldered mother, his purple faced alcoholic brother, his rigid boned best man and finally Heather, a tissue squeezed to her face, others guiding her as if she was blind.

The following Saturday they didn't give me a bowl. Banished me to the boundary where I was insulted from the crowd. I could've won the game. Where the grass on the pitch was worn back to little more than a man's three-day growth I could've spun the ball out of those spaces with the surprise of a card trick. I thought there would've been the chance of rebuilding. I would tell them I had no idea this could happen. That Gary told me it was not my fault. It was the bank, I was only the messenger. Nothing meant more to me than the friendships I had here. But after the match they drove away before my shoes were unlaced. When I roughly folded my long white pants away I found a note tucked into a pocket. "Don't come back" was all it said. I looked at it a long time before tearing it into pieces.

Landings

I hear the jet coming. Lift up arms and wait for its roar to fill the hollows inside me. Turn my face up into a flush of heat and air gusting with smells of aviation fuel. It's a 737. Two minutes ago it was nothing more than a gritty trail turning against the horizon. Now I watch it land. Black smoke twirls from tyres. Where is it flying from? Hypothermia during a northern hemisphere winter? Evenings of heatstroke and mosquitoes in Cambodia? Convulsions from flickering neon lights in Tokyo? Confiscated credit cards in Las Vegas?

There's a silence between planes. Sometimes brittle grass presses flat under winds. Tiny cicadas click from stalks laden with seed pods. Other people arrive. They haul children from cars, holding them up into rushing tail winds. Amusement park fear clenches kid's faces.

I'm here whenever I can. I have this instead of friendships. My world is not planting lines of tomatoes. I don't slow cook legs of pork or try on imported suits. I never order frappes at cafes or drape over back fences telling neighbours their lawn looks great. No one wraps themselves around me at night.

They brought me here for my tenth birthday. Back in the time of Fokker Friendships and Ansett. After that we came here the way families go to church. Hot water from a thermos was poured to make tea the colour of old puddles and sharp cornered three point sandwiches laid out. My father sat in a trance in the driver's seat as planes roared over. The windscreen was dabbed with spots of dried rain. "Wait for the reverse thrust," he exclaimed excitedly. My mother shook out the picnic blanket, last week's crumbs lifting off like sand. While eating she stared emptily out at flat distance and grey horizons.

They fought where we parked. Their voices probably reached the tarmac, maybe they were watched through binoculars from the control tower. She stood in ridiculous stilettos with the tendons in her legs bulging. "All we ever do, sick of this place, what about him? Don't you think he wants to play with other kids?" My father's shouting of 'shut up!' almost drowned out as the next plane swept over.

I wonder if the pilots can see me. The police do. They used to keep stopping, asking for my license, would I mind opening the boot? But they know me now. They ask what I will do if someone invents vertical take-off. Go and watch trains? Build model planes?

At times my parents argued away from the car. Face to face they shouted, close enough to see veins in each other's eyes. A decade before their faces must've been close like that, resting lightly together before kissing. They later stopped caring if I saw the fights and argued around me. There was the time when my mother put her hands on the bonnet to lean across and insult him but her palms burnt against the duco. She cried hysterically, beating him off with small fists. A passing car stopped and a man came over, asking her if she needed help. He said he could take her somewhere. My father stood still, his shoulders heaving like slow pistons. Then a jet shrieked over and he tilted his head up, eyes alive again and following its decent.

Sloping rain with the texture of smoke bends against distance. I will the rain closer. First drops will coat my face like an onset of pins and needles. I love the whirls of spray as jets land. They unleash cyclones that spiral briefly.

There were long drives home in the car. Hours of sulking silences. Paddocks flat as runways skimmed by windows. A whiff of baby powder and I'd know my mother had eased off shoes. At home my father vaulted from the car.

Once from the front seat she turned around after he'd gone to the door, facing me. She told me never to treat anyone like that. That he made her so unhappy she wanted to sleep in my room. Lie on a couple of those square cushions off the couch and drag spare sheets and a dressing gown over her. There was nothing worse than being trapped. All she could do was keep ironing those primary school shirts, overalls and cook endless mixed grills. Maybe all that fat would give him cancer. Then she could at last leave. She seized my arm. Her other hand darted to her mouth. She breathed in through fingers.

"I'm sorry. Please don't tell anyone I said that."

It was only my father and I that last Saturday. We drove in the same heavy silence. The first plane was a 707 with *Lufthansa* emblazoned along the side. Normally he'd swoon at those four engines but he was as blank as when I spoke about school.

"Your mother won't be there when we get back," he said later in the fumes of another jet. I had worked it out. It was in his dulled eyes, how he drove too fast and hadn't brought a thermos or sandwiches. He concentrated more than ever on the planes that day, most likely so he could forever play them through his mind. He never took me back there.

It's not that different now. The planes are quieter. None have propellers. I tell my father about them in his wheelchair while he looks through me. He asks about my mother. I say I don't know. Maybe when I'm watching them one of these days she'll appear. She'll say she can't believe it's me. Incredible that I still visit there. And because in the beginning there were happy times, one day she decided to come back. I'm still waiting for that.

The Protest

All the photographs were black and white. Dates and places scrawled in lopsided writing across the backs. Fingerprints ribbed over their gloss. I lay them on a table. One of me holding a placard was out of focus. In another my arms linked with Carol and a line of protestors. In the next a policeman dragged a man from in front of a tram. A picture folded through the middle showed my mouth open as I chanted.

Grace glanced from behind my shoulder. She told me to let her know when I finally started living in the present. The revolution was over. Grace said I obsessed over those pictures. It was more than fifty years ago. I'd turn into one of those people in nursing homes with only long term memory, talking as if it was 1969.

Sixties music often throbbed down our hallway. In its crescendos lay memories of old dance steps, shouting at my father, calling 'no more war' and long rambling conversations with Carol. Some nights I sang those songs in the shower's drumming water tasting of warmth and lead.

Grace picked up a couple of photographs, shaking her head. She placed them neatly together and passed them back. She asked me to return the pictures to the box under the stairs when finished.

Our hottest week in fourteen years the newspaper said. I prepared a coffee from our espresso machine, jetting steam into milk. A spray of milk prickled my skin like heat rash. Outside I sat at our glass table covered in drifts of orange dust blown in from north of grasshopper plagues.

Sun lifted over the house behind. A constant, flat note of bees hummed from flowers along the back fence. Grace came out, barefoot and wrapped tightly in a dressing gown. A belt trailed behind her. She drank deeply from my coffee. She asked what was left to talk about. Kids had left home and weren't even calling by to drop off washing. Our house was like an old gold rush town where everyone left and only empty buildings remained.

I asked Grace what she wanted our futures to look like. We'd speculated how we might retire. Tow a caravan an option, driving before finally stopping when enough locals said the fishing was good. Grace wanted to visit Venice, her life only complete when listening to the quiet gliding of a gondola along canals. My tastes were simple. If there was a fish and chips shop that sold bait I'd be happy. Grace drained my coffee, leaving dark lines around the inside like rising damp marks along a wall.

My first protest was in 1969. When we assembled Carol said we were the first generation to think for ourselves. We had to be patient. It'd take time for older people to understand. Never trust anyone over thirty Carol said. She looked around at the swelling crowd. Carol asked if I could feel the change. It was in the music, universities, streets and theatre. Her voice lifted two octaves when she spoke like that. Others looked at her, leaning in to listen, at times nodding intently. When we marched Carol and I were in the second row. The rhythm of hundreds of steps tapped through the walls of my stomach. We turned into Swanston Street, a giant sweep of people chanting.

"One, two, three, four, stop the Vietnam war!" I joined in, roughly in time with the crowd. Later if I faced a mirror and angled the yellow light of a torch down my throat it would be streaky red from yelling. But for now I shouted until I felt volts of pain every time I raised my voice. At the end of the march people sat in front of a tram. It grinded to a stop. The driver half leaned out the door and signalled them out of the way.

"Come on!" Carol said. She took my arm, long fingers gripping around a thin muscle. She propelled me into the crowd, wedging us between two sitting protesters. The police dragged people out but they scrambled back. I called out in my raspy voice, re-joining the chant. Police on horses arrived, edging forward into the crowd.

Later we walked home. All we needed to change things were loud voices and placards I told Carol. She smiled, more inwardly than at me.

Carol lived in a squat in Carlton. We crushed into her bed upstairs. I was so squashed against her I joked my skin would grow over her like a graft. She pasted images onto posters; pictures of soldiers, burnt children, dead babies and a Vietnamese grandmother with the tip of a gun barrel trained on her head. A local printer ran the posters off and we lugged them along Faraday Street, taping them to telegraph poles. I held the posters over splintering wood while Carol taped them into place.

At home that night my father spoke to me.

"You turned into a communist? We fought the Japanese and the Germans for the freedoms and liberties you abuse. Maybe you'd enjoy facing a firing squad in a communist country." My mother braced for another shouting match between us.

A storm was going to break the heat. I stood in the front yard watching distant soft lines of rain plummeting. I breathed it, a smell of turned earth before planting vegetables. Then I walked down the side of the house, my greyhound pressing her nose to my bare legs. Martin was scraping the barbecue. Rolls of fat curled in front of the spatula. He flicked them into the garden.

"My dog will eat that," I said. "She's going to have to share my cholesterol medication."

Martin was about to retire. He'd planned it meticulously. His investments planned out so his wife and he could afford two cars. In a few weeks they'd move to Byron Bay. I pictured him on the varnished timber veranda he talked about. He'd lie on a lounge, leather skinned and drinking craft beers. His face turned into sea breezes that probably started as storms out to sea. He told me he loved it because the hippies at the beach reminded him of his youth.

"I was surprised at you all those years ago," he said. "After all that protesting. Thought you would have gone into environmental law. Something with a social justice side."

It was true. In the beginning I believed I'd change the world from a courtroom. Along the way I side tracked into employment law. In my first case I defended a local council against an action brought by employees spraying herbicides. They claimed constant migraines and skin infections from the sprays. The Agent Orange of the suburbs a local paper called it. I won the case when residents testified the council workers removed their masks while spraying. Afterwards the magistrate took me aside. He said he had no choice but to give the ruling he did. He added I'd better never stand in his courtroom and claim compensation for anything more serious than a paper cut.

That night Grace opened champagne, toasting my legal career. Half way through my third glass I wondered if Carol was somewhere, hearing it on the news and wondering what brought me to change sides. Grace said we should buy a new lounge suite to celebrate.

"What happened to it all do you think?" I said to Martin. "We were changing society. Then nothing. It all ended. For a year or two we demonstrated against uranium mining. After that we faded away. We turned into foodies or renovators, depending on what reality television show was on. Now we're faced with climate change, more war, erosion of freedom and all we get angry at is whether we can find a parking spot."

"We grew up," Martin said. "Our cause became comfort. It's time for the next generation to do the work. They get to save the earth or bring down the banks. If they can get off their mobile phones for long enough."

After our next march Carol was charged with trespass and interfering with a police horse. They drove her away after one of the police blocked me from pulling her back. Finally I brought her home in the still heat of night. Along the way she ripped down one of the posters we'd put up.

"It's not enough!" she said bitterly. "People pass these every day. How many of them change? How many of them do anything? Every time I put up posters I use pictures that are more and more horrifying. My Lai massacre, burning monk, execution in Saigon, children burned by napalm. They keep walking past them as if the pictures are just Christmas decorations. Nothing changes."

I pushed back my hair. It was almost as long as Carol's now. In her room she sat at the table, head bowed. A half chilled cask wine stood on the table.

"All the marches and posters in the world won't change anything," she said.

I arrived home at the time my father was leaving for work. He brushed past, odour of his shaving soap whisking over me. Humidity pressed out of the house. My mother tentatively asked where I'd been. She followed me down the hallway, telling me I was disappointing my father. My steps were wide, clunking and echoing along the hallway while her worn down slippers scuffed along. I stood on the bed, reaching into the space above the wardrobe, dragging down a suitcase. Wads of dust floated to the floor. I said I was leaving. I'd return the suitcase. In a few Sundays I'd try to come by for lunch. Her hand, shy and unsure, settled against my back. I felt the outline of her fingers fanning over my skin.

"Please don't go," she said. Her voice barely reached me. She trembled right through to the points of her fingers so they touched my skin like soft Morse code. I could not look into her eyes. Only years later as a parent myself did I realise how much that must have hurt her. A couple of times I half turned towards her as she spoke. I jammed a stack of perfectly folded t-shirts into the case.

I kissed my mother lightly. Then I walked by her, suitcase wobbling in my hand. She stopped me, hooking fingers around my arm.

"I'll drive you," she said.

I told her she could drop me at the station near home. Then I trailed her out to the car. She kept glancing sideways at me as we drove. Her small knuckles lay pink on the steering wheel.

"We'll go one more station. Please. For me," she said. Each time we passed people waiting on a platform she repeated that. Her face was rigid, concentrating on traffic. Finally in a shy voice she said she was too nervous to drive any further. She let me out four railway stations along our railway line. Then kissed me goodbye on the side of my face gently.

The carriage jolted and clacked through suburbs. Lately men in suits stared at me, sometimes muttering. That day I returned their gaze with my best mocking smile. They looked away out the dusty windows. I leaned against the gently warm glass. The rounded outlines of plane tree trunks flashed past.

I walked slowly through Carlton. Pavement heat burned through my thongs. Inkblot clouds foamed along the horizon. My feet thumped up the wooden steps to Carol's door. It was open as it usually was on hot days. I never knew if that let heat in or out. Carol was sitting on the bed smoking. As I walked in she stood, running towards me, arms lashing around my body. She said my name over and over, except more quietly each time.

Grace said we needed a pool.

"You could dive in from here," she said, feet together and hands clasped, arcing in air towards where she pictured water. For a moment I saw it too, ripples glinting along the surface. "We could have a palm tree here," she said, standing at attention, smirking as her hands waved the way fronds floated on wind currents. "Here you are on a towel." Her hands shaped a place on our dying grass. "This is where you'll give me a neck massage after I have done a few laps." I glanced in the direction she was pointing.

Carol held my face in her hands. Her breath heated against my face. She told me there was a way to change everything. People in America had already started a group called "The Weathermen." They'd declared war on their government. As long as bombs were dropped on Vietnam, Cambodia and Laos they'd fight back. Banks and office blocks were already blown up. Her hands squeezed against my cheeks so hard I felt the dips in her palms.

"It will make them listen," she said. "Government supports violence. So let them suffer it. Let them see what it's like. The war will be here. They will realise they have pushed us too far. We cannot allow injustice to become law. How can we run a system based on people going to jail for murder while government bombs kill thousands?" I dragged my face out of her hands so fingertips drew along my skin.

I asked how she was going to organise that. There was no popping down to the hardware store to pick up a few sticks of dynamite and a timing device. I was happy to march, even throw red paint over politicians. But this idea would end up with someone in jail or dead.

"I don't need bombs or guns," Carol said. She looked exasperated. "There's other ways. We can use petrol. It's easy to buy and can do a lot of damage. I don't care about throwing paint. The impact of that will last as long as it takes a dry cleaner to get the stains out." She stared evenly at me. "I've already talked to some of the others we marched with. I was really counting on you."

That night I unpacked. Stuffed my clothes alongside hers in the three drawers she had. Heat swelled timber around the windows and now they jammed open. Mosquitoes whined around us. Street lights shone dull squares on walls. Carol pulled a sheet over our bodies. She kissed my mouth, ribs squeezing into me.

I slept in until mid-morning. Sitting up in bed I saw Carol at the table writing and concentrating. A male voice asked if she wanted honey in her tea. I saw him bend over her, setting down a cup. He caught my eyes.

"Don't mind us," Carol called to me. "We're just planning to end a war. You get your sleep." I stood, pulling a shirt on. I recognised the man she stood with from a demonstration. We shook hands briefly. He lifted a shirt and showed me a bruise.

"A cop did that," he said. "At the last march. Don't worry, I'll get them back. Great fire of London will be nothing compared to what we do." He grinned. Carol looked intensely at him. When she spoke it was in a low voice, tense and breaking. She said our first target would be the public service building opposite the park. We would wait until the weekend, late at night, staying out of headlights. She pointed at four cans of petrol on the floor.

"Used in lawn mowers. Highly flammable," Carol said. "We're taking a walk up there now. Just to look around. Make some plans. Want to come?" For a second I held her gaze, waiting for her to flinch with doubt.

"Sure," I said, trying to sound convincing. "Will see you there. Want to put a couple of things away first." They stood. Carol said the best part was the letter she was writing. After the attack she was mailing it to politicians. The last line promised more to come if the war didn't stop.

I watched them hurry down stairs. From the stuck window saw the tops of their heads bobbing down the street. Then I pulled my suitcase out from under the bed, reefing clothes out of drawers. Rolled them into balls and flattened them in the case. I stood and hurried out, slamming the door shut behind me. My feet seemed to blur down steps. Then I rushed across the road and leapt onto the side rail of a moving tram, gripping it hard as the conductor shouted what the hell was I doing.

Martin was leaving tomorrow. We had a final beer outside my back window. A pyramid of soil was piled next to a deep hole. A man working the excavator said they had dug past the line of earth there would've been in 1970. He told us we might find fossils of Janis Joplin records and flared pants. He laughed, stepping over the mangled plants I used to hear bees from gouged out along the fence. I told Martin there were probably fossils of Carol in me. The way she tasted of roll-your-owns. Her mania when she talked about how the world had to change. The hushed way she once said my name when dreaming. The shifting of muscles in her back when she turned over in bed. Martin watched me, frowning. He called inside to Grace that if things didn't work out in Byron Bay we should expect to see him lolling by our pool one day.

When I arrived at my parent's house after leaving Carol it was quiet. It always was. There was never music. My parents rarely spoke except to remind one another to change out of those dirty shoes or bring in the mail. When I walked in they were sitting at dinner. I set my suitcase against a wall. No one said anything. I pulled out a chair and sat where I normally did. My mother stood, lifting a plate off a stack in the pantry. She placed it next to hers, sliding mashed potato off her plate onto it. She sawed at a chop, halving it and pushed a portion onto the plate. Then, smiling shyly, she set the food down in front of me.

Twenty Six Dances

Lorraine stood in the doorway, swaying slightly. I'd noticed her at other times moving like that. As if she carried the dying rhythms of a song played at a nightclub in her bones. Her outline was barely lit in gloom. I sat up in bed. Lorraine bent to lift a suitcase. She didn't answer my question about what she was doing. Her footsteps measured and precise clomped towards the front door. A draught of cold air burst through the house as she stepped outside.

That was the last time I saw her. Weeks later I took down the photographs. Lorraine with the wedding veil turned back, eyes glistening and loving. Lorraine with an off the shoulder top, her body rounded as if a sculptor had chiselled curves into skin. Lorraine on a hill top in Noumea, facing out over ocean so blue it'd tint our eyes if we swam in it. I dropped the framed pictures into a box, hard enough for them to break.

I kept working. If anything drove myself more, staying at the office later. A couple of staff asked who I was trying to impress and what promotion did I want. Sometimes I fell asleep at my desk, stirring awake later to accents the cleaners spoke.

People often described mornings as the most beautiful time of day. They didn't do anything for me. I lay rigidly in bed after the alarm went off. Body heat lifted off me softly as evaporation when I kicked back sheets. Light grey as skin without enough circulation touched windows. Drove along the freeway, orange overhead lights flaring by. Eventually I queued behind brake lights. Turned up the radio, listening to news of economic downturns and crime.

Late in the day the dull shine of computer screens lit the faces of people still working, making them silvery and bloodless. Then I followed the traffic home.

Lorraine and I managed that one holiday in Noumea. We picnicked on a cliff top looking so far into distance the horizon dipped at the edges. We stood so close to each other it was as if I was dunked into the heat of her breath. When we walked along the beach the friction of sand warmed my feet. Clouds broke up, threads thinning and disappearing. Lorraine constantly photographed me. A picture of me bent in concentration, examining herbs in a market. Another one in a cane chair reading. In one picture I was diving into surf. Airborne droplets of water hung suspended.

After she left I joined a gymnasium. Finished each session with the rowing machine. My fringe knotted like dreadlocks and prickled into eyes as I exercised. It felt as if the bones in shoulders tore through skin. One of the instructors knelt beside me.

"You're pushing yourself too hard," he said. "Build up to it. You might be able to sustain that kind of effort in a few months. You trying to punish yourself for something?" He shook his head slightly. "Neither of us wants you to need CPR so take it easy." I slumped forward as he stood, waiting for my breath to come back. The next week I joined a theatre group for singles. We gathered in the foyer on Friday nights. Someone met us, introducing each person and handing out name badges. We sipped pre-show drinks before they led us off to where we'd watch the performance. The first three shows were musicals and I could barely sit through them. Musicals belonged in the 1950s when the world was about Doris Day and the cold war. In the third week I sat next to Abbie. At interval we stood in silence after realising we had nothing in common.

'Learn to dance.' The sign dangled over double doors between where I lived and netball courts. My Saturday mornings were umpire whistles shrilling and spasmodic applause. I'd walked past that door over and over. Usually passing during the slow jogs I began after giving up smoking. One day I entered into the building's cavern darkness. A woman sat behind a desk, her outfit Spanish. She mimicked a Spanish accent, facing me with a full smile when I asked questions. Yes, there were different packages. Lessons twice a week and a little practice between wouldn't hurt. I was welcome to attend alone. Who knows, I might meet someone special. It was a great way to have fun. Be a little sexy.

I signed for the largest package. Twenty six lessons. Decided I might as well do it properly. I walked home pleased, feeling I'd done something positive. Sun glared off passing cars.

Tuesday night was our first lesson. In the doorway stood the Spanish impersonator, smiling glossily as I arrived. The class stood shyly in the middle of a room of dull floorboards. A man came out, clapping hands so that a split second later the sound echoed, cracking against the back wall. He rested hands on hips, inspecting us.

"So, you want to learn dancing?" he called. He stared challengingly around the room. No one spoke. He moved between us, pausing sometimes to study someone before taking them by the arm and depositing them next to another person. Eventually we all paired up. "These are your partners. You may love them. You may leave them for another in the group. You may go through the motions with them. You may be passionate with them."

My partner was Veronica. She smiled quickly at me, dropping eyes. The instructor signalled to someone. Music started.

"Show me!" he called over it. "Dance with your partners. Do whatever you think goes with the music."

I danced the way I did at weddings. Veronica and I spun out of time and a dirty window bumped through my corner vision as we turned. She smiled tightly. The instructor walked between couples as they jerked around him. Now and then he shook his head. He watched us pass him. One woman beamed at him as she hobbled by, as if convinced she was gifted at this.

"Stop!" he said. The music finished abruptly. He looked across the room. As if he had used telepathy the woman doing her best to be Spanish flounced over to him. The music snapped on again and they took off, hips together perfectly as two bones in the same body. They swept across the room. She arched over at crescendos of the music and he caught her, lifting her so she spun away and then swivelled back to him. After a few moments they stopped. She pouted at him and for a few seconds they hung there, breathing heavily.

"Can you do that?" he said, looking in our direction. We stood in silence. His partner's head straightened from where he held her, spirals of hair falling across her face. "At home dance with pillows, lampshades, strangers, chairs, whatever will follow you."

The house was loud. My footsteps amplified through the large rooms. Central heating warmed corridors, oxygen watered down by gusting heat. From the windows a "For

Sale" sign illuminated in the front yard. How long would it be before it was tagged, some meaningless scrawl drawn over the real estate company name? Lorraine and I would split the proceeds. I half expected her to come by, checking I was keeping it pristine for the inspections. That I'd cleaned up crumbs. Sheets on the bed tucked in. Bedside table clear of snotty tissues and dust.

I made it to lesson eleven. I was so uncoordinated I made up a story about having a hamstring injury. Stepped on the edge of Veronica's foot so she yelped and looked pleadingly at the instructor. After that I stopped going. During the time the next lesson was due to start I lay in bed imaging Veronica sashaying around the room, her hands cupping empty air as she followed the music.

The next Saturday a van pulled up outside the house. I looked out, the rough idle of its motor vibrating through walls. They are coming for Lorraine's things I thought. What we haven't agreed on I'm going to have to argue about with removalists. To my surprise they started unloading furniture.

"What's this shit?" I said, striding down the footpath. "I live here. Who's moving in?"

"No one far as I know," the driver said. He nodded towards a number of chairs being stacked on the nature strip. "This is furniture to help present a house that's for sale. Your wife organised it, didn't you know? There's also pictures to hang. There'll be an interior designer coming to set it up. They'll bring flowers as well. Talk to them if you have a problem."

I stood back. Everything was carted in and piled in the hallway. I was asked to sign something and refused. The driver shook his head and walked off.

Soon after the interior decorator came with a couple of assistants. She went from room to room telling them where to locate the furniture. She told me I didn't have to do any of the thinking, my wife had arranged everything. She said I could use the furniture but it had to stay clean. Absolutely no marks. They lugged away our other furniture.

"Storage is arranged," she told me. "Soon as the house is sold we can take back all this."

Work had become a pretence. Morning after morning I woke, staring at the gap in curtains where there'd be a strip of flimsy light around 7 AM. I dragged on suits stretched out of shape by endless dry cleans. Then I joined the lines of cars. Once I arrived at the office, forced myself to begin. I smiled through the meetings. Offered ideas. Tapped keyboards with two fingers to write up reports. I was pleasant to everyone. But the whole time, somewhere deep where the real me lived and cowed, I seethed about my life.

When I arrived home men worked in the garden, planting clumps of lavender roughly into holes. One trimming a tree nodded at me as I came up the driveway. I stood so motionless I could hear the whine of Tinnitus in my ears. Someone was taking out the bulbs I'd planted years ago, one by one. He wrenched the stalks like snapping a chicken's neck. From the backyard a mower chugged into life. I smelt cut grass, something I once associated with Sundays and the beer that was certain to follow.

I went inside and changed clothes. It was the time I used to attend dance lessons. Left the house and hurried down the road. Busy traffic nosed by. Rain mottled footpath. I rushed up steps into the hall and music throbbed towards me. The lesson was ending. I was just in time to see their final steps, beautifully in time as they floated along the perimeter of the dance floor. They landed together, finishing in the same pose and holding it, sinews of arms stretching, legs pointing out. In the middle of it all Veronica caught my eye, holding my gaze for a second before the slightest of smiles crossed her face.

The Lighthouse

That wind could blow Leigh's eyes shut. Vault him back two steps in mid stride. Give him a taste of sea salt as if he'd received mouth to mouth from someone who'd swallowed seawater. Leigh used to retreat into the lighthouse on days like that. He stayed downstairs, walls trembling when winds gusted. The winds usually blew two or three days, coming across paddocks like avalanches. Leigh read out of date newspapers or slow cooked meals to pass time. During mornings he sat by the window with a coffee, boots braced against glass, watching surges gliding through ocean. Occasionally it snowed, tiny flakes billowing like cinders ahead of a fire. At nights he turned on the light and it pushed out from the lantern room into darkness.

Leigh noticed rotors thudding from the horizon. He could pick that sound that went under the howl of wind or waves slinging themselves onto the jet-black rocks. Each week the helicopter came, dropping off supplies. Leigh was the only remaining lighthouse keeper. The pilot announced that when he last arrived. He said the lighthouse at Maatsuyker Island was now powered by technology. The rumours were Leigh's lighthouse was about to close, no longer needed with GPS systems on ships. It could be anytime.

"They'll pay you out at least," the pilot said. "What about us? The two of us have been taking it in turns to fly out here for years. Ray one week, me the other. Weeks go by without seeing each other so we're leaving notes around reminding each other what needs to be done. But if we stop these flights, there's nothing. I might as well ditch our chopper into the sea. At least that way we can claim insurance. That's what we'll have instead of superannuation."

"Get a job flying tourists around," Leigh said. "Fly them over suburbia. They'll all fall asleep from boredom. You won't have to talk during the tour."

"Hate bloody tourists," the pilot said. "All they want to do is pick up a koala and ask about spiders. Anyway, pack your toothbrush and a few changes of underwear. Keep them handy for the day they'll send me out here to bring you back to the mainland." The pilot laughed, shaking Leigh's hand. Then rotors shredded air. He never stayed for the cups of tea Leigh offered. Even when satellite pictures showed clear skies he still worried about weather changes with downpours squalling in and cutting visibility.

The island was at its best in late spring when the winds dropped. It took three windless days for the sea to calm. Leigh could still hear the ocean at night but the rhythm quietened. On those days he lay on the grass, feeling it prickle against his arms. At times he woke to the air cooling and clouds like threadbare cloth swirling by. In the lighthouse he turned on heating that filled the small rooms.

Two years ago Leigh came here to be alone. He walked out on a secure job, marriage and mortgage. He left behind predictability right down to what he ate on Tuesdays and the exact minute he woke mornings. He took the lighthouse over from a seventy something man who the helicopter pilot said spent so many years on his own he'd forgotten language. Leigh found bottles of after shave with lids rusted on and light bulbs blown in every room when he moved in.

Leigh planted a vegetable patch. Eventually he dug up a few spindly carrots but little else grew. Leigh also tried to build a shed with leftover materials. Overnight the two walls he put up blew down.

Leigh lay in bed. He balanced the laptop on his knees. He went through the usual websites; weather, sports results and Wikipedia to check that day in history. That night he clicked on a site to meet singles. He looked at the pictures and read the captions. "The time is right for Mr Right." "Christian ready to meet clean living man." "Rebound with me." "Be my Chapter Two." "I don't know what to say here as I'm new to this." He started keying shyly. "Looking for a non-smoker who doesn't mind a remote location." Leigh read it over. He decided the intimacy of hand writing would make it easier. He picked up a pad, testing a pen, zigzagging it across paper. He started again. "Polite and respectable man seeking woman interested in getting away from it all. No suburbs, peak hours, trains running late or crime." Methodically he keyed it in.

The wind was hard and dry on his face next morning. Leigh turned his back to it and made his way to the beach. He was surprised at what washed up. Sometimes coconuts bobbed out past waves, eventually tumbling into shore. Pieces of timber lay on the sand, disappearing after the next storm. Tangled fishing lines often spooled between rocks, hooks rusted as if at sea a long time. Seaweed heaped up and stunk when the sun came out. Pieces of fishing nets and plastic piled up. There were no messages in bottles.

Helen came in on the helicopter. Leigh had been weeding an area where he hoped for better success with growing vegetables. Earlier he'd cleaned up, making the bed over and over so blankets smoothed perfectly flat. He'd taken out saucepans he'd once been content to let blacken at the bottom and scrubbed them until the hairs on the brush mangled.

He heard the helicopter pulsing from distance. He watched it skim over shifting waters. Leigh stood back from the rotors downdraught as it banked and descended. It rocked slightly as it touched down, rotors swishing as they slowed. Leigh crouched slightly, running to it. The door slid open.

Helen was thin. He hadn't pictured her like that. Her photograph on the dating site admittedly was only from the shoulders up. She'd posed in a park, barely smiling. Something in that picture made him imagine her shorter, and not as thin. Leigh felt the circular bones in her fingers as she offered her hand. He wondered how she might stand up to the winds, whether she would be able to push through them the way he sometimes had to, face clenched, chin tucked to chest. He watched her eyes dart nervously around.

"How was the trip?" he asked.

"How was the trip?" the pilot mimicked over the top of Helen's reply. "Don't ask her that. Of course it was great. I could reverse park this chopper up my armpit if I wanted to."

Leigh glanced at Helen. She was transfixed, staring out at light changing as it broke from between clouds before dimming. He'd been like that when he first arrived.

"You could give us a hand with these boxes," the pilot said. "Going to have a curvature of the spine lugging these potatoes. Hope you're not allergic to carbohydrates."

Leigh placed Helen's bags inside the door. He went back to the helicopter, reefing a box out from a shelf.

"She doesn't say much." The pilot said quietly, shrugging and watching her walk ahead. "I suppose that won't matter to you. You came out here for silence. You'll probably get plenty of that from her."

As usual Leigh offered the pilot a cup of tea. He gazed out as if sizing up the likelihood of weather changes. He shook his head.

"When those old football injuries ache it only means one thing. Low pressure trough. Isobars falling. Trust my old joints before any satellite images."

They watched the helicopter lift and make a half turn, tilting before beating away. Leigh felt the wind chilling against his teeth, aching in old fillings. He asked Helen what she thought. She looked around, slowly taking it in. She said it wouldn't take a lot of time exploring. Leigh smiled. He led the way to the lighthouse, holding the door open while wind buffeted around the entrance. Dead blades of grass spun in eddies of breeze. Leigh bent and reached past Helen's legs, hauling up one of her bags.

"This way," he said over his shoulder, smiling back at her. She followed him to the tiny bedroom he'd used as a storeroom. He thought she gasped as they walked in, pausing to take in the view of rough slate coloured sea, shadows of black cast by clouds.

"This is what you wake up to every morning," he said. Helen looked past him. Salt had built up on windows, fogging the view slightly.

Leigh said he would let her unpack. He said to come down when she was ready. He'd made lunch. He headed into the kitchen. Leigh had already planned the meal when ordering the ingredients. Mushroom sauce tossed through pasta stuffed with truffles. She would have to be impressed.

Leigh listened to Helen coming. Her steps were slow, pausing at times as if distracted. He heard her stopping now and then, looking out windows. He started cooking, adding extra garlic as if the smell would lure her down. Leigh opened the chardonnay he'd been chilling. Condensation misted the bottle. When she sat he poured, the wine quietly gurgling into the glass.

"Hope you'll be happy here," Leigh said. He stirred pasta. Bubbles of olive oil turned with it through water. "You have to remember to stay back from the cliffs. You're also better off inside when the winds are over fifty knots. There's an anemometer you can see from the door that tells you how fast it's blowing. Have you heard of one of those before? Oh, and the rocks on the beach? They can be slippery. You don't want to be down there with a broken ankle when the tide is coming in."

Helen nodded. Leigh spooned pasta into a bowl. It'd been used for so long a pattern on the bottom was almost gone, just the slightest outline of a chicken. Leigh passed the bowl to her. Thin steam curled from the meal. He served himself, sitting opposite her. They started to eat, so that there was only the ring of spoons and forks for a few seconds. Helen asked him about the lighthouse. Was it lonely? What did he do in his spare time? Did he see ships? Were there seals? Did he talk to himself?

Leigh told her he loved the satellites. They glided over as dusk darkened into night. Occasionally space junk or meteorites fragmented across skies. On some nights a glaze of cloud drifted across the moon. During the day jets left long white lines of exhaust that slowly faded away.

Occasionally he noticed ships lit at night on the horizon. They didn't seem to be moving, like seeing lights in a house.

Helen said the pasta was perfect. She carried their plates to the sink. Wind hurled against the window. Leigh took her outside, walking around the perimeter of the island. Sometimes he raised his voice to be heard over the rushing wind.

At night Leigh demonstrated turning on the beacon. Helen watched mesmerised as the light swept through sky. It took him back to when he saw it for the first time. It turned through mist rolling in, an outcrop of rocks and lines of flotsam in the distance.

A week later he wondered what he'd remember of her. How he might look back at his time with Helen if they were no longer together. It might be the taunt skin of her back, or how her skin was flawless, as if never exposed to sun or wind. Perhaps it would be the thinness of her arms with their surprising power when they wound around him. It could be the roundness of her hips where they strained through skin. The quietness of her hands as she traced small circles on his back.

When afternoons were still Helen went down to the water. He followed her along an eroded path. She walked awkwardly, her feet used to shoes now tentative over flinted gravel and sharp angles of rocks. She relied on Leigh to tell her if it was safe to swim. He stood on the sand, concentrating on the water's undertow, studying which way the rip was running. At times he said not to, it was too dangerous. Then they would sit on the rocks that could be warm if the sun had been out long enough. If Leigh said it was safe, she dragged off her blouse, plunging in and standing up dramatically, looking back at him while wiping water from eyes. She said it was freezing but still taunted him to come in. Leigh folded arms, shaking his head. Helen said it would be good for circulation and skin. Leigh said he would prefer a cardiac arrest to swimming in there. She swam breaststroke. Through waters Leigh watched her limbs fanning out in smooth circles. He told her to turn back in case she caught hyperthermia.

The next day they dug together where the vegetables were to be planted. Clumps of black soil broke and rolled aside. Helen trailed a watering can along mounds of earth. After soaking the ground she planted seeds, pushing one at a time into the earth. Before dinner that night, she slid hands inside his. Leigh's hands were dry with broken skin that caught on the insides of sleeves when pulling shirts on. He warmed his hands with hers, letting the heat find its way up through his calluses and life lines.

At first the plants looked hopeful. They broke ground with corkscrew stems, leaves straining against strengthening winds. Within two days they died. Leigh inspected them brown and collapsed. He called Helen down, telling her they had to be planted deeper. She said it was probably because of salt in the air. It burnt back new plants worse than frost. Leigh told her she hadn't been on the island long enough to know that. It took months of watching the elements, until you were so sure of what would happen next it was as if the weather was obeying you. Helen swung away, striding inside. Leigh kicked dirt over the dead plants.

Leigh had already predicted what the email would say. He wasn't surprised the wording was blunt. He didn't appreciate the tone of 'it has been decided.' Felt offended by 'take only clothes and personal items, bulkier possessions will be collected at a later date'. New technology was the reason. Safer passage for ships the email claimed. If Leigh was an angry man he may have decided not to switch the light on to protest.

The winds became cyclonic. They couldn't go outside. Leigh and Helen sometimes started short conversations. Leigh told stories about going to school and throwing his school bag over the brick wall before scaling it, running to the creek where he dozed, head on a jumper while he was meant to be at woodwork class. Helen spoke about tedious years living at home, her parents arguing so hard she thought visitors to the house days later would be able to sense the menace and the dying echoes of shouting.

Leigh and Helen's conversations eventually faulted and became quiet. They didn't have as much in common as Leigh had thought from how Helen described herself on the dating site. Her interests in photography, books and gardening only amounted to silence.

"It's not what I expected," Helen said days later. It was over breakfast, wind hitting windows like someone breaking down a door. He passed her eggs with bacon still sizzling. He nodded. She'd gone from looking outside and taking in the rhythms of the island to now staring out as if hating the place. He told her it was only because they were cooped up. The winds wouldn't last forever. It was a low pressure trough moving slowly. Once Helen felt that sun again she'd be fine.

Helen told Leigh she wanted to leave. She said she was sorry. She took his hand in both of hers, kneading his thick veins with thumbs. Explained they didn't have as much in common as she hoped. Leigh snatched his hand away. He said she wasn't trying hard enough. This was real life, not a profile on a dating site that could be altered when it wasn't working. Quietly she told him she'd believed life in that dreary suburb had not been for her but now realised neither was this.

Light cut a turret out into the night. It swept through smudges of mist, illuminating an outcrop of rocks. Leigh listened to Helen moving up the stairs, step third from the bottom creaking faintly. She'd rejected him. He even sensed it now in her strides away from him. When the email came, he'd considered how to tell her. Maybe sit with her over coffee, seeing if she'd accompany him back to the mainland. He considered explaining while tossing the ingredients of a pasta dish. Inviting her to go with him over the wafting smells of chives and cream. But now he made a different decision. Leigh listened to Helen's shoes thumping across floor upstairs before she shed them.

The barometer rose. Leigh already knew the weather was improving. Light streamed down in the west before an orange sunset. Wind was easing too, weakening like breath from a collapsed lung.

Inside Leigh spotted Helen looking at the calendar. Behind her he asked what was she checking. He said all their Saturday nights were free with no visitors expected. She half turned, saying she wanted to be ready for the helicopter.

"There," he said. He stubbed a finger at a date on a calendar. "In two days." Helen drew a careless circle around the day.

"So you aren't going to stay with me?" he said.

"No," she said so quietly he momentarily leaned forward to hear. "I'm sorry if I let you believe I was going to remain here. Originally I thought I might. But it's so lonely." Leigh said she may as well pack. Then he sat down, listening to the rustlings of her clothes being folded.

Leigh still lay next to her in bed. Aside from brushing her when turning over they didn't touch. During previous nights he'd gathered her to him, once while her hair was still damp from the sea. Now he was close enough to feel her heat but not her skin. Leigh lay awake through the long hours. Moonlight angled through windows. On and off he slept, peering through darkness at the digital clock each time he woke, wishing the night away.

During first light Leigh sat up. He dressed quietly, up on toes around the room. Early sky was faintly pink. He went to the kitchen, heaping powdered coffee into a cup. Steam from boiled water mushroomed into his face. Methodically he made breakfast, scrambling eggs so that the colour was better than anything in a cook book. Helen came down, her face tired. She pushed a fringe back. Leigh gestured her towards a chair. Light was stronger now, radiating out of the horizon. He said it was a perfect day, ideal for a swim. She smiled although he could see she didn't mean it. Leigh pushed a plate of food across the table to her, positioning a coffee in front of where she sat. She thanked him sleepily.

"Have a final swim before you go back. Who knows what it'll be like tomorrow. You'll be packing anyway."

Helen asked if that meant he was accepting her leaving. He shrugged.

"I don't have a lot of choice do I?" he said. They finished the meal in silence. Leigh stood to pick up plates.

Later Helen padded through the room. She clenched a rolled up towel under an arm. He told her to go ahead and he'd join her soon. She passed him so closely he smelt the deodorant she often turned her body into when spraying. Leigh stepped over to the window, watching her descending the carved out path to the beach. She was poised and sure of herself without shoes now.

It only took a few minutes. There was hardly anything to take. Nothing to be sentimental about. No favourite fountain pens, personalised coffee cups, journals full of lines with his slanting writing like a fence tipping over or photographs. He shoved a few clothes into a bag. In the kitchen he looked around. There was plenty of food. Even a couple of bottles left of that French oak chardonnay. Enough for her until she worked out where the plugs in the two way radio went he'd yanked out. To find the microphone he'd hidden she would talk into. He checked his watch. Then he went to the window that looked to the east, the window where the sun first appeared during mornings and he could see that strip of pale sand that disappeared at high tide. On the same rock as always he could make out the tidy pile where Helen's towel and blouse were left.

Leigh went outside. Exactly on time the helicopter approached. It stuttered from the distance. He watched it closing in, trailing a vapour of heatwaves. The helicopter circled around, touching down. The pilot's door swung open.

"Need a hand?" he shouted. "Where's your girlfriend?"

"Ray took her back. Didn't he tell you? Must be true what you two say about hardly communicating with each other. She's gone. So quiet Ray probably forgot she was on board. Good luck to her." He climbed in. The pilot shrugged.

"Taking any souvenirs with you?" he said. "Maybe a car tyre that washed up? Piece of jellyfish?"

"Never want to think of this place again. You'll never see me lying on a towel at the beach or doing costal drives."

The helicopter shuddered off the ground. Leigh wondered at what point Helen would realise his lie. Would it be as she looked up from water towards the helicopter? Perhaps it would only occur as she ran through rooms, shouting his name. Eventually she'd find the other calendar, seeing his deceit drawn as an almost perfect circle around today's date, when the helicopter and his departure was scheduled. She'd also realise this was a punishment, something she deserved and brought on herself.

"I'm going to miss coming here," the pilot said.

They ascended so Leigh could see out to grass buffeting and flattening. They turned sharply, passing the lighthouse so he noticed large tufts of moss around windows. Then he was looking out over the sea, water glinting in the sun like the sparks from a lighter before the flame. He might have seen Helen, dragging legs heavily through waist high water, waving frantically, probably frightened, maybe screaming. They flew towards the mainland and Leigh looked back, just the once, so that the island receded; green, grey, the white of waves collapsing on a reef, then nothing.

Dry Cropping

During westerly winds grit slashed along windows like rushes of hail. Sometimes I checked, glancing around into piercing sunshine. There was no need to look. Rain only fell far away, its smell occasionally blustering through in the coarse winds. Oblongs of sunlight glared on the wall like picture frames. When the cleaner came I told her there was enough dirt on the window sill to start a planter box. We could dig in a line of petunias that hung raggedly down like knotted sheets prisoners escape jail on.

At night semi-trailers roared through. They carried logs from a pine plantation that reminded me of Canada when I pulled off the road in their shade. In darkness my room lit up as trucks passed, shadows and glare sweeping across walls. Out past the service station trucks changed down gears. It took forever for their revving to fade away.

The pub owner said I was the first person to stay for more than one night since 2017. And that person was marooned because their car blew three tyres on a cattle grid. I spent most of my time in the room. Occasionally I propped at the bar, drinking until I could barely pronounce the order for my next drink. Some days I walked out into the dry heat. The wind fanned across plains and trees dead from salinity. In the property opposite a lifeless gum tree stood. The tree had been dead so long branches splintered off, spread over ground like the skeleton of an animal.

The plains made me long for rain. I was always thinking I'd just heard it. But it'd be nothing more than winds. Gales sheared through gaps in the window, sounding like long notes on a flute. If rain came I would've stood outside. Opened my mouth into its tastes of crop dusting and bush fire smoke. Let it run down the back of my shirt like how Julia used to trail fingernails down my skin.

I paid for everything in cash. Less chance of being found that way. Credit cards left trails.

My bag was under the bed. I had a rough idea how much money was in there. The number wasn't important. It's what it meant. Never working again. Living in Byron Bay, away from the schizophrenic seasons of Melbourne. No debt. No anxiety when Monday dragged around. Not taking the pathway of working until prostate cancer or heart attack.

On Friday nights people came in from the homesteads. For the first couple of weeks I watched for their daughters and sons. I imagined bored thirty somethings coming in to tap feet to the ABBA impersonators and trying to win the meat tray. But there were none. The town was going to die out with this generation. The next generation had all left for degrees with honours and McMansions closer to the city. Over beers the farmers told me about their dry cropping. Hectares of wheat scattered year after year. They always hoped the rains would break at the right time. For a few days there were hopeful tinges of green, especially on the sides of gentle hills where dew fell. Then the sun burnt it back like the floor of a dead sea.

Thursdays used to be my worst day of the week. I started with a coffee bag, dunking it eight times, the coffee clouding through until black. Then I drank it black and bitter. At my desk I wrote the to do list; 1) calculate the salaries, 2) print off four hundred and nine pay slips, 3) write the cheque to be cashed, 4) ask the managing directors to sign the cheque, 5) meet the armoured delivery van, 6) place cash in envelopes, 7) check cash in envelopes, 8) distribute pays.

We still paid wages in cash. One day I told one of the managing directors we were out of date. It wasn't 1924. We should pay into the employee's bank accounts. I said that before I saw my chance. The best thing he ever did for me was ignore my advice.

"We're thinking of starting a topsoil business," one of the farmers announced. I was wiping the last chip around gravy. "May as well sell it rather than give it away free. That's what happens every time the wind blows. Been enough topsoil blown out of here to pile up a mountain range somewhere else."

I nodded along absent minded. Was preoccupied in fact. I was planning my first trip. Las Vegas appealed to me. You couldn't find a place more opposite to this town. Pavements at night blinking oil slick colours while people sat in bars ordering triple scotches. I'd been told if I met any women I was attracted to, stay away from Elvis impersonators working in wedding chapels.

"So how long you here for? What do you do for a crust? That your car? Where you headed?"

I kept it vague. I studied them during the conversation, looking for signs they suspected something or became too curious.

Months ago I told Julia what I was going to do. I wasn't sure how she would take it. It was during a still and hot night. Dull heat lightening flickered. Neither of us had been able to sleep. She pushed open a window and sat on the edge of the bed blowing cigarette smoke outside. I often asked her not to smoke, telling her it'd blemish her skin. She glowed in the dim light like phosphoresce in breaking waves. A cicada's sound lifted and fell from a tree down the street. I confided in Julia because she often complained about the profits banks made or the enormous salaries of Chief Executives. She'd protested against cutting down old growth forests and the shortage of public housing. So I announced I intended beating the system. She looked at me, jaded by the heat and lack of sleep. She asked what I meant.

I told her every detail. I said the plan was so basic there was no need to write instructions. I explained it right down to the armed guard who stunk of kebabs when he laughed. How his young accomplice lethargically picked his nails while we completed the forms. That there were three copies of what we all signed and mine was green. The guard who always accepted the cheque had tattoos like blades along the white underside of his arm. Julia listened, intrigued.

"So you're going to steal the entire payroll?" she said. "How much?"

"Depends how you calculate it," I said. "Five hundred trips to Las Vegas. One thousand nights at expensive restaurants. Six hundred nights ringing room service from my king plus three royal families sized bed."

I watched Julia's reaction. It occurred to me it was barely a crime. There were no guns or knives. No hacking into bank accounts or fleecing people over the telephone for their credit card number. Insurance would cover the losses. There was nothing more to it than a walk to the car. Then putting a couple of bags in the boot as if packing for a camping trip.

I crawled across the bed to where she sat. There was the gliding smoothness of recently waxed legs. I coaxed her to lie down on her chest. My thumbs rotated in the gaps of her bare back, her bones shifting as if tectonic plates. From the window trickled the slightest breeze, pressing heat to us. I told her we would meet in three months. 28TH March at her place. It would all be blown over by then. I crossed the room to where her calendar hung at an angle, accounts and business cards bulldog clipped to the top. I said watch me and turned from her, drawing a thick circle around that date with a blunt pencil.

"Stay home that day. I'll be coming for you."

It was uncomfortable after a couple of months. The publican kept asking if I was intending to settle here. There was a property about twenty kilometres out of town with a two bedroom homestead that I might be interested in. Before the drought there'd been a lake where people would sit in their tinnies shooting ducks. Now all that remained was the slope of land where water used to be with shell casings protruding from hard clay. He said it'd suit me and if the rains ever returned I might be able to grow something there. I hung on for another few weeks, avoiding him so he wouldn't call me over for conversation. Sometimes he shouted across the bar at me. Did I want kidneys on the menu during the week? How about something Chinese? There was a bookmaker in town next week. Did I want his advice on any twenty to one long shots?

The morning I left I sensed rain. Clouds foamed in the shape of stuffing pulled from cushions. I thought I smelt it too, maybe a flash flood two lines of longitude from here. I dragged out the cash, swinging the bag up and over a shoulder so it hung across my back. The publican looked at me from where he bent over a dishwasher.

"So," he said. "Just as I thought I was going to have to name a cocktail or a room after you, you're leaving."

We shook hands. I almost felt sorry for him. He was stuck in this half town like a spider kept in a box. As I pushed sideways through doors to the car park another log truck swept through, billowing hot air and red dust. I dropped my bag into the boot of the car and started the engine, jetting brown water from the windscreen wipers onto the windscreen. Caked on dust smeared over glass.

I drove through town. Passed half dead plane trees lining the end of the street, the two dollars fifty per litre sign, a few empty looking houses and then dry dams like bomb craters. Electricity towers crossed the road further on, long drooping cables glinting silver in the angling sun. The single track railway came close to the side of the road and I turned off there, shuddering over the corrugated surface, the car trailing dust. The railway station looked old, as if trains never ran here anymore. I parked the car around the back, unscrewing and wrenching off numberplates. I slung each of them high over the paddock, watching their boomeranging across emptiness, chopping into the grassless soil as they plunged to ground.

The diesel shuddered in. Felt its trembling engine inside my neck as it idled, as if I was clearing my throat. I shoved my bag under the seat in front. A couple of bored passengers glanced at me. The carriages jolted and we grinded through the bells pealing at a railway crossing. I fell asleep, at times stirring awake to see a station blurring past.

It didn't feel like March. It was as if June had come early. That autumn warmth soft as body heat must've retreated to the northern hemisphere. Julia's unit overlooked the roofs of passing buses and into the windows of units opposite. Once she told me she could watch occupiers have arguments, share needles or vegetate in front of televisions. I knocked, listening for her footsteps to the door although I never really heard them when inside. She was always barefoot, walking so quietly it was as if she haunted the house rather than lived in it. The door swung open, gusting a puff of breeze over me, light as exhaling. I leaned into her space, kissing her intimately on the cheek, keeping my lips there and feeling the rounded skin on her face. She stepped outside.

"Hi. Three months is it?" she said. "Wow. It went fast."

She glanced past me as if looking for someone else. I almost picked it in her gaze, even half looked over my shoulder expecting to see someone coming up behind me. But there was no one and I changed the bag to my other hand.

"It's done," I said. "You're about to shed the skin of your old life." I pulled her to me, her slight bones pressing into my body like broken springs in a mattress. I started to kiss her but she turned so that my face lay against her hair. Slowly she pulled away.

"I thought about it," Julia said. "I really did. But I can't. I can't live always worrying about a knock at the door. Thinking every car parked opposite is someone watching you. I'm not even sure I can live with someone who could do something like this."

"Christ. Three months ago you couldn't stand the way we'd been made into slaves. Our lives reduced to nothing but deadlines and exhaustion. You said you wanted to live differently." I picked up the bag, roughly unzipping it. Cash bulged through the opening. "Look at that," I said. We both stared down. It didn't look like wealth. It smelt musty. "Touch it," I said. "Just put your hand through it."

Julia shook her head. She said that sooner or later I'd be stopped by a police car or at customs on that trip to Vegas I always talked about. I zipped the bag back up, bending over and struggling as the zipper caught. She stood over me in silence.

"I've got nowhere to stay tonight," I said at last. "Could I at least stop here? Can sleep on the floor if you want. After where I've been I could sleep in a laundry basket."

"No," she said so quietly I never heard it, only saw her lips shape the word. She might have been close to saying she was sorry but I saw it in her eyes anyway. She turned back to the unit. Soundlessly she went inside, closing the door.

I stood there staring at the deeply carved timber of Julia's door. I checked the date, peering into the cracked screen of my mobile phone. Today was the day I'd circled so hard on her calendar the pencil pushed through the page into April and May. I exhaled, imagining my lungs deflating into those wrinkled old balloons still hanging up days after a party. I picked up the bag, hanging it across my back. Its weight was killing me.

The Distance between Loves

Keith predicted the north winds bringing rain. Lines of ribbed clouds flicked with lightening before the downpours. Later as he walked to church chasms of blue sky opened. The grey spire pushed into sky at the top of his street. He sat close to the front, crucifix directly in front. He looked on when communion was offered, watching sombre faces filing past. Finally his row stood and filed out sideways, joining a line before the priest.

"Body of Christ," the priest said, offering the wafer of bread.

After the service polystyrene cups stood in rows, a teabag in each while someone carefully poured steaming water. Keith stood around the table discussing when the heat might break. Someone said they recalled a serious drought in the fifties. Another person said it was worse in eighty three.

He was home by lunch. Afterwards he went into the front yard. On knees he pulled out weeds, roots tearing through fingertips. Then he noticed an envelope pushing out of the letterbox. He ripped open the flap, smudging it with the potting mix he'd used earlier. He flipped open a card. Nola was turning eighty. He'd presumed she'd forgotten about him. He was invited to a party for her. He closed the card. On the front was a picture of Nola as a child, shyly next to a cake with three candles.

Keith felt nervous driving beyond his suburb. Nola lived too far from the bus route. He managed short drives to the shops or bank. He even enjoyed those occasions, at least there was a service assistant to talk to. He could still avoid the impersonal world of automatic telling machines, self-service checkouts and on line bookings.

Keith first met Nola at work. It was almost five decades ago. Nola was studious, filling out forms at her desk. She was so intent he was convinced she never noticed him. But they finally talked in the lunch room. They sat next to the window no one ever cleaned. Keith joked if anyone wiped it they'd discover pollen from extinct flowers. Nola told him she lived with her parents. Most of her time was spent helping around the house. At times she walked the sandy pavements to the beach. There she roughly hauled up jeans to feel ripples of sea water skim over her feet. In July it was cold enough to turn her skin a light shade of blue. In January she let warmth from the waters seep into her skin. She could never stay long. She had to hurry home to cook the next meal.

Keith drew the way into his street directory. Traced it with thick black Texta so when he paused at a bend in the road ink seeped out. He went through his wardrobe. He rarely bought anything. A couple of times he purchased shirts because someone working in the shop said they looked great. He'd returned home and hated them. They were eventually stuffed into a bag a charity collected on Wednesdays. Now he dragged shirts off hangars, trying to find something without loose threads or where colours hadn't faded. Over a dinner of fish fingers that night Keith wondered who might be at the party. After cleaning up he lowered a vinyl record onto the turntable. 'My Sweet Lord' soothed his mind and he sank back, cushions on the old armchair swelling up around him.

He used to write letters to Nola. It didn't seem long ago. He clearly remembered selecting the paper, smoothing it out like a tablecloth. He wrote in his address and the date. Nola once told him she loved his handwriting, his words slanted like the bend in a plant growing towards sun. He wrote carefully, nib of the pen working across the page as if stitching. Then he wrote 'Dear Nola.' He wanted to write it the way he would say it. Spoken softly, fading away on his breath the way some songs ended. He started with what he had done on the weekend. Then he read it back, quickly deciding if it was boring to him, it would also be for her. Letter after letter he tore up.

Under the burning sun Keith strived to save the garden. He wore a hat with a light veil over his face. A neighbour asked if he'd become a bee keeper. Keith directed the long stream of water towards plants. At times a wilted flower fell off and petals whipped away on the jetting water. Soil churned under the torrent. It smelt like rain as water spattered over hot pavements.

Nola's birthday came around quickly. He bought a bottle of perfume for her at the chemist. He chose one of the budget brands and an assistant offered him a smell from a sample bottle. Keith shrugged. He asked if the assistant would wear it.

"Of course," she said. "Is it for your wife?"

Keith nodded vaguely. He returned home. It was too hot for driving. He felt tempted to ring Nola and say he'd suffered heat stroke. Or he could make up an accident. Someone came out from a stop sign. The glare off the road had caused a headache. The radiator boiled.

Keith was overly cautious when driving. He kept below the speed limit. Other cars swept by, drivers occasionally turned and glared. The main road started following the bay and he glimpsed tops of beach umbrellas coloured like toadstools growing under rocks. Smoke haze shaded distance.

Streets became sharp and angular. He turned away from the bay so that it lay flat and grey in his rear vision mirror. Twice he pulled over, tracing with his finger on the map the unsteady Texta line he'd drawn. His hand sweated and ink smeared down the pad of his finger. A few more bends and he was pulling up outside Nola's. He was early so sank back in the seat, winding down windows to let out heat. He imagined heatwaves unravelling from the car, drifting up and folding in mid-air.

Keith was often the first to arrive at events, allowing too much time for the trips. Now he sat, shoulders pushed back into upholstery. He sank down slightly. No one would come outside in this heat. There'd be no kids trying to bowl leg spin on the perfectly flat asphalt, no dads coming out to kick drop punts to their children. Occasionally a car whisked by the end of the street.

Would Nola do the gardening? Perhaps she kneeled on an old cushion to preserve her joints. It was immaculate although patches of grass lay matted brown. Keith decided to wait for someone else to arrive. He sweated through the back of his shirt.

A car pulled up opposite. A couple rummaged around. Keith placed his hand on the door handle but when they stood from the car they went into a different house.

Nola used to write letters back to Keith. Her pages filled with small talk. She described something her mother said. How funny her father was when he watched football. How she might try stuffing mushrooms with cheese. It was the right time to plant for winter vegetables. How she hated washing the car and the joke she kept repeating about whether Keith would do it for her. Keith wanted to peel the words off the page and look under them. What hid there, was there something she really wanted to say?

Keith wished to start letters with 'I've been wanting to tell you how I feel.' He tried 'I have to tell you about what I feel for you.' Once he wrote 'There is something I have wanted to tell you so badly but I don't know how to say it.' He ripped up those pages afterwards.

Nola was promoted the day after Keith tore up four letters. She sat in an office two floors up. Keith was angry with himself. They'd worked together months and still talked as if no more than neighbours. He stared at Nola as she passed his desk, carrying folders to her new location.

People arrived outside Nola's house. He watched them walk slowly up the path. They paused next to white roses, a woman lifting a sagging flower as if tickling a baby under the chin. They rang the doorbell. Keith watched it open and close. Then he gathered up the present and walked to the door. There were whiffs of sweet scents from a rose bush he passed. At the door it was silent. There was no throb of voices, not even an occasional musical note chiming through the wall. He rang the doorbell, standing back. The door grated open. Nola looked blankly at him for an instant before smiling. She said she hardly recognised him.

Keith stepped inside. There were muted sounds from down the hallway. He kissed Nola, feeling her cheek under his lips. She stood back, examining him. It crossed his mind she didn't look well. Her skin was pale. She was even a little stooped. But it was the smile he knew and he followed her down the hallway. They crossed a kitchen and walked outside under a pergola. Shade lay along concrete. Nola asked Keith if he wanted a drink and he nodded. She turned from him, heading towards a line of glasses.

Keith looked around. He recognised a few people he used to work with. They looked so old, would they think the same of him? A couple of men he used to know from work came over. They shook hands loosely. One of them remarked how young Keith looked, what was his secret? Keith shrugged. No smoking, drinking and in bed by ten he said. They smiled at him, glancing between each other as if finding something funny. They asked what he'd been doing since retirement. Keith boasted about his garden. He said he had four front and four backyards. One raised eyebrows.

"It's like that anyway," Keith said. "The garden changes with each season so that it's completely different four times a year. If I left my place in summer and came home in winter I could drive past and miss it. It'd look different."

Someone carried out a cake. Nola hobbled along behind in heels. She smiled shyly into the circle of people.

"Speech!" someone shouted.

Keith had always been glad to see the end of working days. The lift shuddered down to the ground floor, doors straining open. In the street he breathed the car exhaust laden air on his way to the tram stop. One day he reclined in the corner of the lift, feeling the vibrations through his back as it passed the second floor. When it stopped at the first floor Nola stepped in, smiling slightly. She apologised for taking the lift. She said she was tired and couldn't be bothered using the fire escape. Keith looked up. The light glowing next to first floor went off and flicked on beside ground.

"Nola. A picnic. This Sunday, I was going to go on one," he blurted out. "Would you like to come?"

She looked at him as if silently translating what he said. He wasn't sure if she was pink from hurrying to the elevator or embarrassment. She nodded three times before she finally spoke.

"I'd love to," she said.

Nola's speech was ending. She looked around the group, her eyes landing on each person, thanking each of them by name for friendship, gifts, coming and for helping themselves to her drinks. Then her gaze stopped on Keith, resting on him so that he felt her as real as if her palms rested warmly on him. He braced himself. Her eyes softened.

"Thank you Keith for your friendship," she said. He kept looking at her, even after she turned towards the cake. Someone passed her a knife.

"Better pass her an oxygen bottle if she's going to blow out those candles," someone said.

They sang happy birthday. Voices broke and fumbled out of tune. Some reached the end while others were still four words behind.

"You and Nola," one of the men said next to Keith. "We could all see how much you liked her. We could never work out if you did anything about it."

Keith forced a smile and went to the table, lifting a paper plate with a slice of cake. The cake was too sweet, sugar gritty between his teeth. Nola slowly made her way from person to person, smiling up at people, tilting her head to listen into conversation. She started talking to two people they used to work with. Keith heard pieces of their conversation. They started speaking about others they'd shared an office with, most of them now dead. Nola answered a question shyly. Keith knew when she was shy.

Her head bowed slightly, eyes looking away to one side. He might be the only person who knew that about her.

Nola had agreed to the picnic. Keith expected her to make an excuse. Even as she said she would go with him he started thinking about what to take. Would she be happy with plain sandwiches? Should he cut some fruit? What drink should he take? But he relaxed the next day. She passed him in corridors twice, her face turned and shy but there was that smile, now something between them as if they'd spoken their first secret. Keith asked his mother what would impress someone on a picnic. His mother rolled eyes and offered to make cupcakes. She asked him what coloured icing he'd like.

Keith picked Nola up on Sunday. He knocked at her door. Her father opened it, looking him up and down. Keith heard the seriousness of his hello, how it was spoken so gruffly it was like a push in the chest. But she came to the door, hurried and breathless. The heat of Nola's perfume rolled over him. He walked her to the car. At the park hazy autumn sun shone, air barely warm. Keith rolled out the blanket, realising it was so long since it'd been used there was a faintly mouldy smell. Nola sat, adjusting clothes around her. Keith placed out sandwiches, offering them to her. She took one, pinching it delicately between fingers and working it out of the tight fit with others. He wondered if the insides might fall out. After her first bite Nola touched a fingertip to her lips, checking for crumbs. She told him it was delicious. The bread was so precisely cut she said Keith should have been an architect. Or a butcher. Keith laughed, covering his mouth so she would not see what he chewed. Nola told him her ambition was to travel to Fiji. Already in her mind she'd reserved a place on a beach. She imagined it. The trunk of a palm tree slung low over the sand. While lying on a towel Nola heard waves foaming on the reef. She dozed on the sand, waking to the giggle of passing kids. Ten days Nola decided. She would lie in that spot every moment for those ten days. She'd absorb so much salt off that beach that once back in Melbourne every time she perspired she'd smell the sea breezes of that island. Keith nearly said he'd come with her. He almost said he'd roll out a towel right next to her so that after they left the impression of their bodies would be visible on sand, the way sheets moulded to the shape of a sleeping body.

They kissed as the light was fading. He tasted her breath before their faces rested lightly together. She was so unsure, not moving at first until Keith took her face in his hands. He felt the outline of her cheekbones through his palms. Finally it was too cold to stay there. In his car soft warmth enveloped them. They kissed again, leaning over the space between the driver's and passenger's seats. Keith was reluctant to draw back from her. Finally Nola said he should drive her home. He drove slowly back to her place, her hand warmly on his leg.

At lunch the next day they walked through the city. They stopped at the city square, sitting on cold benches. They ate lunches before she slipped her hand in his. Keith glanced around in case people from work might see them. Then he looked down at her hand, fingers splayed over his.

At last Saturday came. Keith waited to be able to make a telephone call in privacy. He stood around while his father went outside to mow grass. Waited for his mother to make that cup of tea she always had half way between breakfast and lunch. Finally he rang Nola, tucking himself into the wall so he couldn't be heard.

"I can't come." When she said that Keith paused, thinking he'd misunderstood. She spoke again, breaking the silence. "I can't see you anymore. My mother is very ill. I'm needed here. I'm sorry." Keith held the phone to his ear, even after he'd heard the click of her hanging up. His mother passed, steadying her cup of tea, smiling mischievously at him as she went by. Keith rang again, waiting a long time for an answer. Nola's father finally answered. Keith listened to his short breath, the way a chain smoker or asthmatic would breathe. Keith hung up.

He went out later, unable to listen to his mother continuing to ask why he wasn't seeing Nola. He stopped at a cafe in Brunswick, drinking a Lebanese coffee and swallowing the sediment at the end. He thought about driving to her house. Maybe it would upset her. Cause problems with her parents. At home his mother asked him again.

"I knew it," she said. "Finally get a decent girlfriend and what do you do? Ten minutes and you've lost her."

On Monday Keith took the tram to work. It banked around corners, wheels scraping. He hung onto a bar, tendons in his shoulder straining as he clung harder through the sharp turns.

"I wouldn't blame you for being angry," Nola said next to him. He hadn't heard her arrive at his desk. "My father needs help looking after my mother. He can't do it on his own. I leave him with food he heats up for her during the day and at night I need to cook. He said it's what I must do. They looked after me all those years and now I have to do it for them."

Keith stood. He was barely taller than her when she wore heels.

"We can still meet at lunch," he said. "Surely we can get together now and then."

Nola shook her head. She smiled weakly and turned away.

"Please Nola," Keith called after her. He watched her cross the floor and wait outside the lifts.

People were leaving. Some didn't want to risk driving in dark. Nola had come up to Keith and asked what he'd been doing recently. He started telling her about the garden. He'd found new varieties of Daffodils, planting them either side of a pathway that led to the front door. For two weeks every August he expected to see their bobbing orange and white flowers. She went to speak. It might have been to say she'd like to see them. It could have been to say she was filling paper plates with cake and would he take one when he left. For a second he saw something else cross her eyes. Perhaps she was going to say what he was thinking. Something about things always in the way, even now because she would never go to his place in August to see those flowers. Someone came into their conversation, brushing Keith, bending through the space between them to kiss Nola. Then everyone was going, piling past, someone taking Nola's hands in theirs, another kissing each of her cheeks, the next person saying congratulations. Keith backpedalled and joined the line, pushing along with it, glancing around the shoulders of the person in front. At last he drew level with Nola, watching her gaze lift off the person in front of Keith and settle on him. She smiled brilliantly and he stood basking in it, even as the person behind bumped him lightly.

"Thank you Keith for coming," Nola said. Right there he heard her voice the way it was when she used to speak intimately to him. Lower and slow, almost breaking but still strong, as if he every word transmitted a feeling in her that hadn't entirely died. It surprised him so much he allowed himself to be jostled along by whoever was behind him, propelling him out the door and into sunshine before he realised he hadn't even said goodbye to her.

About the Author

Peter Farrar is originally from Sydney, moving to Melbourne where he pursued short story classes, unemployment, a Sunday morning breakfast shift on community radio and travelling. This is his second collection of short stories, the first being "The Nine Flaws of Affection" published in 2010. Peter's short fiction has been featured in a range of literary journals and magazines in Australia as well as the United States, some winning awards. He has dabbled in feature article writing on a range of topics including his love of test match cricket.

Through his writing life Peter also worked in a succession of mainly Human Resources positions. His corporate career was never described as stellar or meteoric. Peter is also pursuing interests in writing plays and he has had one short play as well as a full length work staged.

Two greyhounds occasionally check in on him while he works.

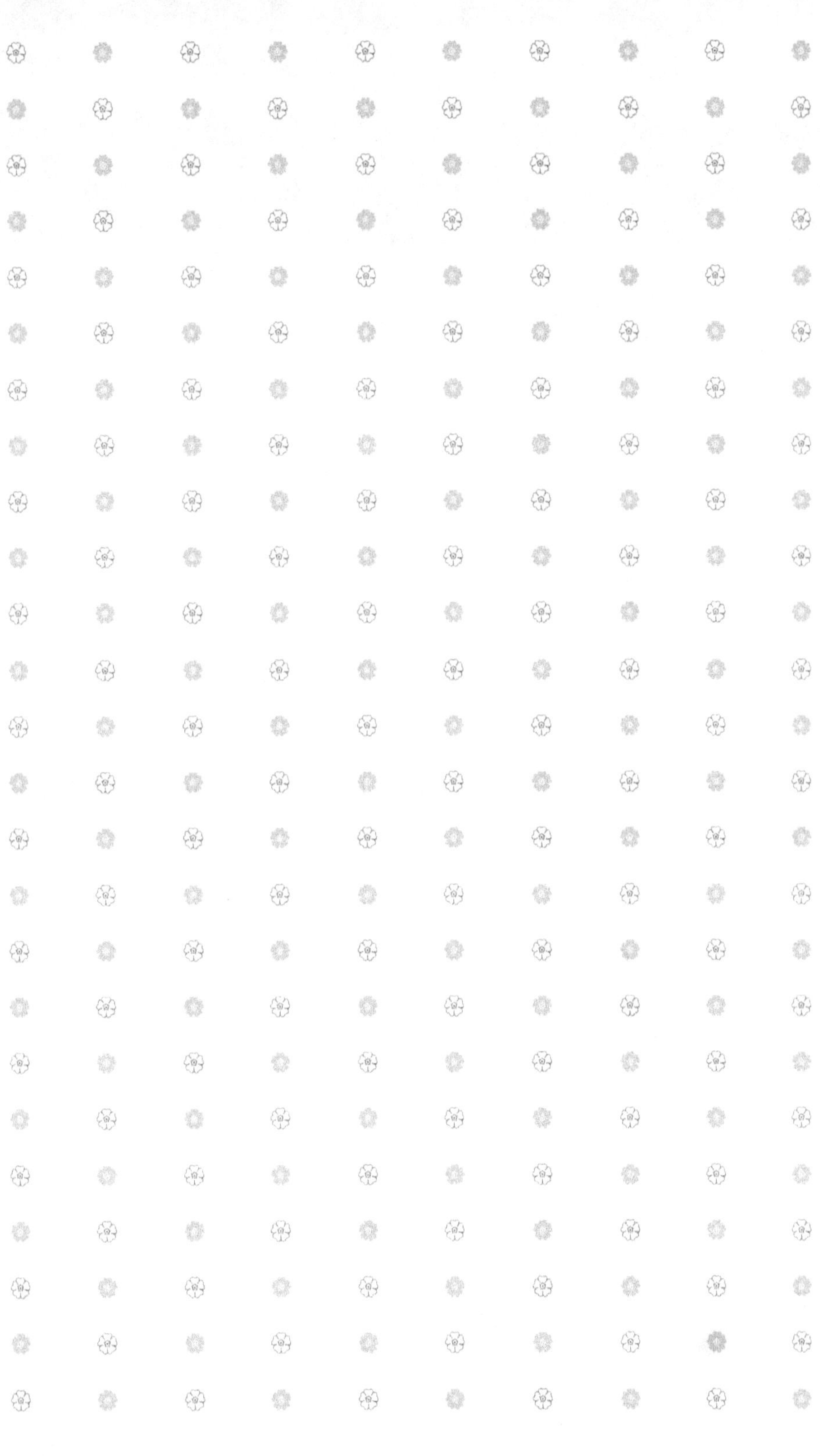

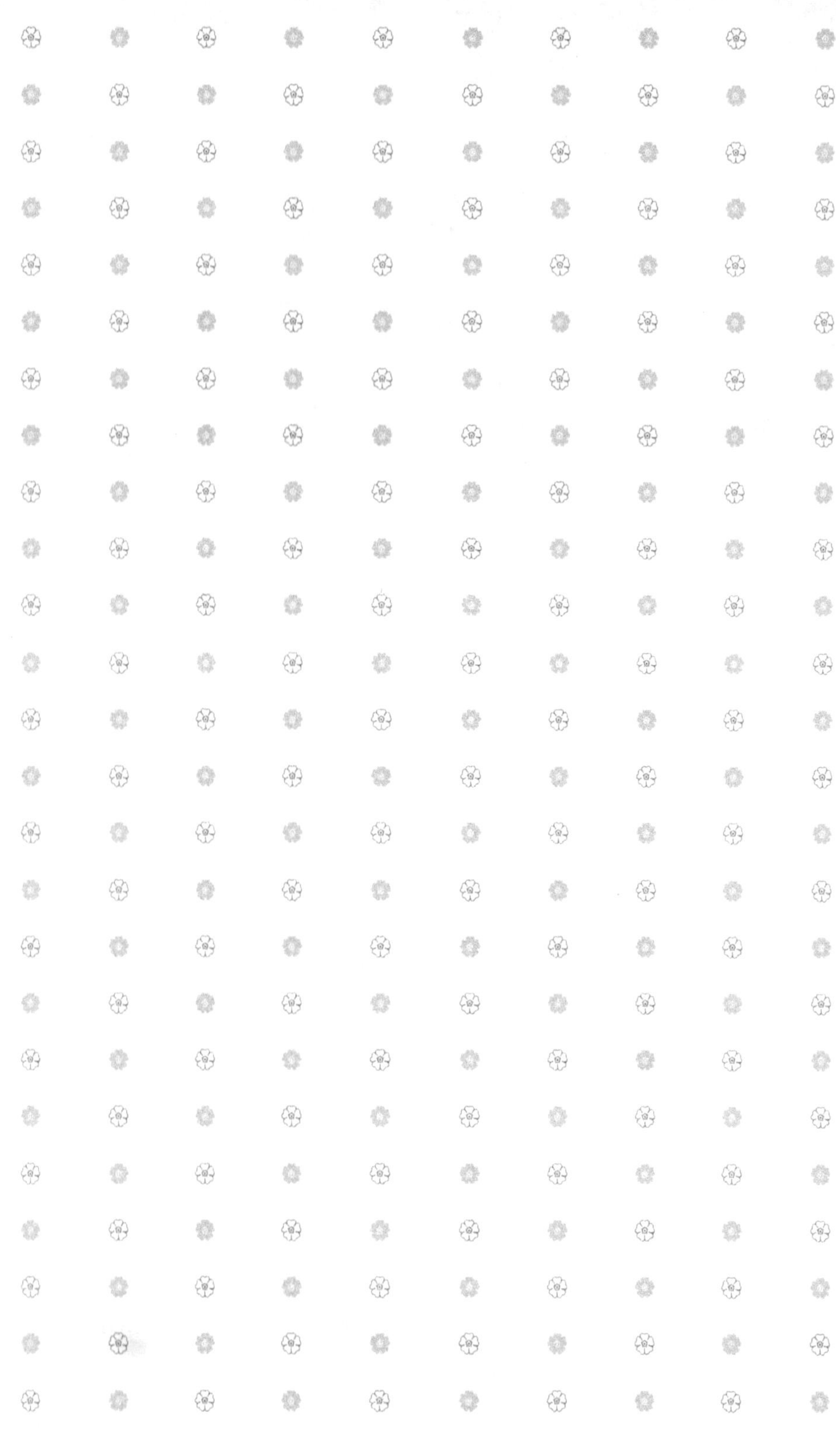